RETURN
TO
WYLDCLIFFE
HEIGHTS

ALSO BY CAROL GOODMAN

Children's and Young Adult

As Juliet Dark

As Lee Carroll (with Lee Slonimsky)

RETURN TO WYLDCLIFFE HEIGHTS

A Novel

CAROL GOODMAN

wm

WILLIAM MORROW
An Imprint of HarperCollins*Publishers*

RETURN TO WYLDCLIFFE HEIGHTS. Copyright © 2024 by Carol Goodman. All rights reserved. Printed in the United States of America. No part of this book may be used or reproduced in any manner whatsoever without written permission except in the case of brief quotations embodied in critical articles and reviews. For information, address HarperCollins Publishers, 195 Broadway, New York, NY 10007.

HarperCollins books may be purchased for educational, business, or sales promotional use. For information, please email the Special Markets Department at SPsales@harpercollins.com.

FIRST EDITION

Designed by Diahann Sturge-Campbell

Nature image © James Casil/Stock.Adobe.com

Library of Congress Cataloging-in-Publication Data

Names: Goodman, Carol, author.
Title: Return to Wyldcliffe Heights : a novel / Carol Goodman.
Description: First edition. | New York : William Morrow Paperbacks, 2024. | Summary: "Jane Eyre meets The Thirteenth Tale in this new modern gothic mystery from two-time Mary Higgins Clark award-winner Carol Goodman, about a reclusive writer who is desperate to rewrite the past" — Provided by publisher.
Identifiers: LCCN 2023042572 | ISBN 9780063265288 (paperback) | ISBN 9780063265301 (ebook)
Subjects: LCGFT: Detective and mystery fiction. | Gothic fiction. | Novels.
Classification: LCC PS3607.O566 R48 2024
LC record available at https://lccn.loc.gov/2023042572

ISBN 978-0-06-326528-8 (paperback)
ISBN 978-0-06-338668-6 (library edition)

24 25 26 27 28 LBC 5 4 3 2 1

To the forgotten girls of the House of Refuge for Women at Hudson

RETURN
TO
WYLDCLIFFE
HEIGHTS

CHAPTER ONE

Like many of the letters that came for Veronica St. Clair, this envelope contained dried pressed violets. Over the last three months I'd been opening them, my desk had become purple with dried violet dust and my hands always smelled like an old lady's closet.

Dear Ms. St. Clair, this one read,

I just wanted to tell you how much The Secret of Wyldcliffe Heights *means to me. I read it for the first time when I was fourteen and it saved my life. I'd never felt like someone really saw me until then, and since, I've reread it a dozen times. Sometimes I feel like Jayne exploring the winding hallways and secret passageways of Wyldcliffe Heights, sometimes I feel like Violet waiting to be released from her tower, and sometimes I feel like Wyldcliffe Heights itself, a big heap of secrets and lies teetering on the brink of the abyss. It's the book that made me into a reader. My only complaint is that there isn't more! I still think about Jayne and Violet and wonder what happened to them after the fire. Have you considered writing a sequel? I would be the first on line to buy it. And maybe*

then you could finally reveal the secret of Wyldcliffe Heights—
ha ha! 😊

> *Yours truly,*
> *A Curious Fan*

I put the letter down. When I started my job at Gatehouse Books as an editorial assistant three months ago, the office manager, Gloria, had explained that I would be reading Veronica St. Clair's fan mail and forwarding all "favorable" letters to her home in the country. *You are never to respond to any of the fans or to send any unfavorable mail to Miss St. Clair,* she told me.

I thought it was a little funny. Why would I write back to a fan? And what "unfavorable" mail? Didn't everyone love Veronica St. Clair as much as I did? When I asked Gloria she'd blinked at me, her eyes owlish behind her black-framed glasses. *Sometimes they love her so much they think they own a piece of her. Miss St. Clair's fans can be a bit . . .* possessive. *Especially when it comes to the subject of a sequel.*

I read the letter again. It was handwritten on lavender stationery with a border of violets in purple ink. I reread the last lines.

Have you considered writing a sequel?

That certainly sounded innocent enough. Lots of her fans wanted a sequel. There were only so many times you could reread a book trying to recapture the excitement of that first read. But what about that last line? *And maybe then you could finally reveal the Secret of Wyldcliffe Heights—ha ha!* 😊 Was Curious Fan suggesting that the book was lacking a satisfying ending? Would

Ms. St. Clair take offense at that? And that smiley face—there was something a little snarky about it. Something almost . . . *threatening*.

Or maybe I'd just spent too much time parsing fan letters and inhaling violet dust.

I gather up this week's letters—twelve besides the one from Curious Fan, all of them gushing love letters to their favorite author and innocent of subtext—stuff them into a large brown mailing envelope, weigh it on our old-fashioned postal scale, and print out the correct postage—a routine that makes me feel like I've gone back to the nineteenth century. Then I write the address on the front even though we have printed mailing labels because it feels like writing to my favorite fictional place—Jane Eyre's Thornfield or the Castle of Otranto.

> *Veronica St. Clair*
> *Wyldcliffe Heights*
> *Wyldcliffe-on-Hudson, NY 12571*

There is one other letter but I don't include it, because it isn't favorable at all. In fact, it sounds rather threatening.

Dear Miss Clare, it began, the misspelling itself a challenge.

> *I don't know how you can sleep at night knowing all the lives you have ruined. My sister was one of your so-called fans. She defiled her body with those violet tattoos and went looking for that trashy life your book made her want. She was last seen on the streets of New York City peddling her body for drug money. I wish you and your book had burnt up in that fire.*

It isn't signed and there's no return address. In fact, it doesn't have a postmark. Someone must have slid it through the mail slot in the door. It wasn't that hard to google Gatehouse Books' address online. Gloria had told me early on to "keep an eye out" when I was entering and leaving the building for any rabid fans or disgruntled writers waiting to pigeonhole an employee about why they hadn't gotten a response about their manuscript yet. That had been unsettling enough, but she hadn't said anything about vengeful family members of St. Clair's readers. And yet, it wasn't the first letter I've read complaining about the effect the book had had on a sister, daughter, wife, or mother. *Your book is inspiring,* a girl who had borrowed the book from her older sister had written, *but sometimes I think it inspires unrealistic fantasies.* A mother had written to say she'd demanded the town library remove it from their shelves because it was *unhealthy and morbid.* A psychiatrist wrote to say it *encouraged suicidal ideation.*

The letters had made me angry at first—*how narrow-minded!*—and then they had made me uneasy. Maybe they knew something about the book I didn't. This letter, though, makes me a little scared. I lay it on top of the larger envelope to show to Gloria, then I look at the time and see it's ten minutes after five. Gloria takes the mail to the post office on Hudson Street promptly at 5:15 each evening. I had just enough time to walk down three flights of stairs to deliver it to her.

As I stuff my things in my tote bag, I am distracted by something Hadley Fisher, the marketing assistant, is saying.

"He called me in to show him how to set up his Instagram account," she says, rolling her eyes. Hadley, the most tech savvy in the office, has barely disguised disdain for our Luddite publisher.

"And he was standing at the window when I came in, staring out at the river. He looked like he was thinking about jumping."

"It's not high enough," Kayla, the publicity assistant, replies. "He'd only a break a leg and the media attention would kill the potential sale."

They're talking about Kurtis Chadwick, our publisher. Four days ago, he'd had a meeting with our accounting firm. I'd brought in the coffee and heard the words "bankruptcy," "merger," and "buyout" as I was shutting the door. Twice since then I've come into his office to find him standing at the window looking out at the river. Each time I'd had the same thought as Hadley.

"Do you think there will be a buyout?" Kayla asks.

"I don't know," Hadley replies, chewing the stem of her horn-rimmed glasses, which I have begun to suspect aren't even prescription but merely accessories to the wool cardigans, plaid skirts, and chunky loafers she wears even in the summer, a nerdy librarian style I've been trying to emulate since I started here. Somehow my old school uniform skirt paired with cheap tops and sweaters from H&M never look quite the same. "He told me there was 'uncertainty on the horizon' and I should consider all my options."

"That doesn't sound good," Kayla says. "My friend at Hachette says there are rumors that they're acquiring us."

"At least that might save the company," Hadley says.

"Yeah, but would the new publisher keep us on?" Kayla asks.

"Not if they saw you gossiping instead of working."

They swerve their heads toward the stairs where Gloria stands glaring through oversized, black-framed glasses. Kayla and Hadley swivel back toward their respective desks instantly, their chair springs squeaking like frightened mice.

"Remember we still have books to edit and promote. Whether the house is bought by a larger publisher or not, we have a responsibility to our authors."

From my vantage point I can see Kayla smirking. Our fall catalog of books is not exactly celebration worthy. It consists of the twelfth installment of a mystery series featuring a clairvoyant tea shop owner and her psychic cats, a history of whaling in the nineteenth century, a memoir of the granddaughter of some World War II general, and a cookbook. *A cookbook!* I'd heard Kayla darkly mutter. *Who buys cookbooks anymore?*

"Kayla, have you notified all the aquariums about the whaling book?"

"Um . . . the aquariums might actually take objection to the whaling book?" Kayla says, but already Gloria's keen predator eyes have turned toward me.

"And you—" She stares at me as if she's forgotten my name even though she writes out my paycheck every week. I know there's nothing wrong with Gloria's memory, though. She does the *Times* crossword puzzle every day in ink and can recite by heart the sales figures of every book ever published by Gatehouse during our weekly staff meetings. I've begun to suspect that there is something about my name—or about me—she finds objectionable. "Agnes Corey," she says now, injecting a tone of disapproval into the four syllables. "Mr. Chadwick wants to see you in his office. Now."

I rise from my desk, upsetting a stack of slush pile manuscripts, and see Kayla and Hadley exchange a knowing look. As the last person hired, and still in my probationary period, I would no doubt be the first fired.

I follow Gloria down the steep attic stairs to the third floor. Gatehouse Books occupies all four floors of a townhouse in the West Village. The first floor is lined with floor-to-ceiling bookshelves of all the books published by the company in its one-hundred-year history. Prospective authors and agents and booksellers are given tea in china cups in the second-floor boardroom. The walls of the third floor, which houses the offices of the publisher, editor in chief, and copyeditor, are papered in a William Morris print and covered with photographs of famous authors. Descending from the attic, where the assistants toil, the smell of mold dissipates into the maple-syrupy smell of old paper and salt from the river—

Which means Mr. Chadwick has his window open.

Gloria must smell it, too, because she pauses on the landing and sniffs, reaching up the sleeve of her cardigan to pull out a tissue to dab her nose. "That damp," she croaks, "from that damn river. It'll be the death of me yet. You go on—" She shoos me toward Mr. Chadwick's office, retreating down the stairs to the hermetic confines of her ground-floor office lined in corkboards and spreadsheets and lit by the green glow of an ancient Hewlett-Packard.

Maybe she just doesn't want to overhear me being fired, I think, heading down the narrow hall filled with framed photographs of authors. Cyril Chadwick, the father of our current publisher, is featured next to one literary luminary after another—John Cheever, John Updike, John Irving—*the Hall of Johns,* I've heard Atticus, the copyeditor, call the passage even though it also includes Arthur Miller, Saul Bellow, Gore Vidal, and even a very old blurry shot of a young Cyril Chadwick with a white-bearded and very drunk Ernest Hemingway at the White Horse Tavern.

At the end of this long hall of men is one woman. It is not, though, an author photo; it's a book cover in the style of an old-fashioned gothic romance—a woman in a flimsy white dress runs from a turreted mansion behind her, one light shining from the tower window like a baleful eye. The woman, her long black hair swirling in the wind, looks over her shoulder as if she hears the hoofbeats and baying hounds of her pursuers. Her profile, partly obscured by her wild hair, is hauntingly beautiful.

"You always stop at that one."

The voice comes from an open door behind me where our copy-editor toils.

"I know it's not supposed to be the author on the cover, but she always makes me think of Veronica St. Clair and what happened to her."

"Actually, you're not entirely wrong." I hear the creak of a floorboard behind me and see him reflected in the picture glass, leaning against the doorway to his office, hands in trouser pockets, shirtsleeves rolled up to his elbows, a blue pencil stuck behind his ear and a smudge of ink on his cheek as if he's been writing with a fountain pen instead of a Mac. Atticus Zimmerman is one of those old-school hipsters who fetishize the trappings of an analog era even as they swipe right on Tinder and catalog the films they watch on Letterboxd.

Thinks he's hot shit, Kayla said once when we all went out for drinks at the White Horse Tavern and he declined because he had a manuscript to copyedit. *Went to Princeton and thinks he's F. Scott Fitzgerald.*

She's just mad because they went out on one date and he never asked her again, Hadley told me when Kayla went to the toilet. *I told her she was lucky; he's a bit of a heartbreaker, our Atticus. He goes through assistants like Kleenex, so watch yourself.*

"Not *entirely* wrong?" I echo, thinking it's the closest Atticus has gotten to saying I was right about something since I started here. Maybe it's being a copyeditor, who's in charge of correcting mistakes; he can't seem to stop correcting people in person.

"There's a story about the cover. When Kurtis Chadwick discovered Veronica St. Clair he went up to her house on the Hudson and stayed there until she finished the manuscript. Then he commissioned a local artist to paint the cover using her house and basing the girl on the cover on her—" He leans over my shoulder to peer more closely at the framed cover. I can smell the old-fashioned bay rum aftershave he uses, and pencil shavings. "You see the way she's turning away? That's to hide the scars from the fire. It was a bold choice to go with a retro gothic look. Who knew a tawdry gothic romance could still be a bestseller in the nineties—or are you one of those girls who thought it was a great masterpiece?"

"I don't know if it's a masterpiece," I say carefully, "but the fans love it and . . ." I try to think of something to say that will sound smart. "All those teens who'd grown up reading *Flowers in the Attic* ate it up and people started comparing it to *Jane Eyre* and *Rebecca*. It introduced a whole generation of girls to the gothic."

"Ha!" he barks his deconstructed version of a laugh. "I remember those girls from high school. They called themselves Wyld girls and tattooed themselves with violets."

"You make it sound like a cult," I say. "Those girls grew up and gave it to their daughters."

I'm regretting admitting to reading the book at all, but then he says, "I stole my sister's copy and read it in one night in eighth grade. I thought that it would be sexier—"

He ducks his head, his hair falling over his forehead, and laughs. As I turn, I see he's blushing. The hallway suddenly feels very narrow and warm. I look toward the closed door at the end.

"I'd better go in there," I say. "He asked to see me. I think I'm about to get fired."

He cringes. "Ouch." He looks genuinely sorry for me but he doesn't try to convince me otherwise. "I'm probably next. If we're acquired the new company will use freelance copyeditors." I see, then, that beneath his hipster pose he's worried—scared even. What will happen to Atticus Zimmerman if Gatehouse Books is bought out? I can't imagine him working in a big corporate office. Where, for that matter, will Gloria go? She must be pushing sixty. As I turn to go, I feel the weight of the house—the literal brick-and-mortar building as well as the figurative publishing house—pressing down on my shoulders like . . . how had Curious Fan put it? *A big heap of secrets and lies teetering on the brink of the abyss.*

My knock is met with a brisk "*Come!*" that sounds like what a captain would say on a ship. And indeed, Kurtis Chadwick is standing at the large porthole-shaped window, legs braced as if against a swelling sea, surveying the Hudson River like a sea captain. Or like a man thinking about throwing himself overboard. When I've stood silently for a minute he turns around and startles, as if surprised to see me even though he presumably asked for me.

"Oh, I thought you were Gloria . . . but . . . good . . . I wanted to talk to you . . ." He gestures to the chair in front of his desk while sitting down at his own, plusher one behind it. He leans back, crossing his long legs and steepling his fingers, resuming the confident ease of a man at the helm of a ship, not one about to jump overboard. I sit up straight. "It's Agnes, yes? Agnes Corey?" He's staring at an open folder on his desk, his head bent so I can make out a few strands of gray in the black. "And you've been with us almost three months now?"

"It will be three months at the end of next week," I say, remembering that's how long my probationary period is supposed to last.

"How have you found us here at Gatehouse?" he asks with a disarming smile. As if he really wants my opinion.

"It's been great!" I enthuse. "Everybody's been . . ." Before I can say "great" again, I manage to *avoid the repetition* (a mantra of our editor in chief). "So helpful! I'm learning so much from Ms. Chastain."

"Diane's a talented editor," he says. "Is that what you want to do?"

"Yes," I say, hoping that doesn't sound too presumptuous. "I mean, I know I have a long way to go and I have a lot to learn—"

"Why?" he asks, looking at me directly.

"*Why?*" I repeat, confused.

"Why do you want to be an editor?" he asks patiently. "The pay's low, the industry's in chaos, writers are difficult to work with—unless what you really want is to be a writer—"

"No," I say, truthfully. It had only taken a handful of interviews to realize that publishing professionals were wary of hiring assistants who wanted to be writers. Luckily, I didn't. "My mother was a writer and I saw how hard a life it was. I want to . . ." I pause and look out the window. A mist rising from the river softens the edges of the West Side Highway and the piers. We could really be on a ship sailing up the Hudson. Maybe that's why

Kurtis Chadwick spends so much time standing at the window; he's wishing he could sail up the river to Wyldcliffe-on-Hudson and relive his first editorial victory when he discovered Veronica St. Clair. "I want to help writers," I say, looking back toward him and finding his gaze firmly locked on me. "Like you do. Everyone says it was your editing that made *The Secret of Wyldcliffe Heights* the masterpiece it is."

His lips twitch, half smile, half grimace. "You think it's a masterpiece?"

"It changed my life." I say, twisting my hands together. They brush against the envelope in my lap and I remember the letters inside. "As it did for so many readers," I add. "We get fan letters every week asking for a sequel—"

He laughs, but it's a mirthless sound. "Ah, that siren song. A sequel! Yes, if Veronica would only write a sequel all our problems would be solved. Personally, I've never understood why they all want one so much—"

"It's the way the book ends," I say impetuously. As long as I keep talking he can't fire me. "I mean, don't get me wrong, the book has a satisfying ending but you've come to love Violet and Jayne so much you want to know what happens to them next. Where do they go after the fire? Does the ghost of Red Bess still haunt them? I mean, we don't even know what the *secret* of Wyldcliffe Heights is!"

His eyebrows shoot up and he laughs, a short bark that startles me and then relieves me. At least I've distracted him from his worries. "I said the same thing to Veronica," he admits with a confidential smile. "And begged her for an epilogue, but she refused. She said she hated epilogues because they tied things up too neatly. *Her readers*"—he's assumed an elevated diction that's supposed, I imagine, to replicate the author's voice—"would appreciate a bit left to their imagination."

"Her readers," I say, holding up the mailing envelope, "would like a sequel."

That confidential smile falters and I see I've lost him. "Unfortunately, it's quite impossible. As you may have heard, Veronica St. Clair is blind."

"She was blinded in the fire, right?" I say, glad I can show off this bit of knowledge. "But why should that stop her from writing a sequel? She could dictate to someone, like Henry James and Milton did. Or she could use voice-recognition software—"

Kurtis Chadwick chuckles. "I can't see Veronica speaking into a machine, and I'm afraid she's much too private a person to endure the intrusion of an amanuensis." He sighs and looks at me sadly. "There will be no sequel to *The Secret of Wyldcliffe Heights*, and without it, I fear, no more Gatehouse Books. Which brings me to the reason I wanted to speak with you. Gloria tells me you've done an excellent job, and Diane needs an editorial assistant. But alas, in the present circumstances—"

He spreads his hands open. "Well, you've probably heard the rumors. We are embarking on a new phase and I've been told that we must trim our sails and lighten our load for the journey. Of course, I'll write you an excellent recommendation. We can continue paying you through next week . . . unless you have other opportunities."

"No," I say, getting to my feet shakily, as if we are really on a ship at sea. "No other opportunities. I have a manuscript from the slush pile I'm reading and Ms. Chastain asked me to write a reader's report for the newest in the psychic cat series. I'd like to finish those if I may."

"Oh yes, those cats," he says with a shudder. "By all means, see what you can do. Maybe the series will get a boost and save the day."

"Maybe," I say doubtfully. I've heard Kayla and Hadley discussing the dismal sales of the psychic cat tea shop mysteries.

He gets up and holds his hand out to me. It's warm and steady, his grip firm, but when I meet his gaze, he's the one who looks as if he's drowning.

CHAPTER TWO

When I come out of Kurtis Chadwick's office, I catch the scent of Chanel Number 5 and hear laughter down the hall. As I walk toward it, I make out the throaty purr of Diane Chastain, editor in chief. It's rare for her to be in this late on a Friday, and I wonder if her presence has something to do with the impending acquisition. When I reach her open door, I see her leaning back in her ergonomic desk chair, long denim-clad legs stretched out in front of her, somehow both elegant and casual in a silky white button-down and burgundy sweater tossed over her shoulders. Her dark silver-streaked hair floats like a cloud over her sharp widow's peak and high cheekbones. A canvas tote bag filled with manuscripts rests on the floor. Embroidered where a monogram usually would be are the words *Book Slut*.

"Hey, kid," she says when she sees me hovering in the hallway. "I heard you were called into the lion's den. How'd it go?"

Atticus, who's sitting on the edge of her desk, half turns to give me an apologetic smile. I blush, realizing they've been talking about me.

"Okay, I guess. I have one more week and Mr. Chadwick says he'll give me a good reference."

"Tough break," Diane says, wincing and taking a long swig of some amber liquid in a rocks glass. "We may all be looking for work soon. I hear they're hiring down at the White Horse. I bartended there in the eighties. Made more in tips in one night than I did in a week as an editorial assistant."

"Speaking of the White Horse," Atticus says, "a few of us are going after work. You should come, Agnes."

"Yeah, thanks, maybe . . ." I can feel a pressure mounting behind my eyes. "I just have to finish that manuscript." As I bolt up the stairs I hear that rich throaty laugh again, echoed by Atticus's drier, deconstructed version. I pass Kayla and Hadley on their way down, Hadley's English schoolboy satchel slung across her chest, Kayla clutching her phone.

"How'd it go?" Hadley asks. "Are you—"

"Still here for a week," I say brightly, squeezing past them. Pressing myself against the wall I feel like my chest is going to explode.

Kayla's eyes slide sideways toward Hadley as if to say, *See, I told you she was being let go,* but Hadley at least has the good grace to look sorry. "That's rough," she says. "Look, we're going to the White Horse. You should come."

"Yeah, Atticus told me, maybe I'll see you there later."

As soon as they are past me, I sprint up the rest of the stairs and then slip behind the stacks of manuscripts on my desk, grateful Gatehouse is so old-school that they still print out manuscripts instead of having us read them on screen. They form an effective blockade against any prying eyes as the tears begin to fall. *Stupid,* I tell myself, digging for Kleenex in my bag, *you knew it was too good to last.* This job had felt like an answer to a prayer. I had already been in New York for six months, looking for a job in publishing, living in a rented room the size of a closet, burning through the money it had taken me three years to earn as a teacher at a juvenile reformatory upstate. It had been a steady, dependable job that I should have been grateful for, but sometimes when I walked down the drab, cinder-block halls and looked out the barred windows at the perpetually gray skies I felt as trapped as the girls sent there by the state. I wanted something more—the glamour of the city, yes, but mostly the magic of books and getting to work with them.

When I said that at interviews, though, the editors and their assistants smiled pityingly at me and asked again where Potsdam was and why had it taken me so long to finish my degree there and what kind of school was this Woodbridge Institute I'd worked at? The other applicants, I soon learned, had gone to better colleges and had already done internships. Then, while riding the elevator up to an interview at Random House, I heard two of my rival applicants talking about an opening at Gatehouse Books.

"My English prof at Vassar emailed me about it," a young woman in plaid and cashmere said, "but it's so small and old-fashioned. They haven't had a real bestseller since that big gothic romance in the nineties."

"*Wyldcliffe Heights!*" her male companion, impeccable in a three-piece suit, gasped. "I read it three times in high school. But yeah, so nineties. I'm surprised they're still in business."

I ignored their disparagement and presages of doom and the fact that at almost thirty I should have moved beyond assistant jobs. I dropped off my résumé that day. I received an email the next morning asking me to come in at 10 a.m., which barely left me enough time to queue in the hall for a shower, iron a shirt in the laundry room, and speed walk the eight blocks downtown. At least I knew the way. I'd scouted out their offices when I first got to the city, immediately recognizing the four-story townhouse from the publisher's logo on the spine of *The Secret of Wyldcliffe Heights*. Pushing the brass doorbell, I felt as if I had arrived at the gatehouse of Wyldcliffe Heights itself. I half expected the ancient housekeeper, Mrs. Gorse, to answer the door. Instead, a stooped woman in a shapeless black dress, square black-framed glasses, and heavy orthopedic shoes opened the door.

"I'm here about the assistant's job?" I said uncertainly.

"Well, are you or aren't you?" she snapped. "You don't sound very sure. You're not one of those millennials who turn every sentence into a question, are you?"

"No," I said as definitively as I could.

"Good, then you'd better come in. Wipe your feet. These carpets are hell to clean."

Maybe she is the housekeeper, after all.

She ushered me through a book-lined room into a cluttered, cork-lined office and gestured to a chair that had a stack of books on it. I was afraid to ask her what to do with them lest I sound too millennial, so I moved them carefully to the floor. She sat on the other side of the desk and opened a thick vinyl portfolio that I presumed held my résumé. I was expecting the same questions— *Why do you want to work in publishing? Why haven't you done any internships? Where is Potsdam?* Instead she said, "I see you worked at the Woodbridge Institute."

"You know it?" I asked, surprised.

"I had a friend sent there," she said, her eyes softening behind the severe glasses. "Are the nuns there still tough as nails?"

"The nuns have mostly all died out. The school depends on lay teachers and interns from the college now."

"Which is how, I presume, you came to work there."

I sat still for a moment. Her voice had not gone up at the end. It was not a question. The brown eyes behind the glasses held mine for a steady beat and then she went on.

"Can you type?"

"Eighty words a minute."

"Make phone calls?"

"Of course—"

"A lot your age can't. Read cursive?"

"Yes—"

"The nuns taught you grammar?"

"Every day," I said before realizing I'd given away having been an inmate at Woodbridge, not just a teacher.

"Good," she said, slapping the portfolio shut as if closing the book on my misspent youth. "When can you start?"

She had hired me out of pity because she knew the kind of girl who ended up at Woodbridge and how few doors ever opened for them. It was unlikely I'd find anyone else willing to take the same chance on me. Besides, I didn't want to work in one of those huge office towers. I'd found my place here in this tiny corner of the publishing world, tucked beneath the attic eaves in my papered hideout.

I raise my head, eyes stinging from the salt breeze blowing through an open window. Ink-blue clouds have massed across the river, the sun setting below them flashing off car windshields on the West Side Highway like a pebble skipping over water and landing on my desk to turn the dull brown envelope the rich ochre of ancient villa walls. I'd forgotten to give it to Gloria to mail. I hadn't even sealed it. I take out the letters now and inhale the scent of dead violets. What had Kurtis Chadwick said?

If Veronica would only write a sequel all our problems would be solved.

But Veronica St. Clair was blind. She wouldn't recite her book to a machine or to a stranger—

But what about a reader?

Like Jane Eyre, the narrator of *The Secret of Wyldcliffe Heights* ended the book by addressing her reader, only instead of *Dear Reader, I married him* she finished with *Dear Reader, what more would you have me say?*

She'd ended, millennial style, with a question. No wonder we, her readers, were still waiting for an answer. What if she could give that answer to a *reader*?

I open my desk drawer and take out a sheet of Gatehouse letterhead—old-fashioned stationery with a letter-pressed logo of the townhouse—and find a pen. As I begin to write I pause. Veronica St. Clair is blind. She wouldn't see this. But she must have someone to read it to her.

Dear Ms. St. Clair,

Forgive the impertinence of writing to you directly. I work at Gatehouse Books and have been reading letters from your devoted fans and now, since it's my last week here, I must add my own voice to theirs. We all want a sequel! We all want to know what came next for Jayne and Violet. We all want to return to Wyldcliffe Heights. I understand the difficulties that face you,

*but if you could tell the story to a sympathetic reader—as you
told* The Secret of Wyldcliffe Heights—*mightn't you be able?*

I stopped and considered if I should say more. Should I tell her
that Gatehouse Books might close without her sequel? That I'd
be out of a job? But it seemed unfair to put the former on her head
and petty to put the latter.

I hope you will consider my proposal, I conclude. And then I
sign it.

Your devoted reader, Agnes Corey

Before I can change my mind, I slip the sheet into the envelope
along with the violet-scented letters, lick the gummed strip on top
of the envelope, pinch shut the tin clasp fastener, and seal the
envelope. Then I shove it in my tote bag along with the psychic cat
manuscript and head downstairs to take it to the post office myself.

WHEN I GET outside, I'm surprised at how dark it is, that last ray
of sun I'd glimpsed from my attic window extinguished by a bank
of fog rolling in off the river. The street, usually busy, is nearly
deserted. *It's not summer anymore,* I remind myself as I turn up
the collar of my light denim jacket and head east toward Hudson
Street. When I'd started in July the neighborhood was always
teeming. Now, in October, this funny little corner of the West
Village, lined with old townhouses and paved with cobblestones,
feels as though it's been forgotten by the twenty-first century.
Tonight, with the edges of the buildings softened by fog, it's like
the turn of the nineteenth century down to the clip-clop of hooves
on cobblestones—

I pause, listening to the sound. Not hooves, but footsteps. And not far behind me. But when I came out of Gatehouse, I didn't see anyone on the street. I must have missed them in the fog. I reach into my jacket pocket and grip the penknife I always carry and walk faster—

The footsteps speed up.

Someone is following me. Someone who was waiting outside Gatehouse Books. Maybe it's one of those angry fans—or the person who blamed Veronica St. Clair for their sister's fate. *It has nothing to do with me,* I'll say, *I don't even have a job there anymore.* The lights of Hudson Street seem dim and far away. I walk faster, my heartbeats keeping time with my footsteps and their echo over the slick, uneven cobblestones, the fog clammy as a hand over my face. All of it—the fog, the invisible pursuer—reminds me of a recurrent childhood nightmare I have of being chased through an impenetrable fog. In the dream I always fall—

My foot slides between two cobblestones and I lose my balance, my ankle twisting. Just as in my dream I am falling and I can hear a mournful wail as of a pack of hounds ready to pounce on me—

Then there's a burst of noise from Hudson Street and a group of young, laughing women careen around the corner. One spots me and calls out, "Hey, is this the street that Carrie Bradshaw lived on?"

"That's over on Perry and Bleecker," I say, glad I went that time Hadley wanted to show me the *Sex and the City* landmark. I hurry to join them on the corner and point them in the right direction. Buoyed by their boozy goodwill I turn to face my stalker, but there's no one behind me. The street is empty. I hear that wailing sound again and recognize that it's a foghorn from the river. *It was just your imagination,* I tell myself, sliding the envelope into the mailbox on the corner, but then someone grabs my arm. I jump, sure the stalker has caught me.

"There you are!" It's Atticus, his breath peaty with aged whiskey. "I was coming back to get you. You said you'd come."

"I said maybe," I say a little too sharply, still rattled by my pursuer. *If there really had been someone following me and it wasn't my imagination.* His face falls and I feel instantly sorry. "But yeah, sure, I could use a drink."

The White Horse is cheerfully crowded, warm, and bright as we come in out of the damp. Kayla and Hadley are crammed into a corner table beneath a portrait of Dylan Thomas with Serge and Reese, two college friends of Atticus's. They squeeze over on the banquette to make room for us. Reese pours us both a foamy beer from a nearly empty pitcher while Serge continues recapping something he saw at the Film Forum, where he works as an usher. Hadley is listening intently but Kayla's busy scrolling through her phone. I look over and see she's looking at an anonymous Instagram account that posts snarky memes about publishing.

"Did you finish the manuscript?" Atticus asks.

For a second, I don't remember that's what I told him I was doing. "Yeah," I say, recovering quickly, "but it was so bad that the entirety of my reader's report will be *No.*"

Kayla looks up from her phone. "You have to give editorial more so they have something to say on the rejection letter."

"Don't they always say the same thing?" I ask, slurping a mouthful of beer foam.

"*Although this had promise I found ultimately that I couldn't relate to the characters,*" Atticus intones in a dead-on imitation of Kurtis Chadwick's upper-crust voice.

"*But others may feel differently,*" Kayla and Hadley singsong in unison like the evil twins from *The Shining.*

"Sometimes," I say, "I think it would be kinder to say, *This is really bad. You have no talent. Find another way to make a living.*"

"You're just burnt out," Hadley says. "It's hard not to be with all the extra work we're expected to do for such low pay and having to read so much dreck. I mean, some days I don't even *like* books anymore."

"Yeah," Kayla says, "publishing is kind of over."

"That's because of the paper supply issues," Reese says.

"Actually," Hadley corrects, "it's Amazon that's killed the industry."

"Cell phones," Kayla says. "And TikTok. No one reads books anymore."

"Yeah," Atticus says morosely, "sometimes I think we might as well be hatmakers and JFK has just gone hatless, killing the industry in one sartorial swoop." He holds up his beer as if toasting the end of the industry that employs most of us. I take a large gulp. "You're probably well out of it, Agnes," Atticus says, not unkindly.

A silence settles over the table as everyone looks down at their glasses in mourning for the publishing industry—or at least the end of my career in it. "Mr. Chadwick said the company would survive if Veronica St. Clair wrote a sequel," I blurt out, desperate not to be the target of so much pity.

"I don't understand why anyone would want to read more of that maudlin trash," Hadley says.

I stare at her, shocked that she would disparage the book our own publishing house is most famous for. I had assumed that everyone at Gatehouse Books must work there because they love the book as much as I do.

"Gawd, yes," Serge says. "I remember all the girls who went crazy over it at boarding school. They weren't exactly geniuses."

"Hardly," Hadley says, rolling her eyes. "And the worst of it is that half the plot is stolen from a 1920s tabloid murder case that took place a few blocks from here at the Josephine Hotel. I researched it for the true crime book I'm writing."

"You're writing a true crime book?" I ask, surprised. I'd thought it was verboten to admit you wanted to be a writer if you worked in publishing.

"That's where the money is," Hadley replies. "Fiction is kind of over."

"Yeah," Serge agrees, "I only read nonfiction. What's your book about, Hadley?"

Preening under Serge's attention, Hadley leans in to tell us the gruesome details. "There was a notorious serial killer called the Violet Strangler who used a violet ribbon to strangle young girls who sold violets. One of the violet girls went mad and slaughtered all the girls at a settlement house and claimed it was the Violet Strangler who did it. She was convicted of murder and sent upstate to a women's prison, where she killed the warden. Her name was Bess Molloy but the tabloids called her Red Bess—"

"That's only the backstory to *The Secret of Wyldcliffe Heights*," I interject. "Veronica St. Clair's grandmother was Josephine Hale, for whom the Josephine Hotel is named. In the book, Jayne thinks Red Bess is the ghost haunting the house—" I shiver, recalling the moment earlier on the foggy, empty street when I thought I was being followed. It had felt, I realize now, like a moment from the book. "What difference does it make if the novel is based on a true crime story? So was *Crime and Punishment* and 'The Mystery of Marie Rogêt.'"

Serge goggles at me, appalled. "Are you comparing Veronica St. Clair to Dostoyevsky and Poe? Have you even read them?"

Before I can tell him *yes, believe it or not I read classic literature up at SUNY Potsdam,* Atticus intercedes. "A sequel to *The Secret of Wyldcliffe Heights* might save Gatehouse but"—he gives me a pitying look—"it'll never happen. Diane was telling me—" He lowers his voice and we all lean in. "Veronica St. Clair lost her mind years ago. That's why she's a recluse. Some assistant wrote her a letter asking for a sequel and St. Clair demanded he be fired," he finishes, but then he sees the mortified look on my face. "Oh! You didn't—" He must be recalling the big envelope I'd mailed on the corner. "You didn't write a letter to Veronica St. Clair, did you?"

Out of the corner of my eye I see Hadley and Kayla exchange an amused look. "What difference does it make?" I ask, feeling the press of tears behind my eyes. "I've already been let go."

"Yeah, but I assume you want a reference," Hadley says as if I'm a simpleton. "And Chadwick is pretty strict on that rule."

"I thought it was Gloria's rule—" I begin but I'm cut off by a barely suppressed giggle from Hadley.

"Chadwick *is* fanatic about no one bothering St. Clair," Atticus says with a pitying look that pushes the tears up my throat. "But hey, maybe she won't get the letter before he writes you a recommendation."

"But you'll still never be able to list Gatehouse as a reference," Hadley adds, barely able to keep herself from smiling. The tears, so close to falling, vaporize, replaced by a boiling anger that threatens to erupt. Before I can say or do anything I will regret, I rise to my feet and push my way out of the bar.

CHAPTER THREE

The crowd, as if sensing my anger, parts for me and I'm soon outside. Hudson Street is still crowded and I'm tired of having to squeeze myself around people. I head down Eleventh Street, walking fast—

And hear for the second time tonight footsteps echoing my own. This time I turn, ready to challenge my stalker. But again, it's only Atticus.

"Hey, wait up, there's no need to get so upset."

"No?" I spit back at him, turning to continue west on Eleventh. "Hadley as good as told me that I'll never get hired in publishing again and she looked pretty happy about it. And don't tell me it's my imagination Serge doesn't think I could possibly have read Dostoyevsky because I went to a backwater state school or Kayla and Hadley don't smirk every time I open my mouth and you—"

"What am I guilty of?" he asks as I turn north on Washington Street.

"You think *The Secret of Wyldcliffe Heights* is *tawdry*." It bursts out of me before I know it's what I'm going to say. "And anyone who likes it . . . what did Serge say? Isn't exactly a genius."

"Serge is a jerk," he says automatically, and then, three paces later, "I guess I am, too. I didn't mean to call it tawdry. The truth is . . ." He pauses and stays quiet for half a block. This far from the busy avenue the street has gone quiet save for the distant hum of traffic on the West Side Highway and the mournful dirge of foghorns coming from the river. For the second time tonight, I have the feeling that I've slipped back in time and the modern world has fallen away. Perhaps Atticus feels it, too, because when he breaks his silence, he speaks in a tone I've never heard from him before. After a second I recognize it as humility.

"The truth is that *The Secret of Wyldcliffe Heights* scared the crap out of me, which was really embarrassing considering I borrowed it off my kid sister. I just wanted to see what all the fuss was about. I thought it was about sex—and there is all that simmering tension between Violet and Jayne—but what got me was the ghost of Red Bess stalking the halls, trailing blood and dead violets in her wake. And then there was that scene when Jayne awakens and finds Red Bess hanging over her bed—"

"*Her neck broken by the hangman's noose,*" I quote, shivering at the image that had haunted my nightmares throughout my childhood and teens, "*her eyes still wide with the terror of her last moments—*"

"*—reflecting back the black pit she saw in her first moments of the death that she had always felt stalking her,*" Atticus finishes the quote. "*That* was what got me, the idea that your death stalks you from the day you are born. That you can't escape it."

"What got me," I say, "was that Veronica St. Clair wrote about Red Bess burning down Wyldcliffe Heights and then she was nearly killed when her own house caught fire. It was like she knew what was coming for her."

"Or that she wrote Red Bess into existence," Atticus says. "I've sometimes wondered if that's why she stopped writing—she was afraid of bringing her back."

It's such a terrible thought that I can't help looking over my shoulder, afraid I'll see the broken-necked phantom emerging from the fog. When I turn back, I see with relief that we've reached my street.

"So, you made fun of the book because it scared you?" I say, stopping under the streetlamp on the corner.

"That's pretty much how I deal with all my fears—mockery and alcohol," he says, ducking his head so that his hair flops over his eyes, giving him a boyish look. "But I'm sorry that I offended you. I don't think you're dumb for liking the book, just a lot braver than me."

"Yeah, well, I've seen some worse horrors than what's in *The Secret of Wyldcliffe Heights*. This place, for instance—" I look up at the building looming out of the fog behind an iron railing. It could be one of the haunted castles on a gothic romance cover. "Living here feels like being walled up in a convent sometimes."

"You *live* here?" he asks. "Isn't this the Josephine Hotel—the place Hadley was talking about?" He looks at me strangely. "Why didn't you say something when Hadley mentioned it?"

"And interrupt Hadley's lecture on her *research*?"

He laughs, and I'm relieved that he's bought my explanation and I don't have to tell him that the real reason I didn't say I lived here was because I was ashamed. "It's a sort of hostel now, run by a nonprofit charity."

His face, under the streetlamp, is lit up now. Of course, this would be his kind of thing—retro, underground, and a bit arcane. I've gone up in his estimation within seconds and it thaws something inside me even though I've earned it unfairly. If he knew how I got here the admiring look on his face would change to pity. Before that happens, I break the number-one rule of the Josephine.

"Do you want to come in?" I ask.

BEFORE I COULD rent my room I had to sign a three-page agreement with the residence manager: no candles, no hot plates, no food in the room, no smoking, no drugs, no drinking. And no guests, not ever. It was like Woodbridge all over again, only outside the doors lay New York City and I could leave anytime I wanted to—except there was no place else in the city I could afford. If I got thrown out for bringing in a guest, I'd have to leave the city.

Luckily, Atticus must sense the need to be quiet as I let him in the lobby because he whispers his awestruck "Wow!" as he gapes at the art nouveau tiled ceiling, palm-crowned columns, and stuffed peacock spreading its plumage over the reception desk. "This is like stepping back in time."

"It was built in 1908," I say in a low voice, "as a hotel for *indigent ladies* and then in the twenties it became a settlement house. Josephine Hale, the grandmother of Veronica St. Clair, was a progressive reformer who worked here and gave so much money to the place they eventually named it after her. There's her picture hanging over the front desk—" I point to a framed sepia-toned portrait that has faded so much over time that it's hard to make out the features of the woman in it. "Come on, I'll show you the ballroom." I lead him into the big room at the rear of the hotel, hoping that Alphonse, the octogenarian night guard, is tucked up in the manager's office watching old movies on YouTube. I leave the lights off until I close the door behind us just in case he's not. Our footsteps echo in the dark, high-ceilinged space, and for a moment I can imagine the Josephine ballroom in all its incarnations. Before I turn on the light, I want Atticus to see it, too.

"Old photos show that it was fitted out like a Victorian parlor. Aspidistras and flocked velvet settees and doilies and tea sets. Josephine Hale believed in the civilizing properties of tea and etiquette. She thought that women who spent their days working in sweatshops or walking the streets would become ladies if they learned how to pour tea and play the pianoforte."

I can hear Atticus breathing softly beside me and sense that he's picturing it, too—girls in starched white shirtwaists and Gibson girl poufs leaning over their needlework, listening to thin, tinkling music.

"Unfortunately, etiquette and tea weren't enough to keep underfed, penniless girls off the streets or out of the hands of the men who would take advantage of them. So Josephine founded a women's refuge upstate on the grounds of her family estate so that women caught shoplifting or selling themselves could be removed from *pernicious influences* and placed in a safe, homelike environment. After Red Bess's rampage—as the tabloids called it—the Josephine went downhill. It got a reputation for housing prostitutes. By the late twenties, Josephine Hale wiped her hands of it and it became a speakeasy and bordello. The pianoforte was replaced by a jazz band, the teacups held gin, and the girls dressed a bit skimpier."

"Poor Josephine must have been appalled to have her name connected with such an establishment," Atticus says.

"It was called JoJo's in those years. In the Depression it became a soup kitchen and flophouse. In the forties, the navy commissioned it as a training school for WAVES and used the ballroom for USO dances—"

"I bet they had a swing band and soldiers danced their last dances with their sweethearts," Atticus says in a soft voice. Although I can't see his face, I sense he's stirred by the same images I'm seeing.

"Those were the last dances for a while. The hotel fell on hard times after the war and by the sixties it was a welfare hotel, infamous for drug overdoses and knifings. In the eighties and nineties the ballroom became a venue for punk goth bands— Siouxsie and the Banshees, the Cure, Bauhaus, Skeletal Family, the March Violets—"

Atticus is standing so close to me I can feel heat coming off him and hear his heartbeat as if we're crammed into this dark space by a teeming crowd dancing to a hard beat. "In the early aughts it was bought by a developer who tried to make it into a boutique hotel but they hit a rough patch after 2008 and it went downhill again. It was bought up by the nonprofit that runs it now. I guess some places always revert back to their true natures."

I reach over to the wall and flip the light switch, laying bare the room as it is now. No aspidistras or velvet settees, no gin in tea-cups, no teeming crowds. The floor is stripped and shellacked like a high school gym, the only furniture a few threadbare, lumpy couches and stacks of folding chairs for weekly AA meetings and poetry readings. The only touches of glamour left are the cast-iron mezzanine railing and the stained-glass light fixture in the ceiling. I turn to Atticus, expecting to see the same deflation I feel, but instead he's looking at me as if I were one of those women I've conjured from the past.

"How do you know all this, Agnes?" he asks, a look of awe on his face. "And how did you find this place?"

Instead of answering either question I say, "I want to show you something else."

I take him up the iron staircase to the mezzanine, where there's a gallery of old photographs. I lead him past the sepia-toned ones of young women in shirtwaists marching for suffrage and labor reform, flappers with bobbed hair and dropped-waist dresses kicking up their heels, the WAVES lined up in naval uniforms, then a dreary series of nuns and social workers posed with politicians and businessmen, to a dozen or so black-and-white arty shots of punks with jagged hair, torn T-shirts, leather jackets, and safety pin piercings. Atticus stops to point out a few recognizable faces—Patti Smith, Deborah Harry, Richard Hell, Joey Ramone. I keep going until I reach the last photo. It's taken from the mezzanine gallery, where we're standing, looking down at the stage. The ballroom is packed, a seething mass of upraised arms and upturned faces, all focused on the stage where two young women lean into one shared mike. The stage lights hit the face of the one closest to the edge of the stage while the second woman, standing a few inches behind her, recedes into the shadows, her face a dimmer reflection of the other woman's. They're both wearing dark chokers around their necks so that their pale faces seem to float disembodied.

"Wait," Atticus says as he leans over my shoulder. "That looks like—?"

"The woman on the cover of *The Secret of Wyldcliffe Heights*. I thought so, too. Look at the tattoo on her arm."

Atticus peers closer. "Is that—"

"A violet? Yeah, I think so, just like the one Jayne gets in the book. And then there's this—"

I take the picture off the wall and turn it over, prying loose the prongs that hold it in its frame. I lift the cardboard backing to reveal the underside of the photograph and show Atticus the faint pencil lines.

"*Violet and Jayne onstage at the Josephine, Summer 1993,*" he reads aloud. "Holy crap! It is her. And look at the date—one year before she published *The Secret of Wyldcliffe Heights*. None of this is in her bio. Forget about a sequel, Agnes, what I'd like to read is the real story of how Veronica St. Clair went from that"—he taps the glass—"to the author of *The Secret of Wyldcliffe Heights.*"

"I think it had something to do with a girl who died here at the Josephine—" I begin, turning to Atticus. He turns at the same time and for a second our faces are as close as the two singers' in the photograph, as if we, too, are sharing the same song, lips close enough to kiss—

But then a voice breaks into the silence, as discordant as reverb.

"Miss Corey, please escort your guest to the front entrance and then report to my office immediately."

CHAPTER FOUR

Roberta Jenkins, the residence manager, telling me off is bad enough; the look on Atticus's face when I let him out is worse. All the glamour I'd gained in his eyes is gone. He looks at me as if I were an inmate.

"Are you in trouble?" he asks at the door.

I shrug, assuming a casual tone. "Nah, they just have a lot of rules here . . . I'll see you on Monday."

I close the door before he can ask me what kind of rules and why would I live somewhere with them. I make my way to the back office, past the bulletin boards with notices for AA meetings and counseling services and the whiteboard with chore assignments. This is the drab reality. It's no longer the Josephine Hotel, it's Josephine House, a residential halfway house for the detritus of the social welfare system—recovering addicts, paroled inmates (as long as they're not sex offenders), teens who have aged out of foster care, anyone who has fallen through the cracks and needs a safe berth. Beyond the lobby, the back offices share the same smell of chalk and industrial-strength disinfectant with every halfway house, group home, and correctional institution I've ever been in. I can feel my spirits sag, tugged down like a kite from the flights of fancy I'd taken with Atticus. Back to the familiar—*where you belong,* a little voice says inside my head.

Mrs. Jenkins is seated behind her desk when I come in, her hands laid atop an open folder. For the second time today I'm sitting down in front of a desk with my life spread out before me—only this time the file is thicker and Roberta Jenkins is a lot sterner than Kurtis Chadwick, the lines burned into her face by decades in social services giving her a look of long forbearance, as if she's seen all the foolishness of the world and mine is just the newest disappointing iteration.

"Agnes Corey." She says my full name like a judge passing sentence. "I know you didn't forget the rule about outside guests. Did you wake up this morning and decide you were tired of living here and were ready to get kicked out?"

"No, Mrs. Jenkins," I say, beginning the familiar catechism I'd learned at Woodbridge. "I don't want to get kicked out of the Josephine. I'm very grateful to be here. I'm sorry I broke the rules. It won't happen again."

She narrows her eyes at me, scanning for sarcasm. It makes me feel like I'm fourteen again, sitting in the warden's office, caught smoking; or fifteen, caught sneaking out; or sixteen, caught running away. I abide her scrutiny, washing my face clean of any guile, until she lets out an exasperated sigh and shakes her head. "Then why did you do it?"

This is the part I dislike the most—having to retrace the steps of my mistakes back to the moment I went astray—a mea culpa without the privacy of the confessional.

"One of my coworkers walked me home and he was interested in the history of the Josephine. I-I just wanted to show him what an amazing place it was—and still is. I wasn't going to take him to my room or anything and we weren't doing . . . *anything.*" I blush, remembering that moment when Atticus's face was so close to mine. Had he been about to kiss me?

"Uh-huh," she says with heavy skepticism. "So it was just a history lesson?" She looks down at the file on her desk and flips a page. "Well, I do see here that you were good in history at Woodbridge . . . and also that you have some history yourself."

I steel myself. Although a juvenile's records are sealed, in order to be eligible for residency at Josephine House I had to sign a release making my records available to the residence manager.

"Although a good student you ran away six times." She purses her lips and whistles. "Where were you trying to go?"

"I don't know," I lie. "Just—away."

"Didn't you like it at Woodbridge? I know some of these places can be rough, but I've heard from former residents that it's better than most."

"It is," I say. "There are worse."

"And you liked it well enough to go back to teach there after finishing college."

"Yes," I say, "they offered me a job and it seemed like the best way to pay off my student debt and save up some money—"

"To come to the big city and work"—another glance at the file—"at a publishing company. I see you got a job three months ago at"—she glances down again—"Gatehouse Books. How's that going?"

My heart sinks. "I met with my boss today and he said he's been happy with my performance. In fact, I have a manuscript I'm supposed to be reading—"

"Uh-huh," she hums, not fooled by my diversion. "And . . . ?"

"I've been let go—but only because the company is in financial trouble and may be acquired. He said he'd give me a good reference."

"So, you have to start looking for work again. Remember, it's a condition of your residency here that you maintain gainful employment."

"I remember," I say. "Atticus—who I was showing the ballroom to—told me he's got some leads for me."

"Well, that's very nice of Atticus," she says. "Just tell him no more midnight visits."

"I will, ma'am."

She smiles wryly at the "ma'am," closes my file, and swivels her chair to pull open the drawer second from the top of the filing cabinet beside her desk. It opens with a jarring metallic screech, like an animal hungry for my mistakes and sins, and closes with a satisfied groan when it's consumed them. I wait until she starts to rise to get up, too. As she does, she frowns. "Gatehouse Books? Weren't they the ones that published that book that was so popular back in the nineties? *The Secret of Wyldcliffe Heights*?"

"Yes," I say, "it's still their biggest seller."

I'm expecting her to say something disparaging about the book. Most of the social workers I've met have disapproved of it. Instead, she lets out a hoot. "I read it three times while I was doing my residency at Bellevue just to have something to take me *away*. You tell that boss of yours he ought to bring out a sequel."

It rains for the rest of the weekend, as if reproaching me for my misconduct. I stay in my room, subsisting on weak tea and canned soup from the hall kitchen, my only company the clanking of the radiator pipes and a pigeon fluffed up on my windowsill sheltering from the rain. I huddle under a scratchy wool blanket in SUNY Potsdam sweats and finish reading the manuscript Diana gave me. After a dozen failed attempts to draft a reader's report, I pick up my old and tattered copy of *The Secret of Wyldcliffe Heights*. It's the copy my mother gave me when I first went into foster care—a gift my foster mother scoffed at as "too mature" for an eight-year-old until I demonstrated I could read it. Of course I could; I knew it by heart. Even now when I run my hands over the tattered dust jacket and yellowed pages and stroke the violet ribbon my mother left as a bookmark, I can hear my mother's voice reading aloud.

It begins simply enough with our heroine, Jayne, traveling by steamboat from New York City to the old house on the Hudson River where she has taken a job as a teacher. She frets about whether she'll be up to it. She's apprehensive, but excited, too, so eager to arrive that she escapes the confines of the stuffy ship's cabin and braves the rain and wind to stand on the deck, peering through the fog to catch her first glimpse of Wyldcliffe Heights—

I pressed myself against the railing, straining to see through the mist as if it were my future I sought—and then, as the ship rounded the last bend, there it was! Gray stones materialized as if hewn from the fog, standing sentinel on the steep headland like a medieval fortress. A single light shone in the tower—a beacon drawing us into port—into safety, I wondered, or was it a warning to stay away from the rocks below? Either way, it was too late. As the ship drew into port, the tide hurrying us to shore, I felt the glare of that single yellow eye fixed on me. "I see you," it said, "and I claim you as my own."

I read all of Sunday and late into the night, swept as inevitably into the story as Jayne's ship is pulled by the river's tide, following her into the great gothic mansion Wyldcliffe Heights, presided over by the charming but controlling warden, St. James. Jayne's students are well-behaved but oddly suppressed, as if drugged by the violets they pick in the glass houses to be shipped down to the city. At night Jayne hears mysterious sounds coming from the attic and she catches the girls whispering of a ghost named Red Bess, a housemaid who had murdered her master and then hung herself from the tower.

Mysterious signs appear—stones arranged in patterns, dead violets pressed between the pages of her books, cracks in mirrors, and cryptic messages etched in windowpanes. At last, Jayne discovers that there is a prisoner kept in the attic, a girl named Violet who turns out to be the illegitimate daughter of Red Bess. When Jayne confronts St. James with what she's learned he claims that the girl has inherited her mother's violent propensities and she must be locked up for her own safety.

But as Jayne spends more time with Violet, she sees she's sensitive, gentle, and intelligent. She eagerly reads all the books Jayne gives her, devouring the fairy tales of captive girls—"Beauty and the Beast," "Bluebeard," "Rapunzel"—but when Jayne gives her *Jane Eyre*, Violet becomes distraught.

"I am Bertha," she cries. "I am the madwoman in the attic."

In a blind rage, Violet sets the house on fire and Jayne risks her life to save her. They escape out onto the roof and climb down a trellis to safety, but as they struggle through the smoke and fog they hear the baying of the guard dogs and run toward the cliff. St. James appears out of the fog, badly burned and raging, aiming a pistol at them. But before he can fire, he sees a shape appearing out of the fog and—screaming "Red Bess!"—falls to his death.

Jayne and Violet walk to the edge of the cliff and look over to see St. James lying on the rocks below, his neck broken. "You're free now," Jayne says, turning to Violet and holding out her hand. She sees Violet hesitate, still afraid to leave Wyldcliffe Heights, the only home she's ever known. "*We're* free," Violet says, taking her friend's hand as they step over the edge of the cliff.

To climb down the cliff path and cross the marshes to the train station and a new life in the city? Or to plunge to their deaths? Fans have argued for both readings. Veronica didn't say, instead ending with the cryptic line *Dear Reader, what more would you have me say?*

I read the last lines through bleary eyes and fall asleep to the sound of rain from the river and dream of *The Secret of Wyldcliffe Heights.*

I am on the headland, running through the mists, following the call of the foghorns to the river, my feet bare, my skimpy nightgown—a garment unlike any I have ever owned in my waking life—in tatters. Behind me I hear the thud of footsteps coming as fast and hard as my heartbeats, gaining ground, coming closer—

I turn to look over my shoulder and there it is—a yellow eye glaring at me, only the yellow eye twins itself in the mist, turning into the eyes of a ravening beast that gathers itself and leaps—

I awake Monday morning in a tangle of bedsheets, feeling as if I've been running all night. It's not the first time I've had the dream about the fog-beast. My psychiatrist at Woodbridge, Dr. Husack, said the fog-beast represented all my fears and that the dream came in times of stress. It's not hard to pinpoint the *stressors* looming over me right now.

I haven't finished the reader's report for Diane.

I've sent a letter to Veronica St. Clair that will lose me a reference.

I'll be out of a job in a week—

Or sooner if Veronica gets that letter and calls Kurtis Chadwick to complain.

And then not only will I be unemployed, I'll be thrown out of the Josephine. I'll have no place to live and I'll have to go crawling back to Woodbridge.

I suppress the urge to cry in self-pity and pull myself up to shower and get dressed. After I fill up my travel mug in the lounge, I walk briskly down Washington Street, joining the early morning commute. I've loved feeling part of the great throng of the city's workforce—from the restaurant owners putting out their chalkboard signs to the office workers in smart outfits and the galleristas in artful ensembles.

I walk quickly so I'll be early enough to type up my reader's report before Diane gets in. Gloria is already here, of course; I sometimes think she sleeps in the office, tucked in between the filing cabinets. She peers out of her office as I come in. I wave, hoping I can get to my desk without engaging in conversation, but I hear the shuffle of her rubber-soled shoes before my feet hit the third step.

"You didn't give me anything to mail on Friday," she says, "but I remember quite a few letters coming for Miss St. Clair. Did you forget about them?"

I pause on the stairs, caught. "You were already gone when I came out of Mr. Chadwick's office so I mailed them myself."

Not an outright lie, I remind myself, just one of omission. Could she already have received a call from Veronica St. Clair? But she only says, "Good. You did the right thing. You may not think a writer as famous as Miss St. Clair cares about fan mail, but I happen to know she depends on those letters from her readers."

"Of course," I say, wanting to sink through the floor. "Well—there's a reader's report I need to type up—"

"You don't have your own laptop at home, do you?"

"No—" I begin, feeling as if I've been caught in another lie. I'm sure I must have told her at my interview that I did.

"Or a smartphone?"

"Just a dumb phone," I say, my cheeks burning. "I can't really afford a fancy one."

She gives me a rare look of sympathy. "I'll talk to Mr. Chadwick about keeping you on for a few more weeks. Buyout or not, we'll be here for a bit longer and there's room in our budget for your modest salary—don't go looking for a raise, mind you!"

Then she turns abruptly away before I can thank her, as if she's embarrassed by this unusual act of sentimental kindness. I'm left feeling worse than ever as I climb to the attic. I should have told her about the letter I sent to Veronica St. Clair. When Kurtis Chadwick finds out it won't matter that Gloria's found room in the budget for my modest salary; I'll be out on my ear without a reference.

I sink miserably into my chair and write up my reader's report then attach it to an email to Diane.

I get through that day and the rest of the week without being called down to Gloria's office, flinching at each creak on the staircase, every ping of incoming email raising an alarm in my head. *Now they know Now they know Now they know.* Kayla and Hadley are polite but distant, as if they don't want any association with someone who's broken company policy. And Atticus—

I'd been afraid that he'd act embarrassed by our *moment* in the Josephine ballroom, but he acts as if nothing happened at all, which is worse because it means nothing *did* happen. It had been my imagination. He doesn't even ask if I'd gotten into trouble for sneaking him in.

On Thursday, just before five o'clock, the call comes in the form of an email from Mr. Chadwick himself with the subject line: *Please come to my office IMMEDIATELY.* I can feel Kayla and Hadley's eyes on me as I gather my belongings into my tote bag. If I'm being fired, I don't want to have to come back up.

As I walk down the stairs I hear voices coming from Diane's office but when I hit the creaky last step on the landing they abruptly stop. By the time I pass Diane's open door Gloria is stagily discussing the spring production schedule and she, Atticus, and Diane are all studiously avoiding looking at me. *They all know,* I think, shifting my gaze to the wall where I catch the eye of the woman on the cover of *The Secret of Wyldcliffe Heights. If I were you,* I can almost hear her telling me, *I'd make a run for it, too.*

Kurtis Chadwick is at his desk when I come in, hands clasped in front of him, head down as if in prayer. Maybe he's praying for patience; I don't think he's praying for me. I stand awkwardly for a moment until he looks up at me.

"Agnes Corey," he says, then looks back down again as if matching me to a picture in the folder. "I've been reviewing your résumé again and I had a few questions. This Woodbridge School you taught at, isn't it some kind of reform school?"

"They don't call them that anymore," I say automatically. "But . . . yes, basically. It's a juvenile detention center."

"And how did you come to teach there?" he asks.

I could tell the story I usually tell, that I interned there while going to college, but I can already guess where this is going and I might as well get it over with. "I was a student there—a resident—from age thirteen to eighteen, placed there by the state."

"I see," he says, leaning back. "And may I ask how you came to be 'placed there by the state'?"

In fact, I think, *he's really not supposed to ask.*

Your juvenile records are sealed, my social worker assured me when I turned eighteen. No employer, school official, or police officer has a right to ask about it. I could tell him this but when I look up, I see that he's leaning forward, hands clasped, brow furrowed, a look of compassion on his face that nearly undoes me. After the tension of thinking I was about to be exposed for writing to Veronica St. Clair, his regard feels like slipping into a warm bath. The truth just spills out.

"I was placed there after running away from three foster homes," I confess, "and getting picked up for vagrancy and shoplifting when I was on the run."

"That must have been terrible," he says, leaning back. "I can only imagine what those homes were like. How—again, if you don't mind me asking—did you end up in foster care? What happened to your parents?"

"It was only ever my mother and me," I say. "I never knew my father. And my mother . . . she wasn't really well. She had mental health issues. We kind of moved from place to place for a while and then she was institutionalized and I was put in foster care."

"What a rough start to life, Agnes," he says, shaking his head. "I'm impressed with how far you've come . . . what about your mother? Is she still . . . in an institution?"

I shake my head and feel, to my horror, a tear streak down my face. "She was released three years ago. The last time she tried to contact me I told her I didn't want to see her anymore, which I know sounds awful—"

"Not at all, Agnes," he says, pushing a box of tissues toward me. "Sometimes we have to protect ourselves from toxic people in our lives. You're a bright young woman with a lot of promise. Which is what I was writing in my recommendation letter for you, but then I received a most peculiar letter."

"A letter?" I parrot dumbly.

He shuffles the papers on his desk, looking for the letter as if he received dozens a day—as if anyone wrote letters anymore—and finally produces a sheet of typescript. He chuckles. "Dear Veronica, such a Luddite! She insists on corresponding by snail mail."

I suck in my breath and cross my arms over my chest, digging my nails into my arm.

"She says here that you wrote her a note asking for a sequel."

"I-I did," I admit. "I'm so sorry. I know I shouldn't have. Gloria said not to and I know you didn't want anyone bothering her."

"No," he says gravely. "You see, poor Veronica, she's never been very . . . *stable*. Who can blame her, growing up in that secluded old house? And then the fire . . ."

"I'm so sorry I wrote her," I say again, dangerously close to tears once more. "I'll understand if you don't feel you can write me a recommendation—"

"No, I won't be writing you a recommendation," he says, confirming my worst fears, but then he adds, "because you won't be needing another job. Veronica St. Clair has offered to employ you as an amanuensis, which is—"

"Someone to take dictation," I finish before he can explain the word.

"Well," he says, smiling indulgently, "a bit more than that. It's someone with a feel for language. Someone Veronica would be comfortable with and trust—and whom *I* could trust would be up to the job. Gloria tells me that you are an excellent typist, have good handwriting—apparently a rare skill amongst your generation—and are always polite and punctual, all of which are just what's needed to be an amanuensis. So, what do you say," he concludes, flinging one hand toward the river as if my ship were waiting there for me. "Are you willing to go up to Wyldcliffe Heights and get that sequel from Veronica St. Clair for us?"

CHAPTER FIVE

Reader, I said yes.

What else could I do when he was offering me a chance to meet my idol and be the first person to read—to *hear*—the sequel to *The Secret of Wyldcliffe Heights*? Never mind that it was a job offer and a chance to get out of the Josephine.

"Good," he says briskly once I agree. "Gloria will go over the arrangements with you. She has moved some things around so you'll be able to stay on the payroll here at Gatehouse, and I expect you to keep us apprised of the progress of the book. Gloria is arranging to get you a laptop. Emailed pages as you type them would be ideal. Then I'll be able to judge the shape of the book and make plans accordingly." He smiles. "If all is going well, I may be able to avoid the buyout and offer you a permanent job here when you're done. How does that sound, Agnes?"

I tell him it sounds very good indeed. When I get up, he stretches out his hand. "Thank you, Agnes," he says, squeezing my hand. "I'm not sure you really understand what you've taken on, and I would feel myself unwise in placing such a burden on your young shoulders if I wasn't completely confident that *you* are the right person for the job."

I leave him feeling as if I'm the one doing *him* a favor by taking the job.

When I step into the hallway I hear voices coming from Diane's office that once again halt as I reach her door. This time, though, they're all looking at me.

"Is everything okay?" Gloria asks me.

"Yes," I tell her. "Mr. Chadwick says I'm supposed to see you about the . . . 'arrangements'?"

"So you're going to take it?" she asks.

"Of course she is," Diane says. "I knew you would as soon as Gloria showed me the letter from Veronica. What a clever idea, Agnes," she says, looking at me with newfound respect, "writing to the dragon lady herself and demanding a sequel. That took balls!"

"I didn't exactly *demand*," I say, glancing uneasily at Gloria to see what she has to say about my infraction, but she's busily straightening a pile of books on Diane's desk and doesn't meet my eye.

"I'd better go downstairs and get things ready so you can leave tomorrow," Gloria says.

"Tomorrow? Mr. Chadwick didn't say anything about going tomorrow."

"Unless you have a previous engagement?" Gloria asks, raising one eyebrow above the rim of her glasses.

"N-no . . ." I stutter, feeling Atticus's eyes on me.

"Miss St. Clair has advanced a sum to pay any expenses involved in your relocation and travel. When you've gotten your belongings, come down to my office and I'll explain everything."

She brushes past me, leaving me standing dumbstruck.

"Don't mind Gloria, kid," Diane says. "She likes to do things by the book. This is great news. A sequel to *The Secret of Wyldcliffe*

Heights will save the company. That was gutsy of you to write to Veronica."

"Thanks," I say, basking in the warm glow of Diane's approval. So what if Gloria is peeved at me for breaking a silly rule. *Rules are for the unimaginative,* my mother always said. "'Fortune favors the bold,'" I say aloud, finishing what my mother would say just before doing something reckless.

I glance at Atticus, hoping to see the same warmth and gratitude that had come from Diane, but he looks nervously away. "Well," I say, "I'd better get downstairs to finalize the arrangements with Gloria."

Atticus follows me out the door. "Hey," he says, catching up to me at the stairs. "Can we talk a moment?" He's raking his hair back off his face, clearly nervous. Is he thinking about our *moment* in the ballroom? Maybe he doesn't want me to leave.

"Sure," I say. "What's up?"

"I just wanted to make sure you've thought carefully about what you're doing. Are you sure you want to take this job?"

"Why wouldn't I?" I ask, surprised. "I'll get to meet Veronica St. Clair and work with her on the sequel to *The Secret of Wyldcliffe Heights.*"

"Do you really want to be stuck up in that old house—" He lowers his voice and gestures for me to move closer. "I told Hadley about the photograph you showed me of Veronica St. Clair at the Josephine and she said she's done some research for the book she's writing and learned there were rumors about Veronica in the clubs back then. She was into that goth scene in a really hard-core way, like seances and sacrifices and black magic—"

"That was thirty years ago," I say, trying not to show how upset I am that he talked to Hadley about the photograph. What else had he told her about what happened at the Josephine? "It was part of that whole scene. It wasn't supposed to be *real*."

"No? Did you know that she was involved in a girl's death? She would have gone to jail for it but her father was a wealthy doctor who ran a mental hospital upstate. He was able to get her remanded there instead of going to jail. That's the real Wyldcliffe Heights—a mental hospital. She wrote the book while she was a patient there and then, when her father died—in a fire many think *she* set—she inherited the estate. She closed down the hospital, boarded up the burnt-out tower, and went on living there. That's where you're going, Agnes, to an abandoned mental hospital presided over by a madwoman and murderer. If you don't believe me, talk to Hadley or look up the stories online."

When he's done, he sucks in a long breath, puffing out his cheeks, and blows it out as if exhausted by his speech. I stare at him, stunned and betrayed, not just because he told Hadley about the photograph but because he's stumbled upon my worst fear and made it real.

"Maybe that's where I belong," I retort. "Anyway, I've been to worse places." Then I turn on my heel and leave before he can see the tears fall.

I STOP ON the second-floor landing thinking about what Atticus said. There was something to it. I've seen rumors on fan sites about the history of the real Wyldcliffe Heights—that it was a women's training school and then a mental hospital and even that Veronica St. Clair had been a patient there. But I've always chosen not to focus on that part of the author's biography. While there were scores of references to madness and confinement in the book— halls laid out like the meanderings of a disordered mind, spiral staircases tightening like the arms of a straitjacket—I had always thought they were metaphorical. Perhaps, though, they were references to the real mental hospital that the house was based on.

On the landing where I stand there is a bookcase. It doesn't take long to locate a copy of *The Secret of Wyldcliffe Heights*—a large-print edition with a glossy violet-bestrewn cover. I flip to the back jacket flap. There's no author photo, only a threadbare author bio: *Veronica St. Clair grew up in the Hudson Valley in the real-life Wyldcliffe Heights, where she still lives today and is at work on her next novel.*

Over the years I've googled my favorite author's name but have found little more. There are fan sites aplenty with conjectures and rumors—that she came from an old family related to the Astors and Montgomerys, that she had a sheltered childhood and was privately tutored, and that she inherited the family estate and still lived there. Maybe there were rumors that she was connected to a girl's death at the Josephine and that her father ran a mental hospital, but there were also rumors that she was descended from witches, that she was really a man, that she wrote erotica under a pseudonym, and that there was a hidden message encoded into the book that revealed her true identity.

The theories tended to get more outlandish the deeper one dug on the web. Hadley's story was no doubt from one of those sites. *But what,* I ask myself, putting the book back and continuing down the stairs, *does it matter?* If Veronica St. Clair had been there when some punk rocker died and her father whisked her away to his private clinic, that was thirty years ago. It wasn't a hospital *now.* I am going to Veronica St. Clair's home as an *amanuensis,* not a patient.

I find Gloria tapping away at her computer, her glasses reflecting the green letters on the screen, her ancient printer spitting out sheets of paper. "That's your contract," she says. "Take it and read it."

I quickly scan the paper. It says I'll be working as a personal assistant at a rate of $1,000 a week, twice what I made as a teacher at Woodbridge, for a period of six months with an option to renew.

"Six months?" I ask, signing the contract.

"With an option to renew, but frankly, if we don't have a book by then we'll be underwater," Gloria says, tapping away at her keyboard. Another sheet spits out of the printer. "That's your NDA. You have to agree not to divulge any personal details of Ms. St. Clair's life or post any pictures of her or her house on social media."

Another sheet spits out as I'm signing the NDA. "That's your train ticket. You leave Penn Station at 9:03 tomorrow morning. I've wired a thousand dollars into your bank account and"—she swivels her chair ninety degrees, opens the bottom drawer of her desk, and removes a gunmetal-gray box—"I'm authorized to give you two hundred dollars from petty cash for travel expenses."

She deals out ten crisp twenties from a stack of bills like a Las Vegas croupier, then counts them again before holding them out to me. Only then does she look me in the eye. "Any questions?"

A million, I think, but then I recognize the look in her eyes from a dozen social workers over the years. She took a chance on me by giving me this job and I disobeyed her by writing to Veronica St. Clair. "No," I say, taking the money quickly so I won't have to see the look of disappointment on her face any longer, "I think you've answered them all."

On the way back to the Josephine I stop at an ATM to verify the wire transfer and take out another $300. Then I go to the fancy grocery store on Bank Street where Kayla and Hadley always get their lunches and buy a can of fizzy wine and a gourmet cheese and fruit plate. I stash them at the bottom of my bag so Roberta won't see them and know I'm planning to defy both the no alcohol and the no eating in your room rules. *Rules are for the unimaginative,* my mother sings in my ear, *fortune favors the bold.* Roberta Jenkins is on her way out when I get to her office but she sits back down at her desk when she sees me.

"Here's the back rent I owe," I tell her, handing her $460. "I got a job upstate and I have to leave tomorrow. I know I'm supposed to give two weeks' notice so I've included two weeks' extra rent." I wonder why I'm more nervous now than I was with Kurtis Chadwick and Gloria, and when she lifts her head, I know it's because I am waiting for a look of approval. But all I get is puzzlement and worry.

"Are you in trouble, Agnes, is that why you're leaving town in such a hurry? And where'd you get this money?"

I try to laugh off the sting of her first assumption. "I told you—I got a job. Upstate. And it comes with a stipend."

"A *stipend,*" she repeats. "Fancy. What kind of job is this? And where exactly upstate? Are you sure you know what you're getting yourself into?"

She must think I've answered some sketchy ad on Craigslist. "I'm going to Wyldcliffe Heights to work for Veronica St. Clair," I tell her. "Remember we were just talking about her?"

"To Wyldcliffe Heights?" she asks skeptically. "Honey, that's not a real place."

This is not going the way I had imagined. Now she thinks I'm delusional. "Actually, it is," I say, sounding as pedantic as Atticus.

"It's the home of Veronica St. Clair in a town called Wyldcliffe-on-Hudson a hundred miles north of here. I'm taking the train tomorrow." I fish out my ticket and hand it to her. "I'm going to be her assistant while she writes the sequel to *The Secret of Wyldcliffe Heights*."

Roberta Jenkins studies my train ticket and then looks up at me. She still seems skeptical. "A sequel? After all these years? And you'll be helping with it? Well, isn't that something. If you're sure, Agnes. Can you give me an address to reach you at? And a phone number?"

I give her the mailing address I've written dozens of times but tell her I don't know the phone number. I promise to email it to her when I get there. She looks at the address I've written down as if I've given her the directions to Narnia, but then she arranges her features into an expression of supportive belief that seems at war with her habitual skepticism.

"This looks like it could be a good opportunity for you, Agnes. I hope you make the most of it. But just in case, I'll hold on to your two weeks' notice money as an advance on your first two weeks rent if you should decide to come back."

THE WINE AND cheese don't taste quite as celebratory as I thought they would. The wine gives me a headache and the rich cheese sits in my stomach like a stone. I drift off to sleep with Atticus's melodramatic warnings echoing in my head. *Look up the stories online,* he'd said.

I wake up in the dark with Atticus's words repeating in my head. Easy for him with his smartphone and tablet and laptop. All I have is a cheap pay-as-you-go flip phone. There is, though, a computer downstairs in the lounge for the residents' use. Maybe it's not a bad idea to do some research on the place where I've just agreed to live for six months.

I take the stairs down because I don't trust the Josephine's rickety old elevator and let myself into the lounge, which smells like burnt coffee and stale baked goods. The hulking IBM computer is older than the one in Gloria's office and takes forever to boot up. The Wi-Fi connection is weaker than the coffee. I type *Wyldcliffe Heights, Wyldcliffe-on-Hudson, NY* into the search bar and wait so long I expect to get no results but then, finally, a page opens with three links. One's for a restaurant in Wyldcliffe, one's for a wellness center in the Berkshires, and one's for a site called Haunted Hudson Valley. I click on the last one. A sepia-toned photograph of a decrepit stone building covered with ivy, glimpsed through shaggy overgrown trees, appears. Scrolling down I find an old-fashioned illustration of a stately imposing building labeled "The Magdalen House for Wayward Women" and an entry in florid Victorian type.

One of the most haunted locations in the Hudson Valley can be found behind stone pillars, brick walls, and overgrown forest on a promontory overlooking the river. Wyldcliffe Heights was built by the Hale family in 1848, converted into a Magdalen refuge in the 1890s, and then a women's training school in the 1920s by progressive reformer Josephine Hale, who had inherited the estate. One of its most notorious inmates was Bess Molloy, aka Red Bess, who had been convicted of murdering six young women in a settlement house. In the 1960s it became a psychiatric treatment center for troubled teens run by Dr. Robert Sinclair, who subsequently married Josephine's daughter, Eliza Bryce. Dr. Sinclair's methods, which relied on hypnotism, past-life regression, and electroshock therapy, were called into question in the 1990s after he was killed in a fire set by one of his patients. His daughter, author Veronica St. Clair, inherited the house and still lives there today. Many believe her neo-gothic novel The Secret of Wyldcliffe Heights *was based on her experiences as her father's patient and in the goth scene in New York City. As for ghosts, take your pick! There's Red Bess, said to have hung herself in the tower; the mad Dr. Sinclair, burning through eternity; or perhaps Veronica St. Clair herself, who some believe died in the fire and now haunts her decaying ancestral home. No wonder she's never written a sequel to her bestselling novel—*Dead Women Tell No Tales!

I grow cold reading this loathsome entry, but more with anger than fear. When I try to click on the site's home page the link fails . . . and then the Wi-Fi goes down entirely. The modem is in Roberta's office, which is locked, but I know she keeps a spare key on top of the door ledge. *It won't take a minute to restart the modem,* I tell myself, walking down the dark hall, and Roberta would want me to find out everything I can about my new job.

Halfway down the hall, though, I'm arrested by an ear-splitting screech coming from Roberta's office that raises the hairs on the back of my neck. It sounds like an animal caught in a snare, but when the sound comes again, I realize it's the noise those old filing cabinets make. Someone's in the office. Could it be Roberta, come back because she forgot something? But Roberta lives in the Bronx and I can't picture her riding the subway all the way here in the middle of the night. Besides, wouldn't she have turned the hall light on?

I take a tentative step forward, wondering if I should go back to the lounge and call the police, and the rustling in the office stops. Whoever's in there has heard me. I freeze, caught between the desire to run and a spike of anger—*who would dare steal from Roberta Jenkins?* Before anger and fear can battle it out the door bangs open and the hallway fills with a flashlight beam that hits me in the face. I fling my arm up to protect my eyes, anticipating worse, and then I hear retreating footsteps and I'm left in the dark. There's a thump as the back door opens and then the clang of garbage cans falling in the alley. I stay still, listening for returning footsteps, but there aren't any. Finally, I inch forward and go into the office. The only light comes from a streetlamp outside the frosted glass window but it's enough to see the file drawer gaping open. It's the second from the top, the same drawer Roberta had opened to put my file back last week, which could be a coincidence—

But when I check I see that my file is missing.

CHAPTER SIX

I can't sleep the rest of the night thinking about the intruder. Why would anyone want my file, which told a sad, banal story of abandonment, foster homes, petty crimes, and state institutions? All of which would be embarrassing to have exposed, but it wasn't like anyone was going to blackmail me. For a moment I have a horrible image of Kayla or Hadley posting my record, including some unflattering mug shots, on social media on one of those anonymous accounts they're always gawking at, but even in my hyper-anxious state I know I'm being paranoid. Still, someone followed me from the office the night I mailed the letter to Veronica St. Clair and then, the day I got a reply and a job working for the author, my file was stolen. Maybe it's a good thing I'm leaving the city and the sooner the better.

I pack my scant belongings into my backpack and tote bag and head downstairs at first light. I want to be gone before Roberta is in. As soon as she sees that my file's missing, she'll suspect that I took it. After all, I've done it before.

I make one stop before I go—the ballroom mezzanine. I find the photograph of Veronica St. Clair, remove it from its frame, and slip it into my backpack. I feel a twinge of guilt at the theft, but it also somehow makes me feel as if I've got a connection with the famous author—as if we were both once wayward girls at the Josephine. And, I admit, now Hadley won't be able to get at it.

I'm two hours early for my train but I'm used to making myself invisible in train and bus stations. I buy an overpriced coffee and pastry and find a quiet corner where I can sit, cradling my backpack in my arms and scanning the crowds for anyone who could be my stalker. The crowd queueing for the 9:03 Ethan Allen Express looks bland and innocuous, as if they've stepped out of the pages of an L.L. Bean catalog in their corduroys and padded jackets, backpacks and canvas totes, loafers and rubber boots. I wait until the line starts moving to join it and look over my shoulder on the escalator and on the track until I get to the furthest car. I sit backward in the last aisle seat next to a teenage boy in a Bard sweatshirt reading Aristotle and keep my eye on the door at the other end of the car for anyone threatening.

I have a bad moment when the train goes into the tunnel and the lights flicker off, but then the train comes out and I see the Hudson, flowing gray beneath overcast skies, and the swaying of the train lulls me to sleep—

I am at the prow of a ship plowing through a thick fog, my face wet with mist, my wool cloak heavy with damp. I'm peering through the fog, trying to make out a shape assembling itself out of the gray. A light pierces through the murk and my heart leaps—It's a beacon leading us to safety!—but then my vision doubles and the shape gathers itself and pounces—

I startle awake to a man's voice shouting.

"Wyldcliffe-on-Hudson! Next station! Wyldcliffe-on-Hudson! Exit in the rear!"

As we come into the station the doors open and the car is flooded with the smell of the river. I try to peer out the windows but they're blurry with rain. It feels as if we're underwater, as if Wyldcliffe-on-Hudson were really Wyldcliffe-under-Hudson and that's where the fog-beast has dragged me.

I follow the rest of the passengers up an iron staircase and out into a crowded parking lot where taxis and Subaru Foresters jockey to pick up drenched passengers. I find a taxi that isn't occupied and ask the driver if I can get a ride to Wyldcliffe Heights, but he tells me that he's booked.

"How far is it?" I ask.

"About a mile," he says, pointing right. "Up River Road. It'll be twenty dollars."

"Really?" I ask, surprised. "I think I'll walk it."

He shrugs and starts to get in his cab but then turns back with a worried expression on his face. "Will you need a ride back?"

"No," I tell him, "I'm staying there."

The worried expression deepens. "At the Heights?" He digs a card out of his pocket and gives it to me. "When I get back, I'll take you free of charge."

Why the sudden eagerness? I wonder. I look down at the card and read the name *Spike Russo, Reporter,* New York Sun. He's a journalist—or was one, more likely, as I'm pretty sure the *Sun* doesn't exist anymore except as an online paper. Maybe he sees me as a source to the reclusive author Veronica St. Clair. Recalling my NDA, I say, "Thanks, but I can walk."

"Call me if you change your mind," he says, getting into his taxi. "Or if you need a ride back."

I don't bother reminding him that I'm staying there. I tighten the straps on my backpack and head up the sloped drive to the road. Spike the taxi driver hadn't told me that the mile to the Heights was all uphill and the road—narrow and bordered on one side by a high stone wall topped with iron spikes and towering sycamores on the other—has barely any shoulder to walk on. The pale, splotchy tree trunks look like bones covered with moss. The canopy, thinned by falling leaves, offers little protection from the rain, and the leaves, turned a rusty brown from the rain, are slippery underfoot. I'm drenched by the time I reach a pair of iron gates.

Which are locked.

I rattle them twice to make sure, getting nothing but rust stains on my hands for my trouble. Then I notice a flash of bronze on one of the pillars. Brushing wet leaves aside I find the words *Wyldcliffe Heights* inscribed above a metal grill and a recessed button that's so corroded it's hard to believe it will work, but I push it nonetheless. After a few seconds I hear a voice as rusty as the gates.

"Yes? What do you want?"

"I'm Agnes Corey," I shout into the grill, "the new assistant."

The only response is the grating sound the gates make, slowly inching open as if pushed by invisible hands. While I'm waiting for an opening large enough to step through, I notice there's another plaque on the pillar, all but obscured by corrosion. I peer closer to make out the words . . .

Psychiatric Treatment Center

So there had been something to Atticus's story.

The gates yawn open now, inviting me to step through. *To commit myself.*

You can leave anytime you like, I tell myself. *It's not like Woodbridge. You are here of your own free will.*

But it doesn't feel like that. It feels as if an invisible hand has been at my back ever since I wrote the letter to Veronica St. Clair, pushing me along to this precipice, and that one more step will begin a fall that I won't be able to stop—

But where else is there to go?

I've hesitated so long that the gates begin to close. As if they know I don't have any other choice. At the last moment I bolt through the narrow gap, catching my sleeve on an iron spike. I jerk my arm free and smell blood. When I pull back my arm, I see a long red streak as if a ravening beast had caught me in its jaws.

Only rust, I tell myself, *from a corroded spike.* Not blood, not the teeth of the fog-beast.

The driveway is even steeper than the road from the station and longer. It, too, is bordered by sycamore trees, which get closer as I ascend, hemming me in, their bare white branches reaching for me. When I pause at a turn in the drive and look back all I see are trees—no train station, no village; I can't even see the gate. *The forest wall,* Jayne calls it in *The Secret of Wyldcliffe Heights. We could hew it down every night and it would grow back by morning.* I take a breath to steel myself against the claustrophobic panic clawing at my throat and turn around—

And the house appears, as if the trees had parted to reveal it or some spell has been broken to make it visible. It's huge, built of stone that's more black than gray, and seems to be hewn from the cliff. A lone tower like the one where Jayne sees the ghost of Red Bess juts up to the sky. There's no one standing on the tower now, but as I start walking, I feel as if I'm being watched. When I look up again, I see that a light has appeared in the window. The final touch in the gothic romance cover. Am I supposed to flee now, clutching a tattered negligee to my bared breasts?

No, I think as I put my head down and continue my trudge up the hill, *I'm not going to be scared by atmospherics.* That light feels like a challenge that spurs me on over the rutted and overgrown drive, past a ruined fountain where a headless marble girl pours nothing into a dry cracked basin, to the foot of the tower—

Which is a ruin, a stone skeleton hollowed out by fire. Patches of sky show through its charred ribs. The light I saw is a reflection of the sun in a piece of broken glass in the window. It clings to the rest of the house like an atrophied limb. When the wind stirs, I smell wet ash and rotting wood. Who would choose to live with this reminder of death and disaster?

As I walk up the steps to the front door, I remember Haunted Hudson Valley's suggestion that Veronica St. Clair had really died in the fire and now haunts the decaying house. The hollow echo of my knock sounds as if the house is an empty shell. The woman who opens the door could be a ghost—pale, gray hair combed so tightly back from her face that her head resembles a skull, wearing a knee-length gray skirt, white button-down blouse, and a gray cardigan.

"I'm Agnes," I say, holding out my hand.

"Laeticia. I'm the housekeeper," she says without taking my hand. "You're wet."

"It rained," I say, stating the obvious. "And there were no cabs at the station."

She sniffs as if clearly both circumstances are my fault. "It rains often in the Hudson Valley. You'd best get used to it. And Miss St. Clair expects punctuality. Please wait in the atrium while I tell her you have arrived." She opens the door wider for me to pass but when she sees my backpack she shudders. "Leave your . . . luggage on the veranda. Syms will bring it up to your room."

I'm not happy letting my backpack out of my sight in case I need to make a hasty retreat, but I can see there's no point arguing with her. I step across the threshold and she erupts. "And take off your shoes! They're filthy!"

I shuck off my sodden sneakers and pad after her in wet socks across the cold marble floor of the cavernous atrium. She leads me to an equally cold marble bench and tells me to sit there, then glides toward the rear of the house, opening a glass-paned door that lets in a gust of damp air that swirls around me like an inquisitive ghost. When she closes the door behind her the glass panes shiver, setting off tremors in the wooden stairwell above me. I look up and see that the staircase loops upward into an elliptical spiral seemingly into infinity. It feels like being inside a nautilus shell.

"Miss St. Clair will see you now." The housekeeper has appeared from the opposite direction from which she went, as if we really are inside a spiral shell and she has crept, snail-like, around the outer loop. She leads me through the glass-paned door into a long room with tall arched windows framing a spectacular view of the Hudson River and the Catskill Mountains. The fog has lifted, but low ink-blue clouds hang over the mountains threatening more rain. I'm so absorbed in the view that I don't notice the woman until she clears her throat.

"Come closer."

She's sitting on a high-backed green velvet couch at the far end of the room, wearing a green velvet jacket and slacks that camouflage her like a woodland creature. Even her glasses are tinted green. As I approach, I can't help but compare her face to the one in the photo taken at the Josephine. Thirty years have aged her but she's still arresting—beautiful, even. Her hair is still mostly black except for two streaks of gray that spring from her smooth brow like the wings of a silver bird. Her skin is taut and unlined except for a mask of white scar tissue around her eyes.

I saw a statue once of a woman whose face was covered by a veil. That's what her face looks like—as if muffled by a sheer silk scarf. Her eyes—or what's left of them—are invisible behind the green lenses. She looks both older than her fifty-something years but also somehow timeless, as if she were indeed a statue. She doesn't move until I stop a few feet away and then she removes one hand from her sleeve and points to a straight-backed chair directly in front of her, quickly tucking her hand away, but not so quickly that I don't see the scars.

"So, you're Agnes Corey," she says, her voice a rusty rasp, as if she wasn't used to speaking.

The green lenses are turned directly toward my face and despite knowing that she is blind I feel seen when she says my name.

"Yes—" I swallow the *ma'am* that rises in my throat. "Ms. St. Clair. Mr. Chadwick said you wanted an assistant—"

"*You* wrote to me saying you wanted a sequel," she counters querulously, as if it's my fault I'm here.

"Lots of your readers do," I say. "I sent you the letters—"

A hand flutters in the air like a moth that has escaped her sleeve. "Yes, they all *say* that," she says, her hand dropping as if worn out by its brief flight, "but what do *they* know about what it takes. Why do *you* want it? Weren't you satisfied with the book?"

"Oh yes, of course—only I want *more.* I guess what I really want is to feel the way I felt when I read *The Secret of Wyldcliffe Heights* for the first time."

"And how was that?"

"Like I had escaped my life," I say before thinking.

"Has your life been so very unpleasant, Agnes Corey, that you've had need of an escape?" she asks with a slight tremor in her voice that might be pity or impatience.

I think of the long gray days at Woodbridge—the classes taught by teachers who didn't want to be there any more than we did, the sudden outbursts from girls who'd been pushed past their limits and the quick and brutal retaliation of the guards, a life of boredom punctuated by flashes of violence.

"Sometimes," I say. "But no worse than Jayne's and Violet's lives. I think that's it—I felt when I was reading *The Secret of Wyldcliffe Heights* that I wasn't alone, like when Violet says to Jayne, *Now that you're here I can bear anything.*"

"Has your life been so very lonely that you had need of imaginary friends?"

I study her face for censure or compassion but all I see is my own twinned reflection in her green lenses. I look very small and very alone in their underwater world.

"They felt real to me . . . only . . ."

"Only what?"

"I always felt as if they were keeping something from me, as if there was a story behind the story in the book . . . I suppose that's what I want."

"The story behind the story," she repeats, a slight smile curving her lips. "For that we'd have to go back to what happened before Jayne came to Wyldcliffe Heights."

"You mean . . . like a prequel?"

"Yes," she says, "and you'll have to take it down by hand. I won't tell my story to a machine."

"Of course—" I begin.

"And you'll have to type what you've written each night on a manual typewriter." She gestures toward a desk with a large hulking typewriter on top of it. "I won't have you sending my words out into the ether before they're ready."

"That's fine," I say, "although Mr. Chadwick did say he'd like to see drafts."

"Kurtis can wait like everyone else. I'll tell my story to you, Agnes Corey, and no one else and I'll say when it's ready to go out into the world. You are not to post, tweet, chirp, or whatever else your generation does these days, any of what I tell you."

"Understood," I reply, wondering how I'll explain these conditions to Mr. Chadwick.

She keeps her eyes on mine without speaking for so long I feel as if she's *staring* at me and then she says, "There's one more thing."

What other condition could there possibly be? I wonder. *Will I have to spin hay into gold or carry water in a sieve?*

"I'd like to touch your face," she says, "so I know to whom I'm telling my story."

"Oh," I say. "I'm not . . ." I'm about to say *pretty,* but then I blush, realizing that she can hardly care about that. "All right," I say, "do I . . ."

"Come sit by me," she says, patting the seat beside her.

I get up and lower myself to the couch, gingerly, as if I might injure her. Her hands, released again, hover in front of my face and I close my eyes. They flutter over my forehead, nose, cheeks, chin, the pads of her scarred fingertips as delicate as silk. I wait for her to say something until I realize I no longer feel her touch on my skin. When I open my eyes, I'm alone on the couch. As if it had been a ghost touching my face.

CHAPTER SEVEN

Laeticia is waiting for me in the atrium, standing so still in her gray and white that she might be a statue—*The Silent Servant,* it might be called—until she speaks, that is.

"I will show you to your room now," she says, turning toward the stairs without waiting for a response from me.

"Um . . . my shoes?" I ask, hating how meek I sound.

She points to the marble bench without looking back. Instead of my sneakers I see a pair of worn leather slippers lined up beneath the bench.

"I've left your shoes in the mudroom." She points left to a door leading out of the atrium. "You are to leave your outside shoes there so as not to bring filth into the house."

By the time I've shoved my feet into the too small slippers and caught up to her on the stairs she's gone on to her second dictum.

"You are to enter and exit the house through the mudroom and leave all outerwear there—" She looks over her shoulder and frowns at my denim jacket. "I hope you brought something warmer. It gets quite cold in the Hudson Valley—and damp."

I see what she means about the cold. Although it should be getting warmer as we go up, a frigid breeze follows us up the stairs. It's joined on the first landing by a chill draft emanating from an open door. I peer though it and see a long narrow hallway that seems to extend into a shadowy infinity.

"You will have no need to go into the west wing," she says, leading me up the next flight. "It is closed off and is not structurally sound. By no means attempt to go into it."

"Is that where the tower is?" I ask. "The one that was damaged in the fire?"

"Damaged?" she repeats, curling her lip. "It was *gutted*. Do not go near it. The rest of the grounds are open to you for your exercise and recreation but I would advise staying away from the cliff walk as it has eroded over the years and the drop is quite steep."

"Exercise and recreation" sounds like something granted to prisoners or inmates of an asylum. All of this—the surrendering of my shoes, the list of rules, the unforgiving cold—feels like my first day at Woodbridge.

"How do I get out the front gate?" I ask. "Is there a code to open it?"

She pauses on the third-floor landing and turns to me. "This is not a prison, Miss Corey. There is a button on the inside of the gates that opens them and you have only to ring to gain reentry. You are free to come and go as you please. Miss St. Clair only asks that you do not engage in conversation about her or the house with locals or allow any on the grounds. We have had some trouble with intruders over the years—looky-loos who trespass and then post malicious gossip on the internet about Miss St. Clair and the family."

I wonder if she's referring to the Haunted Hudson Valley site. "How long have you been with the family?" I ask.

I had not thought it possible for Laeticia's skin to go any whiter but at my question she turns a shade paler than the marble bust she has stopped in front of. "I have never been with the *family*. I am *with* Miss St. Clair and have been for thirty years. I nursed her after she nearly died in the fire and I won't let anyone hurt her. Do you understand, Miss Corey?"

She has moved an inch closer to me while delivering this impassioned speech, backing me against the banister until I feel it biting into the small of my back. I'm so shocked by her sudden vehemence, the anger rising off her colder than the draft I feel at my back, that I can't speak. I nod and mouth the words "Yes, ma'am."

She holds my gaze for a moment and then turns briskly away. "Your room is this way."

After Laeticia's draconian warnings I'm expecting a cell of a room, but when I follow her through an open door off the east side of the atrium, I find myself in a spacious, airy chamber. A large four-poster bed, covered with a faded floral quilt, faces a wide bay window, glazed with watery green glass. A small writing desk, with a brass lamp topped by a green glass globe, sits beneath the window. Everything in the room is green or lavender, from the faded quilt to the old-fashioned wallpaper with intertwining vines and pale mauve violets.

"This was Miss St. Clair's room," Laeticia says, moving to the bed to smooth an invisible wrinkle. "She stays on the first floor now because she can't manage the stairs. She particularly instructed me to ready this room for you—" She sniffs as if to question her mistress's generosity. "Not that it was difficult. I regularly change the bedding and dust and air the room."

"That's—" I begin, but before I can voice my gratitude—or wonder why she keeps an unused room ready—Laeticia interrupts.

"Here is your bathroom." She opens a door to a room tiled in green and lavender and smelling of violet-scented bath salts. *My own bathroom.* I've never not had to share one before. I follow her back to the bedroom, where she opens a walk-in closet that's bigger than my room at the Josephine. "I imagine there's sufficient room for your wardrobe." She gives my backpack, which has been left on the floor, a disdainful look and then turns to leave. "Don't forget—eight a.m. sharp in the library."

For all her brusqueness I feel a sudden panic as she prepares to leave, the way I'd felt at Woodbridge when I was on lockdown and the matron would turn the key in the lock. "What's that door to?" I ask, noticing a door beside the bed that's nearly camouflaged by the wallpaper.

"That leads to the attic. You'll have no need to go there." Then she leaves me, closing the door behind her. I listen for the turn of a key but of course there is none. I am not a prisoner here. I am the amanuensis, in a pretty room, the kind of room I dreamed about when I read *The Secret of Wyldcliffe Heights.* A room with a secret staircase to the attic—

Where Jayne glimpses the ghost of Red Bess.

I stare at the door for a full minute and then wrench it open swiftly as if I'm trying to catch an intruder. There's only an empty staircase leading up into darkness. There's no lock on the door, which means I'll have to sleep next to an unlocked door leading up to . . . what? What's in the attic that Laeticia doesn't want me to see?

I head up the stairs before letting myself think about it and come into a long high-raftered room crossed by beams of light that slant in through small windows set in the eaves. The spaces in between the bars of light are dark and dusty. As my eyes adjust to the variegated light, I see that the whole long vaulted attic is filled with discarded furniture, wooden packing crates, cardboard boxes, and, at the far end, a figure staring back at me. All the blood drains from my face in the seconds it takes me to realize it's only a reflection in the mirrored doors of a huge wardrobe. Even then, I still feel cold. There's something about the hulking piece of furniture carved out of dark wood that makes me think of caskets and crypts and old vampire movies. I'll never be able to sleep with that thing lurking up here unless I know what's in it.

I pick my way through the boxes, my reflection in the mirror growing larger as if coming to meet me, until I'm standing in front of the wardrobe, my pale face in the mottled mirror staring back as if through brackish water. It doesn't look like me at all. It looks, rather, as if there were a stranger trapped inside the wardrobe peering out at me.

It's such a horrible thought I have to open the doors to banish it, but when I raise my hand, it's trembling so hard I fumble with the key to unlock them. The whole wardrobe shakes as I turn the key, the old wood and rusted hinges squealing as if someone were inside trying to get out.

I wrench both doors open at the same time—

And find just exactly what I feared: a woman hanging inside, her white throat bared—

The ghost of Red Bess, just as Jayne finds her.

No, not Red Bess, only a long red cloak made out of deep crimson wool, its ermine-lined hood dangling limply as a broken neck, swaying as if she's only just been hung.

I feel stupid having been fooled by the swaying cloak, as if I've been caught falling for a prank, and I make my way back across the attic with studied slowness as if proving to invisible watchers that I am not afraid. I even stop to inspect a few boxes. I find wooden crates with shipping labels from New York, London,

Paris, Rome, and half a dozen European cities I don't recognize. Opening one I see it's filled with crystal glasses. Another holds porcelain doorknobs. Some have been emptied of their original contents—tea, imported cheeses from France, English biscuits— and now hold records from when the estate was a Magdalen refuge, and then a training school, and, finally, a mental hospital. I pull out a file from a box labeled "Magdalen" filled with birth certificates of babies born to inmates of the Magdalen refuge in the 1890s. As I'm putting it back something flutters to the floor. When I pick it up I see it's a sepia-toned photograph of a young woman staring at the camera, her dark hair parted in a straight white line, her mouth unsmiling, her skin so pale she almost fades into the background. Her eyes, though, have not faded with time. They stare out of the photograph as if daring anyone to look back at her. When I turn it over, I find a name and date written in faint pencil.

Bess Molloy, 1923.

For the second time today, I've come face-to-face with Red Bess. I slip the photograph in my pocket and hurry out of the attic before I see her a third time, which, according to legend, is when she kills.

Back down in my room, I find a large rectangular basket on the writing desk. It's one of those fancy hampers that come from England—Diane got one once from a grateful author—but instead of containing caviar and tinned biscuits like Diane's, it holds my dinner and a note from Laeticia.

Miss St. Clair thought you'd want to dine in your room today to recover from your travels. From now on though I will leave your dinner basket in the atrium for you to collect. She expects you in the library promptly at 8 a.m. tomorrow morning.

I start the tub, unpacking the basket while it fills. There's a thermos of soup, a chicken pot pie, a slice of apple pie, a wedge of cheese, warm rolls wrapped in a linen napkin, and apple cider. I end up devouring it all before the enormous tub is three-quarters full. Then, my hunger sated, I sink into the hot water. I close my eyes and tip my head back until the water cradles my scalp. A memory of my mother holding my head in a bath comes to me but I can't remember us ever living anywhere with a bathtub. Mostly we lived in motels, trailer courts, and basement apartments with shoddy plumbing and poor water pressure. I keep my eyes closed to relive the rare memory of maternal tenderness, searching for something to hold on to to prove it's real. As I sink further into the water, I can still feel the hand cradling my head but the water has turned cold. I open my eyes and look up through the water at a face that blurs and wavers as if it's been rubbed out by an eraser—a face that recedes into the shadows like a ghost being dragged back to hell, getting further and further away—

Because I am drowning in the cold water.

I splutter to the surface, clutching the sides of the tub, coughing up bathwater. *I fell asleep,* I tell myself, wrenching myself out of the tub, *and slipped under the water,* which had turned cold. That's why I had that dream, a new nightmare to add to the fog-beast one. I wrap myself in a thick terry robe that's hanging on the back of the door, rubbing the coarse cloth roughly against my skin to banish the cold. It's only because I had seen that picture of Bess Molloy that I gave the woman in my nightmare her face.

CHAPTER EIGHT

I wake up the next morning with a crick in my neck as if it had been broken like Red Bess's. I look at the clock on the night table and see that it's 7:30. I've only got a half hour before reporting to Veronica St. Clair.

I splash cold water on my face and brush my teeth, then dress in my one wrinkled button-down shirt, plaid skirt, and cardigan—my standard work uniform and as close as I ever got to Hadley's retro-librarian look. I pin my hair back with some bobby pins I find in the medicine cabinet. Veronica St. Clair may not be able to see me, but dressing the part makes me feel like I am here to do a job.

Walking down the spiral stairs makes me a little dizzy. When I reach the atrium, I have to steady myself by gripping the carved newel post. A bobby pin slips out of my hair as if it's been undone by my twisting progress. As I lift a hand to push it back I hear a man's voice.

"I wouldn't keep her waiting if I were you."

I turn toward the voice coming from the mudroom, expecting that this will be Syms, who took my offensive luggage upstairs. I'm picturing a relic on the model of a butler from *Downton Abbey*. But the dark-haired man leaning in the doorway, muscular arms folded across a straining T-shirt, looks my age.

"Syms?" I say doubtfully, wondering if I've interrupted a house-breaker. Although he's in the doorway to the mudroom, where we're supposed to abandon our "outside shoes," he's wearing gigantic boots covered with mud.

He curls his lip. "Peter Syms," he says, lifting a vape to his mouth and taking a sharp inhale. "*Syms* was my dad. The old lady likes continuity. And punctuality," he adds, jerking his chin toward the library door. She's in there waiting for you. I brought in the coffee a minute ago."

"Is that your job?" I ask.

He shrugs and takes another pull from the vape. I catch the faint sweetish smell of marijuana. "I'm kind of a jack-of-all-trades. My father was here when this was an asylum and I've stuck around to take care of the property."

"I heard it was an asylum—" I begin.

"I wouldn't bring up the doctor or the asylum to Ms. St. Clair," he says, turning back into the mudroom. "She doesn't like to talk about those days. The doctor," he adds, stopping to look over his shoulder, "was into a lot of crazy stuff. The real stuff that went on here is a hundred times scarier than what's in her book. Good luck if that's what you're here to get out of her." Then he winks and disappears into the shadows of the mudroom.

A door slams, rattling the glass panes of the library door, and I feel a corresponding flutter in my stomach as I cross the atrium to the library. I'm not sure if I'm nervous or excited. My psychiatrist at Woodbridge, Dr. Husack, once told me that anxiety and excitement lived in the same part of the brain. *You can choose which one you want to feel.* I'd scoffed at the idea but right now, my hand on the door, I sense the choice. I can be cowed by the grand dame or excited to be embarking on a new adventure. I *choose* to be excited.

The clock in the atrium begins chiming as I enter the library, keeping time with my heartbeats. I turn toward the green couch and once again I'm momentarily fooled by the author's ankle-length green silk caftan into thinking it's empty. As I walk toward her, I wonder at her habitual color choice. Is it because she's unable to see that she wants to be invisible to the world? As I sit down in the straight-back chair, though, I'm the one who feels invisible.

I pick up the notebook lying on the table. It's an old-fashioned steno pad, with a wire coil at the top and a red line down the middle of the ruled page. There was a surplus of them at Woodbridge; Sister Bernadette used them to teach us shorthand but it had seemed too archaic a skill to bother learning. Does Veronica think I'm going to take down her novel in shorthand? I suddenly realize how daunting a task this will be. *Excited, not nervous,* I remind myself. I uncap the pen and see with dismay that it's a fountain pen. I'm not even sure I know how to write with one.

"Um . . ." I say awkwardly to let her know I'm here. "I'm ready to begin when you are."

"Are you?" she asks archly. "I'm not sure I am. I used to be able to close my eyes and picture my characters in my head but since . . ." Her hand flutters up to her blind eyes. "All I see is darkness."

I feel a stab of pity imagining what it would be like not to be able to look out the window and see the Hudson River running navy blue this morning under a clear sky and the mountains be-yond laid out in folds of autumnal reds and golds.

"How would you begin?" she asks.

"Me?" I shift uneasily in my seat, startled to be asked, but then I think of the photo I found last night. "I suppose I'd start with Red Bess."

"Red Bess?" she echoes.

"Violet says it all begins with her but we never really get her story and growing up here—" I wave my hands at the long library with its rows and rows of books behind glass. I notice that in the recesses between the shelves are marble busts that stare out of the shadows with eyes as blind as Veronica's. She can't see my gesture but she nods as if she has. "I mean, you must have heard stories."

"Oh yes," she says, "growing up here, one would. So we'll begin with Red Bess then. A prologue of sorts. A bloody one."

I GREW UP with a murderess's deeds for my bedtime story—she begins, sitting up straighter, her blind eyes aimed toward the river. Although she speaks in the first person and the story she tells is set in a house much like the one where we are sitting, the house where she grew up, it feels as if another person is speaking. As if she is a medium possessed with an invading spirit and we have moved back in time—*and a murderess's punishment as my lesson book and primer. It didn't matter that my father forbade the servants to talk about her; Red Bess was always on their lips. The creak in the third step was Red Bess stealing out of the house, the spilled flour in the pantry was Red Bess up to her tricks, the wind rattling the windowpanes was Red Bess trying to get in out of the cold, when the guard dogs in their kennel barked at nothing they were barking at Red Bess.*

I had a nanny who'd worked at the training school before my father turned it into a mental hospital. I thought she was ancient but I suppose she must have been in her early seventies. Mrs. Gorse was her name, although I just called her Nanny. My father worried about her working with the new teenage patients because he was afraid she would fall back into the habit of treating them as prisoners, but he knew she'd never make that mistake with me. In truth, she was never anything but gentle, but I don't think he would have left me with her if he'd known that she would tell me about Red Bess. And she might not have told me those stories if I hadn't heard her warning the patients to be good lest they wind up like Red Bess. I begged her to tell me the stories then and she, after a show of reluctance and making me promise not to tell my father, obliged. I think she was still trying to understand herself what had happened. She'd been a young girl when Bess Molloy came to Wyldcliffe Heights—

"When I first laid eyes on Bess Molloy, I was surprised how ordinary she looked. From the pictures in the paper, I was expecting a monster with wild hair and bloodshot eyes, but she was a frail pretty thing with downcast eyes that first day she was led into the atrium and Miss Josephine insisted we treat her just the same as the other girls."

Josephine Hale had very particular ideas of how the training school was to be run. The girls were to be treated like young women from the best families, as if the training school was a fancy finishing school. They were to have real classes to teach them not just useful skills, such as sewing, cooking, and cleaning, but also lessons in the arts, such as drawing, singing, and dancing. "Any girl given the right care and removed from pernicious influences can become a productive member of society. Even a girl who has committed murder," she would say.

Every evening the girls all gathered in the library for tea and an educational lecture given by Josephine or a visiting scholar. Most of the girls had been remanded for minor thefts, vagrancy, or prostitution. Bess Molloy was the only murderer among them, but Josephine insisted she be treated no differently and be welcomed to Wyldcliffe Heights as if she had done nothing worse than stolen a loaf of bread.

In fact, it seemed as if Josephine made a point of favoring the girl. She had her sit by her at tea, singled her out for praise during lessons, and was often seen out walking with her on the grounds. She even gave her a red merino cloak with a fur-lined hood. The girls began to whisper that she was Miss Hale's pet and it got back to the board of directors. They met and voted that there ought to be a warden as well as a headmistress in charge of the girls. Josephine objected at first, but then the board suggested Dr. Edgar Bryce, the doctor who had testified on Bess's behalf at her trial. He came to speak with her and convinced her that he would be a colleague, not a dictator, and that together they would create a better place for "her girls."

The arrival of Dr. Edgar Bryce changed everything. He came with brash new ideas and an enthusiasm Josephine could not help but welcome. At first she seemed to enjoy the intellectual companionship. He praised the work she had done and concurred that it was in separating the girls from pernicious influences that their best hopes of rehabilitation lay.

"The longer they can remain here the better," he advised. As well as comprehensive medical exams, he instituted intelligence tests to better plan for their education. Most of the girls tested below normal range, confirming Dr. Bryce's view that criminality and vice flourished in feebleminded populations.

Together he and Josephine petitioned the courts to prolong the girls' terms. Reading groups and art lessons were abandoned in favor of domestic and agricultural training. The greenhouses were expanded to grow more violets, a thriving trade in the Hudson Valley and the sort of decorous activity suited for her girls.

The only conflict they really had was Bess Molloy. She had scored high on Dr. Bryce's intelligence tests and didn't conform *to his theories of feeblemindedness. Josephine insisted that she be spared the greenhouse (the violets may have been pretty but picking them was backbreaking work) and be allowed to continue with her education. When he agreed, Josephine was so reassured and gratified that when he proposed marriage, she couldn't help but see the sense in it. Married, they could run the training school as equal partners and face down the board together to follow their own vision.*

They married on Christmas Day 1922 in the atrium, attended by the inmates, who wore hothouse violet wreaths in their hair. Josephine carried a bouquet of violets. Bess Molloy was her maid of honor. And then, ten months later on Halloween night, Bess Molloy stole up to the tower room, where Dr. Bryce had his office, and stabbed him fourteen times in the chest and hung herself from the tower battlements.

VERONICA STOPS THERE. I am still scratching away with the finicky fountain pen for several seconds trying to catch up when I realize that she doesn't mean to go further. I uncurl and stretch out my cramped fingers, noticing that my hands are spotted with ink. The page is covered with sloping sentences that would have horrified Sister Bernadette even more than the story they tell. I look up from my pad for the first time since Veronica began dictating and am startled to see the small, stooped figure seated in front of me. It's hard to believe that all of that story has come out of this one small woman. The room had been full just moments ago with so many voices—Mrs. Gorse, Edgar Bryce, Josephine—and it had felt like we had traveled back in time to a remote past. Now she looks like all the air has been let out of her, as if the story has drained her. When she lifts her face, I see that it's wet, as if her blind eyes have wept tears, but it's only perspiration.

The silence is heavy in the room. After the clock ticks off a few more seconds, I shift in my chair, making the wood creak. "Would you like—" I begin, not at all sure what I'm going to offer her for her labors.

"I think that's enough for today," she says in a croak of a voice that is nothing like the one that had filled the room moments ago. "Did you get it all?"

I flip through the pages, counting thirteen, amazed that the story I've just heard could fit on so few. *Did* I get it all? "I think so—" I begin. "It's like you said—it felt like the characters appeared in my head. They felt so real that I kind of lost myself."

When I look up, I see her face is stricken, her hands trembling, and I realize it must have sounded like I was claiming authorship. "Be careful," she says, as she gets up, her voice hard. "Losing yourself inside of a book can be dangerous. Not everyone finds their way out."

CHAPTER NINE

I sit down at the desk and pretend to fuss with the seat angle and position of the copy stand while Veronica taps her way out of the room with a cane. The taps echo in the atrium and then, as they recede, I rest my hands on the typewriter's keys in "home" position, closing my eyes for a second as Sister Bernadette had taught us. When I open them and turn to the notebook on the copy stand the words swim before my eyes as if running in the rain.

What if it's all gibberish? I wonder. *What if I can't read my own handwriting and I can't reproduce Veronica's story?* Already I can feel the echo of her words receding with the tapping of her cane. Then the words snap into focus and I hear Veronica's voice in my head—

I grew up with a murderess's deeds for my bedtime story.

—and my fingers move, striking the keys in time to the voice in my head. I carry on, pausing only to turn the pages of the notebook or feed another sheet into the typewriter carriage, Veronica's voice filling my head as if I had recorded her. I picture the girls in their high-necked muslin blouses and dark skirts, sewing and reading to each other in this very room, Bess Molloy among them, her light hair bright in the lamplight, Josephine's darker head bending beside her to admire her star pupil's work. Then I see

Edgar Bryce appearing on the scene, slim and handsome, casting a sharp-edged shadow across the circle, dividing Bess from Josephine and bringing a new order to the school. What a story to grow up on! No wonder Veronica seemed timeless; it was like she came from a different era entirely.

Threaded into the pictures appearing in my head I recall the inspector who came to Woodbridge once a month. For the first few years I was there it was a middle-aged woman in a wooly shapeless cardigan who spent most of her time drinking tea with the nuns and approving requisitions for more supplies and extra staff. She brought us girls homemade cookies and cast-off books at Christmas. But then she was replaced by a younger, more earnest woman dressed in boxy suits and hard-soled shoes that clicked over the linoleum. She wrote up every infraction and recommended that the old nuns be retired and replaced with lay teachers. She exchanged the old typewriters for computers, which was all well and good until the computers broke down and there wasn't enough money to fix them and the new teachers she'd hired left to make better salaries in balmier climates with less difficult students.

I was familiar with well-intentioned reformers. At least our new inspector hadn't married the head teacher and seized control. I can imagine what Bess Molloy might have felt watching her benefactor marry Dr. Bryce. Did she think she was losing Josephine? Was she jealous? Had something happened that sparked a murderous rage? What could it have been to make her slaughter Edgar Bryce? Had she regretted what she'd done and hung herself from the tower?

I've come to the end of the story as far as Veronica told it, but my fingers, resting on the home keys, are tingling, itching to pound out the rest of the story, as if the answers to my questions are literally at my fingertips, as if the characters I'd pictured in my head were real enough to move on their own.

Veronica's characters, not mine.

I look out the window, frustrated that I can't go on with the story. While I've been typing the sun has crossed the roof beam and cast the shadow of the burnt-out tower across the west lawn. It points like a finger toward the river, as if ordering me out of Wyldcliffe Heights.

Be careful, Veronica had said, *losing yourself inside of a book can be dangerous.*

A breeze blows the long grasses on the overgrown lawn, making the shadow of the tower ripple. For a moment I see a figure swaying in the wind—hanged Bess—

I pull my fingers back from the keys as if from a hot iron. When I look down, I see the last line I typed.

Red Bess cast her hanged shadow across my childhood. My hands had finished the story for me as if directed by some outside agent. Should I strike the sentence out? Retype the final page? But instead, I pull it out of the typewriter and lay it face down with the rest of the finished pages, where it rustles in a faint breeze coming in through the window. I look around the desk for something to weigh it down and notice a collection of smooth gray stones. I place one on top of the pages, but it doesn't seem like enough. They could fly away and be lost and then what? There's no carbon copy, no digital file. And no way to get them to Kurtis Chadwick.

Unless I retype a copy right now.

But before I can start, I hear the library door open. I turn guiltily and find Laeticia standing in the doorway.

"Your lunch is ready in the kitchen," she says.

"I'll just be a minute," I answer, shuffling the pages and making a show of counting them. She doesn't move from the doorway. Finally, I pin them beneath the stone again and follow her out of the library. She stops to lock the door behind us, then leads the way through the atrium into the kitchen in the east wing. My sandwich plate and soup bowl sit at the end of a long butcher block table that might have seated a dozen when the house had a full staff of servants. As I sit, I ask, "Is there really no internet in the house? No computer at all?"

"Miss St. Clair has no use for it, and I believe she made clear that you are not to post anything about her or the house on social media," Laeticia says, filling a kettle at the sink.

"Yes, I read the NDA," I say, noticing that Laeticia has repeated the wording from the NDA verbatim—*Miss St. Clair or the house*—as if they were equal, the house a personage in its own right with its own demands and expectations. "But I have other . . . business I need to do on the internet. Is there someplace in the village where I can use a computer?"

"I believe the town library," she says stiffly, placing the kettle on the stove, "is equipped with such things. Syms can take you into town after you've finished your lunch."

"I can walk," I say, not anxious to repeat my earlier encounter with the surly Syms. "It looks like the rain has finally stopped."

"It will be back," Laeticia says gloomily, striking a match and holding it to the gas ring. The poof of blue flames gives her face an eerie glow. "This is the Hudson Valley; rain is never far away."

AFTER I FINISH my turkey sandwich and butternut squash soup (both delicious; Laeticia may act like a prison guard but she's not feeding me prison fare), I find my sneakers—washed and stuffed with newspapers—in the mudroom. I consider going back upstairs for my denim jacket, but taking Laeticia's warning to heart, I grab a rain jacket off a hook instead and leave through the mudroom door.

I breathe in the fresh air as if I've been imprisoned for a decade and nearly break into a run going down the drive. *Wyldcliffe Heights is not a prison,* I remind myself. And true to Laeticia's word there is a wooden post in front of the gate with a metal box that opens to reveal a button. As I push it I look back over my shoulder as if checking for pursuers, but there's only the house, its dark stone façade closed in on itself against the sunshine like a face steeling itself against grief. *Call it what you like,* a voice says inside my head—*refuge, training school, treatment center—they're all fancy words for a prison.*

I hear a shriek behind me and wheel around, expecting the horrible fog-beast from my nightmare blocking my way, but it's only the gate opening on its rusted hinges. I squeeze through as soon as there's room, carefully avoiding its sharp places, and then take a moment to catch my breath—and to prove to myself and anyone passing by that I am *not* an escaped convict. *I am the amanuensis of a famous author,* I tell myself as I start down the hill, *out for an afternoon stroll.*

The picturesque road with its old stone walls and towering sycamores could be from an English novel. The village below looks like something out of *Masterpiece Theatre* with its church steeple, mansard-roofed train station, and brick-faced and striped-awninged shops framed by the mountains across the river. I see a farm stand selling apples, pumpkins, and apple cider donuts; a church offering godly advice and pancake breakfasts; and a gun club advertising this year's turkey shoot. On the main street I pass young parents pushing strollers, college students vaping at a shuttle stop, and a group of older men sitting on benches in the town square drinking coffee. It could be the West Village only there's more plaid and everyone seems a fraction more relaxed—or at least as if they want to *look* relaxed.

I arrive at the Hale Memorial Library, a low stone building with a plaque saying it was founded in 1928. The bulletin board advertises a Purl Jam Knitting Circle and an It's My Jam-making Workshop. Inside, the young woman behind the counter looks like she could have come out of the twenties in a plaid vintage dress, embroidered cardigan, and cat's-eye glasses. Her name tag reads *Martha Conway*. When I ask to use a computer, she hands me a clipboard with a sign-up sheet. The first available time is in half an hour.

"We're always busy on Saturday," she tells me with a long-suffering sigh. "But you're welcome to browse our collection while you're waiting."

I glance at the New Releases shelf featuring the latest best-sellers and then my eye falls on an alcove behind the bestsellers labeled *Local History*.

"Would there be anything on Wyldcliffe Heights there?" I ask, forgetting for a moment that I'm not supposed to talk about the house to locals.

"Lots!" Martha Conway says with salacious glee as if I've asked to see the porn section. "She's our star attraction."

"*She*?" I ask, with a sick feeling that she's talking about Red Bess.

"Oh, sorry," she says, coming out from behind the counter and leading me toward the alcove. "How heteronormative of me. I think of the house as a woman because of all the women who have lived there. You know it was a refuge for fallen women—as they called them back then." She begins plucking books from shelves in the alcove and laying them on a small table as she talks. "And then a training school run by the progressive prison reformer Josephine Hale. Here's a prospectus printed by the board of managers to advertise the facilities."

She hands me a slim, saddle-stitched pamphlet. "You can see what the girls ate for breakfast and studied in their classes. It makes it all sound very cheery and improving. I suppose Josephine Hale began with the best intentions, but that all changed after one of the inmates, Bess Molloy, killed her new husband and set the house on fire one hundred years ago this Halloween!" she says brightly as if it's something to celebrate. "That's what most people are interested in. We have the reports of the murder in the *Poughkeepsie Journal* and the *Kingston Freeman* and a book by a contemporaneous criminologist positing that Bess Molloy—or Red Bess, as they called her—was feebleminded and corrupted by the pernicious atmosphere of New York City's slums. Then there's one written by a psychiatrist in the fifties theorizing she was a lesbian who formed an 'unnatural attachment' to Josephine Hale." She rolls her eyes at me. "There's even a monograph in here blaming socialists for Red Bess's murderous rage. Are you researching the house for a paper?" she asks abruptly.

I sit down at the table and begin leafing through one of the books to give myself time to think how to answer. She sits down beside me. "Not exactly," I say. "I work for a publisher in the city and I'm doing some background research for a book."

"Is it one of those Haunted Hudson Valley books?" she asks eagerly. "Someone usually does a story on Red Bess around Halloween, and she's always a part of the parade, especially this year since it's her anniversary. Are you staying in the area?"

Mindful of my NDA I dodge the question with one of my own.

"Why are people still interested in Red Bess a hundred years after her death?"

She blinks as if she doesn't quite understand my question but when she answers, her cheeks turning pink, I realize she's offended by it. "Coming from the city you must think it's provincial for us to be fixated on a hundred-year-old scandal."

"No," I object, startled to have put voluble, friendly Martha Conway on the defensive. I realize I've made her feel the way Kayla and Hadley often made me feel, like the naive rube. "I'm not really from the city—" *I'm not from anywhere,* I almost say. Instead, I offer up, like a sacrifice to the Gods of Humble Origins, "I went to SUNY Potsdam."

"Oh, Potsdam," she says, brightening. "Go Bears! I went to Geneseo undergrad and then got my MLS at SUNY Albany." And then, as if our mutual attendance in the state university system has sealed a bond between us, she leans closer and whispers, "The reason people are still talking about Red Bess is because a cloud of bad luck has hung over that house since her death. The girls at the training school claimed they could hear the ghost of Red Bess weeping and saw her shadow hanging from the tower on nights with a full moon. Locals who worked at the house said strange things started happening. The roof sprung leaks, cracks appeared in the walls, the basement flooded. It was as if the house was bent on destroying itself. And Josephine became an entirely different person, a martinet who instituted strict rules—no talking during work hours, no leaving their rooms at night even to use the bathroom, solitary confinement and bread and water rations for any infractions. Before he died, Dr. Sinclair was working on a book about past-life regression and the rumor around here was that he believed one of his patients was the reincarnation of Red Bess."

"That's crazy," I say, pulling back from Martha Conway.

"I know," she says, "but that's what the place does to people. Why do you think Veronica St. Clair has never written another book?"

I'm about to say it's because she's blind but then I remember that I'm not supposed to talk about her to the locals. Martha doesn't seem to expect an answer. "It's because she's afraid of summoning Red Bess back to Wyldcliffe Heights," she says, eyes wide. "Just imagine! It would give anyone writer's block."

CHAPTER TEN

Before I can react to Martha Conway's outlandish theory, she recovers her librarian's decorum and looks down at her watch. "Oh look, it's time for your computer slot. Let's go boot out the youths!"

She has to pry a surly teen off their game of *War Zone* and then she leaves me to check out books for a cluster of mothers with small children. I sign into my email account and see that I've got emails from Kurtis Chadwick, Gloria, and Atticus. The subject line of Atticus's is *Sorry*. I open that one first, smiling smugly that he's apologizing for his behavior on my last day at the office, but the smile soon fades.

Hey, I'm sorry if I offended you. I only wanted to give you all the facts about Veronica St. Clair and Wyldcliffe Heights so you could make an informed decision about taking the job. I didn't realize you would take that as prying. I didn't mean to make you think I was talking behind your back. I know you feel you're saving Gatehouse Books, but I'm afraid you might have been pressured into accepting the job, and frankly I'm a little worried about you. I'm attaching a link to a story about Wyldcliffe Heights that Hadley found. Maybe after you read it,

you'll understand my concern, which was only for your welfare.
I realize that you are new to the city and publishing and I hate
to see you taken advantage of. I hope you'll take this in the
spirit in which it is offered, that you'll take care of yourself up
there, and if your position becomes untenable you won't be
embarrassed to ask for help.

Cheers, az

"What a jerk!"

I hadn't meant to say it out loud, but from the smirk of the
teenager at the next computer and the affronted look from the
mother in the children's nook, apparently, I had. Who could
blame me? *I'm sorry if I offended you* is not an apology; it's him
accusing me of being too sensitive or—worse—delusional. And
he's sorry he made me think he was talking behind my back, not
that he *was*. I can just picture them all gathered at the White Horse
tutting over poor naive Agnes sent upstate on a fool's errand that
she's bound to fail at and then come slinking back with her tail
tucked between her legs.

I hit "reply" and begin an email to Atticus, changing the
subject line to *Sorry, Not Sorry*, excoriating his passive-aggressive,
mansplaining missive. *For your information, I am very comfortably
situated at Wyldcliffe Heights and Veronica and I made a very
propitious start on the sequel this morning—*

I pause, thinking of those typed up pages lying behind the
locked library door on Veronica's desk, pinned beneath the gray
stone. They might as well be at the bottom of the Hudson River
for all I'm able to get them to Kurtis Chadwick. Which I'll have
to admit if he's asked me to send them to him. I save my angry

reply to Atticus in my drafts folder and then open the email from Kurtis Chadwick.

I hope your journey was pleasant and that you have safely arrived at Wyldcliffe Heights. I look forward to seeing what you have uncovered there! Gloria is writing to you with some details that may help the process. Please let her know whatever you may need.

Onward,
KC

Although his choice of wording—*I look forward to seeing what you have uncovered*—makes me feel uneasy, at least he doesn't expect me to have pages yet. I open Gloria's email next.

As you know, Mr. Chadwick has arranged to have a laptop sent to you. However, knowing Ms. St. Clair's views on tech-nology, he has concerns about sending it directly to Wyldcliffe Heights. Please open a post office box in town as soon as pos-sible and let me know the address.

Yours,
Gloria Morris

I'm a little surprised at all the subterfuge—is Kurtis so worried about crossing Veronica?—but at least I'll have something to type the manuscript on. I'm still not sure how I'll sneak a laptop into the library to type the pages into it, but I'll think of something.

Navigating the restrictions and locked doors of foster homes and Woodbridge has made me resourceful (not the naive simpleton Atticus takes me for). I write Kurtis Chadwick that I'll have something for him soon and Gloria promising to send her my post office box today. Then I delete my long reply to Atticus and respond with a curt *Thanks for your concern but it's unwarranted and unwelcome. Cheers! ac*

Then I sign off and cede my chair to the *War Zone* player. As I'm passing the circulation desk, I hear Martha Conway call my name.

"Agnes, do you want these books on Wyldcliffe Heights?"

There are three books on the counter. "Oh, I thought they were reference books . . . and besides, I don't have a library card . . ." *And I never told you my name,* I add to myself. How does she know it?

"No worries, I made one up for you when I realized you were staying up at the Heights."

"How—?"

"Peter Syms and I went to high school together and he texted me to say you were coming down to use the internet."

Before or after you pretended not to know anything about me? I wonder. *Go Bears! indeed.*

"I think you'll find these interesting bedtime reading," she says, pushing the stack toward me. "And if you want help looking through the archives, remember I'm here every day but Tuesday." My new library card is on top of the stack of books. As I take it, I see the title of the slim book on top. *The Bloody Return: The Posthumous Confessions of Red Bess.*

I REACH THE post office and wait on line to fill out the form to get a box, then rush back to the library, slinking past the circulation desk where Martha Conway is checking out books for an elderly patron, to email Gloria its number. The same teen is at the computer, shoulders hunched over the screen, still playing *War Zone*.

"Hm," I say softly, "that doesn't look like homework."

They jerk, bony knees hitting the underside of the desk, and turn bright red.

"I won't tell if you let me on for five minutes," I say.

"You can have it," they mutter, closing the tab while trying to shrug, zip up their hoodie, and look casual all at the same time. I feel a twinge of guilt recalling what it's like not to have any privacy but shrug it away just like they did. They're probably better off getting out in the fresh air than playing video games all day. I open a new tab, sign into my email account, and send Gloria my new PO box number. Then I see I've got a new email from Atticus. I feel a spike of adrenaline as I open it, the way I'd feel at Woodbridge when one of the rougher girls said something nasty behind my back and I knew I'd have to run or fight.

Fight, I think now, tapping the email open. *What have you got for me, nerd boy?*

The email contains two words: *Message received.*

"Fine," I say aloud, feeling the adrenaline drain from my body the way it would when I turned to find the hall empty, my potential attacker slunk away—or maybe never there in the first place. Maybe the nasty words had all been in my head.

That's what Atticus thinks—that I'm imagining the way he and Hadley and Kayla and Serge and Reese all act like I'm an idiot. Like I need Hadley sending me articles about Wyldcliffe Heights. It's probably just a haunted houses site. I go back to Atticus's first email and open the link to confirm my suspicions. It's not a haunted houses site; it's a link to a podcast called *'90s Goth*

Corpses about the punk goth scene in nineties New York City. This episode is about an overdose at the Josephine Hotel. Why would Atticus think this was important for me to know? I already know that a girl died of an overdose at the Josephine.

Then I scroll down and read the teaser for the first episode: *On the night Cannibal Corpse played the Josephine there was a real corpse in the haunted tower room. Sure there'd been lots of ODs at the infamous hotel, but if it was really an overdose why was Dr. Robert Sinclair of the Wyldcliffe Heights Psychiatric Treatment Center in upstate New York called in to consult on the case? And what did his role in this case have to do with reincarnation, hauntings, and past-life regression?*

Dr. Sinclair's name is highlighted as a link. I click on it and follow the link to a Wikipedia entry. I skim through his early bio—educated at Harvard and Columbia, founder and head doctor of the Wyldcliffe Heights Psychiatric Treatment Center, etc., etc., all of which I know. Then I scroll down to the last section, labeled "Controversy," and read that in his later years Dr. Sinclair's methods were called into question by several former patients and colleagues who alleged that he abused his role as psychiatrist to conduct research for his studies in past-life regression.

What the hell?

I follow a few more links to make sense of this allegation and find myself on abuse and survivor discussion boards in which some patients claimed to have been sexually abused by Dr. Sinclair under hypnosis and some assert that Dr. Sinclair saved their lives by opening their eyes to their past-life trauma. These conflicting accounts quickly turn into a debate on the legitimacy of past-life regression and reincarnation, which in turn spirals me down into a labyrinth of conspiracy theories.

What did Atticus think I would get out of this? Maybe he was shocked by these allegations against Dr. Sinclair, but I'd heard worse at Woodbridge. Maybe Veronica's father was a monster, but he wouldn't be the first to abuse his position as a caretaker of vulnerable teenagers. *Big reveal, Atticus!*

I close out of the multiple tabs I've opened, my eyes stinging and my head aching from staring at the screen. When I get out of the library the sky is dark. How long had I spent doomscrolling through the cyber netherworld of conspiracy and innuendo? I check my watch and see it's only 4:30 and yet the bustling Main Street has turned into a ghost town. Bread for the Masses has closed, the remaining mothers are stashing children and strollers into their Subaru Foresters, and only one lonely-looking guy in a long, hooded raincoat is finishing off his coffee in the town square. It's also gotten colder—and damper. A dank wet wind is blowing from the west. Dark clouds are massing over the mountains on the other side of the river, which is coated with a layer of fog thick as foam on a latte. As I start up the hill the fog rolls in from the river, bringing with it a fine, stinging rain. Laeticia had been right; rain is never far away in this damned valley. *Maybe it'll blow over,* I think, looking toward the river, but the fog now blocks the view entirely. When I look back down the hill Wyldcliffe-on-Hudson has vanished like that Scottish village in the movie Sister Bernadette loved.

I continue my climb and find my way blocked by another wall of fog. Maybe Wyldcliffe Heights has vanished, too, and I will be trapped forever wandering in this foggy purgatory, which feels a lot like my dream of the fog-beast. I turn, daring the beast to materialize, and a yellow light pierces through the fog. I freeze, just as I always do in my dream, unable to run. I close my eyes, willing myself to wake up, but the beast lets out a horrible shriek and I can feel its foul breath against my face.

I open my eyes and find myself facing the grill of a car.

"For Christ's sake, I nearly ran you over!" A man emerges from the car, his face hidden by the brim of his baseball cap. He takes it off to wipe his brow and I recognize Spike, the taxi driver from yesterday.

"What are you doing driving on the shoulder—" I begin angrily, but then, looking around, I see I'm actually in the middle of the road. Somehow I must have wandered away from the shoulder. "How is anyone supposed to see in this fog? Should you even be driving in it?"

He heaves an exasperated groan. "I saw you walking out of the village and thought you might want a lift in this rain."

"You followed me?"

He stares at me as if I'm crazy. "I thought I'd keep you from getting wet, not end up with both of us getting soaked. If you get in the car, I'll take you up to the house."

"I'm not spending twenty dollars to drive half a mile."

"It's on me," he says. "Please. I'd feel better knowing you're off this road in the fog. It's really not safe."

The way he says it makes me think of other dangers—like fog-beasts—than getting run over. I study his face, wet from the rain, his beard beaded with moisture, as if I could judge his character from his features. A drop of rain lands under my collar and slides down my spine, setting off a shiver. "Okay," I say grudgingly. And then, a fraction more graciously, "Thanks."

I get in the back seat, grateful for the warm blast of heat from the vents. Spike eases the car forward, leaning toward the windshield to see the road.

"Is it always this foggy?" I ask.

"Not always, but often enough. Whenever the air is colder than the water, fog rolls in off the river, like your breath steaming on a cold day. The first settlers named this town Helbergen because so many ships foundered in the fog they thought it was the infernal smoke of hellfires burning beneath the river."

"Cheery," I say, leaning forward to monitor Spike's progress on the road.

"There's nothing cheery about this spot," he says. "How are you finding Wyldcliffe Heights?"

"It's . . . fine," I say carefully. "But according to my NDA I'm not really supposed to talk about Ms. St. Clair or the house with locals."

"No fear, then," he says, grinning and meeting my eyes in the rearview mirror, "I'm not exactly a local."

"No? Where are you from?"

"Brooklyn," he says. "I worked for *Newsday* and then the *Sun* until it went online and then I came up here in '08. Figured if I was going to drive a cab it'd be safer here than in the city."

"So you've been here fifteen years but you're not a local?"

He laughs. "Nah. I'm still a city person. The real locals are wary of us, going back to the days when rich people came up and built these river mansions and hired the locals to be their servants and grounds people. They didn't like it when the Hale family turned their estate into a Magdalen refuge or when Josephine Hale turned it into a training school or when her son-in-law turned it into a mental hospital for delinquent teens."

"For a nonlocal you know a lot of local history."

He shrugs. "The habits of a newspaperman die hard. Actually, it was writing a story about Dr. Sinclair's treatment center that brought me up here in the first place, back in the nineties before I officially made the move. I had a lead on some sketchy things going on."

"What kind of sketchy things?" I say, thinking about the trail I'd followed on the internet.

"The doctor was into some weird shit—woo-woo stuff like psychotropics, chakra healing, hypnotherapy—there were rumors about what he did to his patients when they were under hypnosis."

"Ew," I say, thinking of prim, upright Veronica St. Clair. What would it be like to have a father who was suspected of mistreating patients under hypnosis? Had he hypnotized *her*?

I grew up with a murderess's deeds for my bedtime story.

What else had she grown up with?

"Yeah, *ew*." We've come to the gate. I suddenly have the urge to ask him to turn around and take me back to the train station. But then where?

"Did you ever publish the article?" I ask, wondering why it didn't come up in my internet trawl.

"Nah," he says, catching my eye in the mirror. "Paper killed it. Relatives of the Hales had some friends in high places who didn't want to see the family's name besmirched. These people usually do." He powers down his window and leans out to speak into the intercom. "Wyldcliffe Taxi," he shouts. "I've got your amanuensis here."

The gates creak open and he drives up the winding road toward the house. As we come around the last bend the fog clears and the house appears as if it's thrown off the misty shroud like a woman baring her face.

I think of the house as a woman because of all the women who have lived there.

I can't help but glance uneasily at the tower where Red Bess hanged herself. There's no sunlight to illuminate the broken glass or cast an ominous shadow, but a light does go on in one of the front windows and I have a feeling of being watched. As if all the women who have ever come to Wyldcliffe Heights are waiting for me. *What,* I'd like to ask, *do they expect* me *to do for them?*

CHAPTER ELEVEN

Laeticia tuts over my wet shoes and clothes in the mudroom and tells me to go take a hot bath. "We can't have you coming down with a cold and passing it on to Miss St. Clair," she says, lest I think her concern is for me. "I'll send Syms up with your supper."

It's barely 5 p.m. but I don't object to the idea of a bath and an early dinner. As I start up the stairs Laeticia calls after me. "I hope you weren't talking to that taxi driver about Miss St. Clair or the house."

"Of course not," I say, which isn't a lie since it was Spike who did all the talking.

Upstairs, I soak until the tub water cools and then, remembering my near drowning experience of last night, get out and wrap myself in a robe. I'd been careful to lock my door so Syms has left my dinner basket in the hall. There are two thermoses—one of sweet milky tea and one of hot corn chowder—warm rolls, cheese, and apples. I eat everything sitting at the desk while sorting through the books Martha Conway picked out for me. There's a cheaply bound history of Wyldcliffe-on-Hudson (*self-published*, I hear Atticus sneering), a thick book in a library binding on the *Conditions of Women Inmates in the Early Twentieth Century*, and a monograph by Dr. Sinclair with the salacious title I'd noted earlier, *The Bloody Return: The Posthumous Confession of Red Bess,* which looks far more interesting. Here, perhaps, will be something more substantial than internet innuendo. I'll start with that.

I don't even make it through Dr. Sinclair's pedantic summation of his academic and professional credentials, all meant to impress upon the reader that he's not some woo-woo hack. I fall asleep halfway between his assertions that he had no interest in parapsychology and a list of psychopharmaceuticals he used to treat his patients. At Woodbridge we called doctors like him Dispensers and compared notes on the best meds, the ones that made you high instead of grinding you down into jelly, and the mocked-up symptoms that would get the Dispenser to prescribe them. Maybe it's thinking about the drugs that puts me to sleep—and sends me into my fog dream.

I'm running, as I usually am, through the fog, but this time I'm climbing stairs and the fog, I realize, is smoke. I'm in a building that's on fire and I have to reach the roof, but the stairs go on forever. When I finally reach the top, I realize from the jagged teeth-like crenellations that I'm on top of the tower, which is on fire. I lean over the side to see how I will get down and realize that the drop is too far. I'll never survive it.

"You'll need this."

I turn to see that I am not alone. A figure has emerged from the smoke, holding out a rope. One end of it has been tied around one of the teeth of the battlement. I can use it to climb down. Only when I take it do I realize that the other end is a noose. When I look up I make out the red-hooded figure, a grinning skull inside the white ermine-lined hood.

I startle awake and realize immediately that I'm not in my bed.

I'm standing barefoot on a cold floor staring at the skull face of my nightmare. I open my mouth to scream but nothing comes out, as if my throat were constricted by a noose. I raise my hand to tear at the rope and the figure in front of me does, too.

It's a mirror, I tell myself, *you're standing in front of a mirror.* Only I don't remember one in my room. I look around and see that I'm in the attic standing in front of the wardrobe, looking at my own reflection. And the cloak . . . only a blanket I'd thrown over my head. I've been sleepwalking—and not for the first time.

IT TAKES ME a long time to go back to sleep. Dr. Husack warned me that if I started sleepwalking again, I should seek psychiatric help right away, but where am I going to find that here? The last psychiatrist at Wyldcliffe burned up in a tower a long time ago.

I only get a few hours' sleep before being woken by a knock at the door and Laeticia's gruff voice barking "quarter to eight." I lurch up, splash water on my face, and dress in yesterday's rumpled clothes. The clock begins chiming when I reach the top of the stairs and I race down the steps so fast I nearly crash headlong onto the marble atrium floor.

"Are you all right?" Veronica asks when I take my chair. "You're breathing quite heavily."

"Y-yes," I say. "I just overslept."

"I hope yesterday's story didn't give you nightmares about Red Bess," she says.

"Oh no," I lie, "but I can imagine that for a child growing up here it must have been terrifying. I think you got that across very powerfully." I notice that she has the typed pages in her lap and that her fingers are stroking the typescript as if it were braille. "Do you want me to begin by reading the pages to you?" I ask, remembering that last line I added. Did I dare read it to her? But she shakes her head.

"I don't think that will be necessary. Yesterday's recital brought me back to that 'terrifying childhood,' as you called it. I think that's where we'll start today."

Once again as she begins to speak it's as if someone—or something—else has entered the room.

THE DOCTOR, AS *we all called him, was a more frightening specter of my childhood than Red Bess. My mother died when I was a baby and I discerned, when I was old enough to discern anything, that the doctor held me responsible.*

"She was too frail to carry a child," I overheard him saying. In my childish mind I pictured my mother trying to carry me and collapsing under my great weight. Certainly Nanny complained when I asked to be lifted that I was too heavy, and the only time in my memory that my father lifted me in his arms was when I strayed into the beautiful violet room that had been my mother's and he grabbed me under my armpits and dragged me into the hall so violently that I was afraid he was going to toss me over the banister and send me hurtling down onto the atrium floor.

"The doctor worshipped your mother," Nanny explained to me later, comforting me in our attic nursery, "and so he doesn't like anyone going into her room."

I knew even then, though, that there was something more—or less—than worship in how my father enshrined the memory of my mother. When Nanny brought me to her church on Sundays there were pictures of the saints and the Virgin Mary with candles lit in front of them, but in our house, there was not a single picture of my mother.

"He destroyed them all," Nanny said. "He couldn't bear to look upon her face."

There were no pictures of me either because I looked so much like my mother and looking at me or my likeness was too painful a reminder to him of what he'd lost. And yet, as I grew older, I often felt his eyes on me. I would be sitting in the atrium playing jacks on the marble floor and the back of my neck would prickle. Looking up through the winding stairs I would spy the flash of light off his spectacles for a second before he withdrew his head. Was it my father watching me, I wondered, or maybe the ghost of Red Bess, who had hung herself from the tower battlements?

After one of those times, he sent Nanny out to bring me to his study. I had never been in the tower as I was never to interrupt him in the study where he saw his patients. At the bottom of the tower Nanny stopped and looked up the winding stairs, her face gray in the shadows. "Go on up," she said, giving me a little push, "until you can't go any further and then knock on the door."

When I got to the top, the door to his office was open and he was sitting behind his desk in the shadows.

"I see you looking up here at the tower," he said to me. "What are you looking for?"

For you, I might have said, but that wasn't entirely true.

I shrugged and felt stupid—and heavy, leaden as the big girls I watched dragging around the lawn on their mandatory exercises. I wanted to prove to my father that I was brighter than those girls who took up all his time.

"I look up because I feel like someone's watching me," I said.

"Do you often feel yourself watched?" he asked. I could tell by the way he asked it that there was something wrong with what I'd said but it was too late now to change my answer. It was as if I'd claimed that I was worthy of his attention—or was complaining that I wasn't.

"It's just the house," I said, remembering something Nanny had said to one of the girls in the kitchen, "up to its tricks."

He leaned forward then, and his face in the light was awful, contorted like one of the stone statues in the Ramble.

"What kind of tricks?" he asked.

"Just . . . things go missing and sometimes there are shadows where there shouldn't be . . . and sounds . . ."

"What sounds? What do you hear?"

"Just creaks and bumps . . ."

"And what do you see?"

"Nothing!" I was perilously close to tears and I knew my father hated tears.

He sighed then and leaned back and wrote something in a book, his pen scratching over the paper. "You'll come see me once a week from now on," he said, "and tell me everything you see and hear."

As I got up to leave he rose, too, and came out from behind the desk and knelt down in front of me. He held me at arm's length and studied me. "You're very like your mother," he said. "Now go tell Nanny to come up."

I knew my mother had been beautiful so I said thank you. His mouth twisted and he got up quickly, motioning me to go. I ran down the stairs and found Nanny outside the door to the tower, as if standing guard. I sent her up and then, because I was afraid to stand alone at the bottom of the tower, I snuck up behind her and waited on the landing. I could hear my father's deep loud voice. ". . . like her mother. Let her stay in the Violet Room and come here once a week." Nanny said something I couldn't make out, and my father replied, "No—not the village school. I'll engage a tutor."

And so, from then on, I was tutored by a retired schoolteacher from Poughkeepsie, Mrs. Weingarten, and once a week I climbed the stairs to my father's office in the tower. On the whole I was happy to have his attention, and I spent a large part of the week thinking up what to tell him. He was most animated when I told him about my dreams, and since I had moved to the Violet Room I had many that I could tell him, made up from the stories in my mother's old books, like The Secret Garden and The Wolves of Willoughby Chase, in which lonely children were banished to ancient mansions like Wyldcliffe Heights.

Those stories, after all, seemed more real to me than the world outside the locked gates and high walls of Wyldcliffe Heights. I was as much a prisoner as the "patients," but at least they had each other while I was not allowed to "fraternize" with them. All I had for companions were my mother's books, and so, moving on from the children's books, I read Jane Eyre and Wuthering Heights, Great Expectations and The Mysteries of Udolpho, stories about girls trapped in great houses as I was. Mrs. Weingarten also brought me her favorites—Rebecca and Mistress of Mellyn and The Silence of Herondale—which had pictures on their covers of women fleeing great houses that looked like Wyldcliffe Heights. All of those women came to their houses from the outside world and they could go back to it. Why couldn't I get away from Wyldcliffe Heights?

When I asked my father, he told me I was too fragile for the world beyond Wyldcliffe's gates, just as my mother had been. "When I came here," he told me, "she was already broken. I thought I had fixed her until—"

I knew he meant until she had me. I thought she'd died having me, but when I asked Nanny she stared at me and shook her head. "Oh no, pet, it was a hard delivery but she survived that. It was after that she took a turn. Some women do, it's called postpartum depression. The doctor said it was particularly bad for her because of her delicate mental health. We had to keep her quiet and calm, he told us, and away from you."

"Why away from me?" I asked.

Nanny looked sorry she had said anything and admitted sadly, "So she wouldn't do you any harm. It was part of her sickness. She'd taken a fancy there was something wrong with you. A taint of her own madness. Red Bess's curse, she called it. She was raving there at the end and fighting us. She got away and found you in the nursery and ran with you to the children's cemetery."

"Why to the children's cemetery?"

"She had a morbid fascination with the place. She would go there sometimes to read the names of the poor babies who were born to the girls here. There was a pair of graves of a mother and daughter at the edge of the cemetery, in a spot overlooking the river, that she used to sit by and say, 'At least they ended up here together. I would never want to leave and know my own flesh and blood had to make her way in the world without me.' I believe she was thinking about those poor souls when she leapt from the cliff with you strapped to her chest. She meant to take you both out of this world, but she must have regretted her choice at the end because she twisted around and landed on her back so you were spared. You can hold on to that, pet; your mother saved you in the end."

It was little enough to cling to. Too little. My mother had been mad. She believed she'd passed her madness on to me and tried to kill me, taking her own life in the process. No wonder my father had quailed when he saw my mother in me. When I tried to ask my father more about her, he said it was unhealthy for me to dwell on my mother's case. But I had to know what lay in store for me.

I waited until he went away for a conference and stole into his tower office and found my mother's file. My father had been called in to treat her by my grandmother Josephine Hale Bryce. He reported that he found a sheltered girl of above average intelligence, who suffered from paranoia and delusions. She believed she was haunted by the specter of Bess Molloy, the madwoman who had killed her grandfather and who, Eliza believed, would return to kill her. She made excellent progress under a regimen of therapy and tranquilizers and was thought to have made a full enough recovery that Dr. Sinclair married her.

The file ended there with no account of her pregnancy, childbirth, and postpartum depression. There were no more answers to be found in my mother's file. As I was putting it back, I saw another file next to my mother's with my name on it. It hadn't occurred to me that I would even have a file. I took it out and sat down at my father's desk to read it. Under "family history" I read, "Mother had a history of mental illness including schizophrenia, auditory and visual hallucinations, suicidal ideation, and postpartum psychosis." Then I read on to my own diagnosis.

"Patient began exhibiting hallucinations and delusions at age 8 . . . lost in a fantasy world . . . early signs of schizophrenia . . . suggest observation and institutional supervision . . ."

As I read it, the words blurring before my eyes, it slowly dawned on me that my father had long ago stopped thinking of me as his daughter and had begun thinking of me as a patient. There were pages of notes detailing each fancy I had confided to him. "Patient believes that inanimate objects such as windows, mirrors, wardrobes, etc. have consciousness . . . patient has experienced hallucinations of ghosts and believes the house is haunted . . . patient believes she is being watched by unseen presences . . . patient exhibits paranoia and delusions . . ."

But was I his patient? Was it even legal for him to treat his own daughter as a patient? I didn't know . . . and I didn't know who I could ask. Mrs. Weingarten had retired and moved to Florida. Nanny was ancient and nearly blind. No one in the village knew me or had ever even laid eyes on me, so completely had my father sequestered me away. I was invisible. It was like I didn't exist.

My hands shaking, I put away my file, but as I did, I noticed a folded sheet of paper stuck between my mother's file and mine. As I unfolded it, I recognized my mother's handwriting from her inscription in her books. "Dear Robert," it read. "Since you will not believe I am well enough to care for my own child I must take her away. This place is bad for both of us—cursed by Red Bess and by all the women whose lives were ruined here. Don't try to stop me unless you want to end up like your predecessor.

—Eliza"

I knew then that my mother hadn't killed herself. She had been running away, with me. She must have fallen as she tried to climb down the cliff. I decided at that moment as I stood in the tower that I had to leave Wyldcliffe Heights. I knew that beyond the Ramble somewhere was the children's cemetery. That was where my mother had gone on the night she had died, to the graves of the mothers and children who were buried there.

I would climb down the cliff she had fallen from—

Or had been pushed from.

CHAPTER TWELVE

"Who do you think pushed her?" I ask before the ink is dry on the last sentence. "Do you think it was your father?"

When she doesn't answer I look up and see that she has turned her blind face toward me. After a long moment that seems to stretch in the sun like a cat she speaks, her voice her own again. "Miss Corey, did you come here for a sequel or a biography?"

I feel an instant flash of heat in my face, as if I've been slapped. *How naive!* I can hear Atticus saying, *to confuse the fictional with the real.* Hadley and Kayla were always laughing over letters from readers who wrote as if the views of fictional characters represented the views of the author and, by extension, those of the publisher.

And yet.

I'm in a house called Wyldcliffe Heights with the daughter of a hypnotherapist who has been telling me—

Her story?

Or Violet's?

"I just . . ." I begin and then start again. "This isn't really a sequel, is it, when the events take place before *The Secret of Wyldcliffe Heights?*"

I catch the ghost of a smile on Veronica's lips—or perhaps it's a shadow passing over her face. Outside, clouds are scudding over the mountains on the other side of the river. "But that book was from Jayne's point of view," she reminds me. "I thought you understood that this was *Violet's* story. I think," she added, "that some of the mysteries will be clearer from Violet's perspective."

"I see . . . so you weren't . . . your mother wasn't . . . ?"

"Mad? A mental patient?" The smile is back but it's a sad one. "And what if she were? Do you believe we are destined to become our mothers?"

"I certainly hope not!" I blurt out before I can think better of my response.

She flinches as if I'd insulted her and her face turns pink everywhere but around her eyes, where the scar tissue forms a mask. "Was your mother so very awful?" she asks.

"My mother wasn't around enough to be awful," I say.

"That's its own way of being awful," she says.

"It wasn't really her fault. She wasn't . . . isn't well. Social services removed me from her care when I was eight and put me in a foster home."

"You didn't have any other family you could live with?"

"No, or at least none that my mother was ever willing to own or that the state could find. We were always on our own and we moved around a lot for as long as I could remember . . ." I pause, recalling that image of lying in a tub and feeling my mother's hand cradling my head, a feeling of being *home*.

"And what became of your mother after you were put in foster care?"

"She wrote me sometimes and came for supervised visits for a while, but she'd get upset when she saw me and she acted so badly on one visit that she was arrested and wound up in a

psychiatric hospital but she ran away . . . she was in and out of
hospitals for the next few years . . ." I pause again to gather breath
to say what I usually say—*We lost track of each other,* as if we
were casual acquaintances who fell out of touch—but that's not
what comes out of my mouth. "When she ran away she would
send me postcards, usually from little towns in upstate New York
or Vermont or Maine, with *Wish you were here* or *I think you'd like
it here!* So I'd go looking for her—"

"Your foster parents let you do that?"

I laugh. "Hardly. I'd run away, following her trail of postcards
until I tracked her down. Sometimes she'd already be gone by
the time I got to the last town she'd written from. Sometimes
she would be there and have a place for us. It would be nice for a
while. She was fun when she was well . . . She loved *The Secret
of Wyldcliffe Heights,* you know; she always had a copy with her
and she read it aloud to me at night. She said she wanted to write
something like it and she would sit and try to write . . ." I falter.
How can I explain to this calm, regal-looking woman what would
happen to my mother when she tried to write? ". . . but it never really worked out for her and she would become frustrated that she
couldn't write. Then she would do something that drew the authorities to us, shoplifting, usually, and I'd end up back in foster
care—or Woodbridge when I was deemed too big a flight risk—
and she'd end up back in a psychiatric hospital until she managed
to run away again. Dr. Husack, the psychiatrist at Woodbridge,
told me she was most likely schizophrenic and bipolar and would
need to be medicated for the rest of her life. I started ignoring her
postcards, but she showed up at Woodbridge and later, she managed to track me down to my college dorm. I moved off campus
and she found me there, too. She always finds me. The last time

I saw her, a few years ago, I told her I didn't want to see her ever again, which I know sounds horrible—"

"You were only trying to protect yourself," she says. "It must have been terrible growing up like that."

"Yeah, well . . ." I begin, shrugging. I wipe my face and find that it's wet. I'm glad Veronica can't see me. "I suppose that's why I loved *The Secret of Wyldcliffe Heights* so much. Violet grows up thinking she's under a curse . . ." I pause, thinking that in the book the curse is Red Bess, but in this new version the curse is Violet's mother's mental illness. "She believes she'll never be able to escape it, but then Jayne comes and finds her and frees her. In the end they're going to escape. I guess the reason I want a sequel so much is to find out if they made it."

"And what if they didn't?" Veronica asks. "Would you still want a sequel then?"

"Oh!" I say, startled at the question. "I don't know . . . I mean, it's hardly up to me." I try to laugh but the expression on Veronica's face strangles the sound in my throat. Her face has gone entirely white, the skin everywhere the same color as the scar tissue around her eyes. It looks as if her face has become a Kabuki mask and her green glasses its dark eyeholes. For one terrible moment I wonder what lies beneath that mask. "Is that why you're telling the story from Violet's point of view? Because she's the only one who's able to tell the end of the story?"

"We won't know that until we get to the end," she says primly, as if I had suggested reading the last page of a book first.

"Of course," I say. "I'd still want a sequel, however it ended."

The white mask of her face quivers like melting wax, but then her jaw tightens as if she's gritting her teeth to keep the mask in place. "Well, then—" She retrieves her cane and taps it briskly on the floor. "You'd best get to work typing. We'll recommence tomorrow morning."

As I TYPE up the pages I hear Violet's voice, not Veronica's, telling the story of her strange, cloistered childhood. Could it be how Veronica grew up here? Kept prisoner in her own house because . . . what? Her father feared she'd inherited her mother's madness? Maybe she had—her mother, after all, had been raised by Josephine Hale, who'd seen her husband slaughtered by her protégée. That would drive anyone mad. Maybe it was this place, I thought, raising my head from the pages and looking out the window. The sun has crossed the roofline and cast the shadow of the tower onto the lawn—Wyldcliffe Heights's very own sundial pointing to noon on the semicircle of the west lawn just as it had in Veronica's story. I looked back at the pages and reread those last lines:

> . . . I knew that beyond the Ramble somewhere was the children's cemetery. That was where my mother had gone on the night she had died, to the graves of the mothers and children who were buried there.

If I could find those graves it would be some confirmation that the story Veronica was telling was based on something true. Laeticia had said I was free to roam the grounds, and there's no reason to go into the village today because it's Sunday, so the library and post office are closed. I could go explore the Ramble, as Veronica called it, if there even was a "ramble" and she wasn't just borrowing the idea from Central Park.

I add the new typed pages to yesterday's and slide them under the gray stone. When I look back out the window a cloud has blotted out the sun, erasing the shadow tower from the lawn. I can still feel it, though, like the needle of a compass deep inside me, urging me forward. *Out. Now.* I don't want to go back through the atrium and into the mudroom in case I run into Laeticia and am summoned to lunch. I look at the floor-to-ceiling windows instead and begin to try them to see if they'll open. They're all painted shut . . . until I get to the last set behind the green couch. These are glass French doors with a latch. As I squeeze past the couch the soft mossy fabric feels like an animal brushing against my legs. I turn and fumble with the latch, afraid I'll find it locked, afraid that if I do I might break the glass in my sudden frenzy to be out—

I'd mostly told Veronica the truth when I said I ran away to join my mother, but what I hadn't told her was how I waited for those postcards summoning me, the pressure building inside me to be gone, and that sometimes I would leave before they came.

The latch is so stiff that when it finally gives, I tumble out onto the wet grass, the glass panes rattling in my wake so loudly I'm afraid they will raise an alarm—

I'm not an inmate, I remind myself, but I'm already running down the lawn, my thin, cheap shoes sinking into the moist earth. From the window the lawn had looked like a fancy green carpet, but beneath its thin veneer of grass and moss the mud sucks at my feet as if nothing grew very deep here. It's cold, too; even though I can see the sun shining on the river and mountains, I can't feel its warmth. When I reach the edge of the woods I turn and see that the way I've come has been in the shadow of the tower. The ground here must never feel the touch of the sun, which is why it's so wet and mossy and not, as a nasty voice in my head suggests, because the shadow of Red Bess's tower kills everything it touches.

THE POSTS ON either side of the opening to the path are topped with crouching lions so worn by centuries of rain and mantled by creeping moss that they look like Chia Pets. The moss covers the path as well, a green carpet that is soft and springy underfoot and seeps a brown, tea-colored ooze over my thin shoes. The path meanders first one way and then another as if it's taking its time. I imagine it was designed that way to lull the inmates into somnolence in the days before psychopharmaceuticals. It's bordered on either side by huge moss-covered boulders and pine trees that flash by at regular intervals like black frames between photo slides, which makes me feel like I'm falling under a hypnotic trance.

I glance back and forth to either side of the path and walk faster, speeding up the reel of tangled greenery between each frame until it all blurs together—pine, shrub, and the moss that has grown over everything, transforming fallen trees and roots and boulders into grotesque shapes—*lions and tigers and bears,* sings the song from another of Sister Bernadette's favorites—*and hounds,* sings another voice just as I turn the next loop and come face-to-face with one crouching in the middle of the path. It's the great gray fog-beast itself, with not just one set of slavering jaws and hollow-pit eyes but three, as if my nightmare has tripled in this hellish labyrinth.

"Meet Kirby."

The voice breaks the buzzing in my head. I turn toward it, not sure which is worse—finding someone else in the woods or finding that the voice and all of this is in my own head. Peter Syms is sitting on a fallen tree just beyond the fog-beast, his legs stretched out, a crumpled sandwich wrapper and Yeti thermos next to him. The smell of tobacco and coffee along with his satisfied smirk pierce the haze in my head; he's too annoying not to be real. I look back at the fog-beast and see it's just a statue.

"Kirby?" I ask.

"Short for Cerberus, the three-headed hound of hell who guards the entrance to the underworld. Never let it be said that the Hale family lacked a sense of humor. Imagine designing the family gardens after a model of hell."

"Yeah," I agree. The statue isn't really like my nightmare beast at all. Where the fog-beast's eyes glow yellow, these eyes are sunken black pits eroded by rain and time. "Must have been quite a laugh for the mental patients on their daily constitutionals."

"Oh, they weren't allowed in the Ramble."

"Yeah, about that, is it named after the one in Central Park?" I ask, showing off a little bit so he doesn't think he's the only one who knows things like Cerberus.

"Designed by the same guys—Calvert Vaux and Frederick Olmsted." He offers me the thermos cup of coffee along with a smirk. I take it because I'm cold.

"So why the hell theme?" I ask, taking a sip and tasting a kick of whiskey in the coffee.

"Jonathan Edward Hale had a puritanical streak. He was the one who turned the estate into a refuge for fallen women."

"And then his daughter, Josephine, reformed it."

"You've done your research," he says, draining the last of the whiskeyed coffee and tossing the dregs into the underbrush. "So what are you looking for?"

"I'm here to help Ms. St. Clair write a book," I say, trying to sound professional despite the squelch that comes as I shuffle my muddied feet.

He laughs and rises to his full height. It's the first time I've seen him stand up straight. He towers over me. He must be around six feet five. It occurs to me suddenly that a real Peter Syms might be more dangerous than imaginary beasts. "I meant," he says, "what are you looking for in the Ramble? Or do you always go hiking in your slippers?" He looks down skeptically at my Mary Janes. He's wearing heavy workman's boots that look like they could kick down doors.

"I was curious about a reference Ms. St. Clair made in her book to something called the children's cemetery, but it's not important . . . I should be heading back—"

"Without seeing what you came for?" he asks. "There's something you might find interesting in the children's cemetery and it's just a little past here." He cocks his head at the statue of the snarling three-headed hound. "What do you think Kirby is guarding?"

As I FOLLOW Peter Syms, I notice the woods here are denser. I'd thought the Ramble path was wild but I see now that it's a construct, a theme-park version of "wild." This is the real wild.

"Why isn't there a path?" I demand, swatting away the branches that snap back behind him.

"This *is* the path," he claims. "It's just overgrown. No one comes here anymore. Do you think blind Veronica could tap her way through this?"

"Aren't you, like, the groundskeeper? Shouldn't you be *keeping the grounds?*"

He barks a short laugh and half turns his head to snip back at me. "Like there's money to maintain this estate. And besides—" He stops suddenly, causing me to run into him. "No one wants to preserve this, least of all Veronica St. Clair."

It takes a moment to make out what he's looking at in the

murky green light. We might be at the bottom of a well, the way the stones slowly emerge out of the gloom like the bones of drowned children. The gravestones are half sunken in the damp earth. I step toward one, my footprints filling with brown water. As I kneel to read the first inscription, I picture the bones buried below, tea-stained in the peaty soil.

Nellie McGovern, it reads, no date of birth or death or cheery epitaph. I move on to the next one, *Jennie Fuller,* and the next, *Mary O'Brien.* "Why aren't there dates?" I ask. But Peter Syms only shrugs, no longer Mr. Know-It-All in this gloomy spot. "Not important enough, I guess. When I asked him, my dad said these were the girls who died in the refuge from dysentery or cholera or childbirth, and there was no one to claim their bodies. Their babies are here, too, and the runaways—"

"The runaways?" My voice sounds hollow and very far away, as if I've become a disembodied echo.

"Dad said that was just a story they told the girls to keep them from running, that runaways would be punished after death by being buried in these woods where no one would ever find them."

I turn around to catch him in a smirk but he's not smiling. His face looks awful in the green gloom, and I realize from his expression that mine must look even worse. "Why would you tell me such an awful thing? Did someone tell you—" I'm about to ask if someone has told him that I was a runaway, but I can tell by the look of sheer confusion on his face that he doesn't know what I'm talking about. "Is that what you thought I would find interesting?" I say instead.

"Never mind," he says too quickly. "It's just a stupid coincidence."

"What kind of a coincidence?" I demand. "Show me."

He shrugs—more of a flinch than his customary loose roll of

the shoulders—and turns. I follow him along the crooked row of tilting gravestones to the edge of the clearing. Through a gap in the trees, I can see the river. I step toward the gap, thinking this is what Peter wants to show me, and find myself on the edge of a steep drop to a rocky inlet below. Is this where Violet's— *Veronica's?*—mother plunged to her death, her baby strapped to her chest, when she fell (or was pushed) while trying to escape?

"Careful," Peter says, his voice so close behind me that I startle. "The ground's not stable and it's a long drop. Runaways have broken their necks on it."

I back away and turn to see if he's smirking at me, but he's looking down at the last stone of the row. This one has a little angel sitting on top. It would be a nice addition if she wasn't missing half her head. "I knew your name sounded familiar," he says, "but like I said, it's a coincidence."

I look down at the stone, the carved name barely visible above the line of earth and so worn I have to kneel down and lean in until my face is inches away to believe what I see. *Agnes Corey,* it reads.

CHAPTER THIRTEEN

s this some kind of a joke?" I demand.

Peter squints at me. "Yeah, sure, I went to the trouble of carving your name on a gravestone and then roughing it up so it looks a hundred years old."

I touch the weathered stone and run my fingers over the letters of the name—*my name*. The surface is granular and softly furred with moss. When I grasp an edge and yank, the stone doesn't budge.

"Maybe you're related," Peter offers, "and Agnes is an old family name. There are dozens of Peters in my family tree. Did your parents ever say if you were named for an ancestor?"

"No," I say. "My mother said she saw the name Agnes in a book and liked it because it was old-fashioned and I wouldn't meet a dozen girls with the same name, unlike her name, Jane—"

"Your mom's name is Jane? That *is* weird."

I think he's going to say something about my mother having the same name as the heroine of *The Secret of Wyldcliffe Heights* but then I notice that he's pointing at a stone behind baby Agnes's. I look down again so quickly that my vision blurs and the soft ground beneath my knees seems to shift unsteadily. The gravestone reads, *Jane Corey*.

"They were probably a mother and daughter," Peter says. "A lot of the girls at the Magdalen refuge were pregnant when they got here and it wasn't unusual for them to die in childbirth. It is a little funny that you and your mother have both of their names."

"Hilarious," I say, getting to my feet. I tear my eyes away from the two gravestones and glance toward the river. This is where Violet's mother came to escape from her controlling husband.

"Is there a way down from here?" I ask, stepping closer to the edge.

"You mean other than straight down to the rocks below?" he asks, coming to stand beside me. "There's a path—" He points to a narrow track that clings to the edge of the cliff. "But it's eroded over the years. I wouldn't try it."

"I won't," I say. *Because I'm not a prisoner,* I add to myself, *and I can go out the front gate any time I choose.* Looking back at the gravestone with my name on it, though, I feel the way I used to when I was caught and brought back to Woodbridge—that no matter how many times I run away I'll always end up back in the same place.

Laeticia takes one look at my shoes and declares them a lost cause. I have a feeling it's her assessment of me as well, as she hands me a pair of moccasins atop a stack of neatly folded clothes—"some old things of Miss St. Clair's"—and sends me upstairs to change before I spread muck around the house.

I don't much like carrying that stack of clothing up the stairs. When I'd come back to Woodbridge after one of my "walkabouts," as Sister Bernadette called them, I'd be made to strip down and given state-issued scrubs while my own clothes were being sterilized and searched for contraband. I suspected that part of the punishment was being forced to wear the rough baggy canvas pants that always chafed my inner thighs and the loose smock tops that made everyone look six months pregnant. Walking back to your room, your pants making that swish-swish noise and carrying a stack of state-issued clothes, was the Woodbridge Walk of Shame. I feel that same shame now as I drop the stack of clothes on my bed. I'm tempted to ignore them, but Laeticia had told me to leave my muddy clothes in the hall for her to collect. If I don't, she'll knock on my door, and I don't want to talk to her. I want to go up into the attic and look through the Magdalen files for the original Agnes Corey and figure out why I have her name.

I peel off my damp clothes and grudgingly try on the pleated tartan skirt, button-down shirt, and cardigan. The skirt has a B. Altman's label that says it was made in Scotland. It has a leather tab that adjusts the waist and a silver kilt pin. The shirt is made of a cotton that feels like silk. The forest-green cardigan is cashmere. It all fits perfectly. When I look at myself in the bathroom mirror, I see that I have finally achieved Hadley's retro-librarian look. All I need is a pair of horn-rimmed glasses. It's the perfect outfit for conducting some research.

I HAUL THE box for the earliest years of the Magdalen refuge over to a rolltop desk in the attic and slide up the ridged top, which rattles like castanets. Inside are tiny drawers and slots that make my fingers itch to explore. I open one drawer and find a collection of glass marbles, another holds a dried corsage of violets, and the last a coil of tattered ribbon. *How lovely,* I think, *to have all these secret places to hide tiny treasures. I bet the girls at the Magdalen had no place to hide.* I open a large, dusty ledger. Each entry has a number, a name, city of origin, reason for commitment, and notes on the progress of the paroled girl after her release. It doesn't make for cheery reading.

> *Lizzie Jones, from Utica, went back to evil ways after a few months.*
> *Anna Hamm, found work at a collar shop, but has been reported cavorting with suspicious characters in Troy.*

I find them in the third ledger.

> *Jane Corey, committed to the refuge for disorderly behavior on the streets of Schenectady, died in 1893 of puerperal fever. Shortly thereafter her daughter Agnes followed her to the grave.*

I stare at the bare entry for so long that the light coming through the west-facing windows reddens. What possible connection could that ill-fated pair have to me and my mother? Then, just as the last rays of crimson fade and darken on the ledger like blood drying, I have a glimpse of my mother walking ahead of me on one of those small-town streets that were always too quiet for her loud voice. She's looking back at me, her face half hidden by dark curls flying loose in the breeze, laughing at me for wanting her to be quieter.

Am I cavorting with suspicious characters in Troy? she teased. *Is my behavior too disorderly for the streets of Schenectady?*

At the time I'd thought she'd picked the cities at random, but now I see that she had mimicked exactly the wording in the ledgers and the only way she could have done that was if she had read them. This was where she got our names, which means my

mother was here at Wyldcliffe Heights, no doubt as an inmate of
Dr. Sinclair's mental hospital.

I READ *The Secret of Wyldcliffe Heights* late into the night, searching in vain for those phrases *cavorting with suspicious characters in
Troy* and *disorderly behavior on the streets of Schenectady* to see if
my mother found them in the book. The words go round and round
in my head and follow me into a restless, shallow sleep in which
I pursue my mother through gauzy curtains of fog as she slips in
and out of sight. We're winding our way down to the bottom of the
Ramble, where I trip over something and land on my knees in the
spongy soil, surrounded by white jagged shapes like teeth—

Gravestones. I'm in the children's cemetery. When I try to get
up the mud sucks me down. I can hear the girls who died here
stirring below me, calling my name. *Agnes Corey, you're one of us,
you belong with us!* A broken half face smirks up at me and bony
fingers encircle my wrist, but I wrench free and reach for a hand
that appears out of the fog to pull me up. My mother has come
back for me! She's pulling me out of the graveyard and toward the
edge of the cliff. *Better to die free in the air than buried here in
the mud,* she says, turning to me at the edge of the cliff, where
the fog that veils her face like a silk scarf slips away, revealing a
bare-bone skull that grins at me as we hurtle over the edge.

I jerk awake, clutching a handful of twisted sheets to keep
myself from falling, my mother's skeletal grin still mocking me.
A gleam of white bone in the shadows. I lie still for a moment,
holding on to that final image, horrible as it is, because it reminds
me of something, some clue to who my mother really was. Who *I*
am. If I can just hold on to the image long enough for those bones
to grow flesh—

A knock at the door dispels the image, the bones sinking back into darkness.

"Seven-thirty, Miss Corey," Laeticia calls through the door.

"I'm up!" I call back, untangling myself from the sheets. I've wound them around me like a shroud, as if I'd spent the night preparing myself for my own burial.

I DRESS IN the tartan skirt, cotton blouse, and cashmere sweater along with warm tights and the moccasin slippers, the outfit making me feel a little bit more organized despite my fuzzy head. As I sit in the straight-backed chair and take up my pad and pen I reflect that I would feel embarrassed to be wearing Veronica's castoffs if she could see me. She turns her face toward me when I'm settled and I steel myself for the sight of that white mask, recalling that moment in my dream when the fog-mask slipped off my mother's face revealing the skull beneath. But Veronica's face does not look like a mask this morning. Her skin, tinged with early morning light, is pink, as if freshly washed. As if some protective layer has been scrubbed away, revealing—

What?

For a moment I think she is on the verge of tears. But then she firms her jaw and, turning her face toward the window, she says, "If you're ready," and begins without waiting for my answer.

I LEFT Wyldcliffe Heights the same night I found my file and my mother's note. Why should I wait? My father was away at a conference and I may never have the opportunity—or nerve—to do it again.

Having never had need of a suitcase before, I found an old bag in the attic to pack my clothes, an ancient brocade carpetbag that might have once belonged to my grandmother, Josephine Hale. Inside was a locket with an enamel violet painted on it hanging from a violet ribbon. I tied it around my neck; tossed my clothes, a copy of Jane Eyre, and the little money I'd saved into the bag; and put on my good coat, which Mrs. Weingarten had bought from Peck & Peck for me last year. As I crept out through the French doors in the library, I felt like Jane Eyre fleeing Thornfield after she learns the secret of the house. As I had. I'd learned that I was the madwoman in the attic.

I stole out in the night and ran toward the woods, the moon casting the shadow of the tower over the lawn, its darkness protection against the eyes of anyone watching from the windows. I knew the night watchman and his dogs would be down at the gatehouse at this time of night. As I ran down the winding paths of the Ramble, I thought of all the girls who had run this way before, their ears pricked for the sound of the alarm, the footsteps of the guards, the baying of the bloodhounds. I crept past the statue of Cerberus as if he might come to life and devour me with his triple jaws, every nerve in my body on fire, my heart pumping so loudly I thought it would wake the dead in the children's cemetery.

As I neared the river the fog rolled in, like a wall blocking my way, and suddenly the woods were filled with light. I thought it was the watchman's flashlight and I'd been caught, but then it passed and I heard the foghorns on the river, and I realized it was the lighthouse beam. It lit my way down the cliff and across the marsh, the wind whispering through the dry reeds like the ghosts of all the girls who had tried to escape Wyldcliffe Heights before me. I was half frozen by the time I reached the station, but I was too afraid of being seen to retreat to the warmth of the waiting room, so I crouched in the marsh grasses until the train came roaring into the station in a cloud of steam.

I'd often heard the whistle of the night train. Mrs. Weingarten, who took the train each Christmas to visit her sister in Buffalo, told me it began in Toronto and continued on to New York City. I had always pictured its passengers as characters out of an old movie—Murder on the Orient Express or The Lady Vanishes. Imagine me walking out of that marsh, in my prim Peck & Peck woolen coat, carrying my grandmother's carpetbag, and onto a train in the early 1990s. It was like walking out of a black-and-white movie into Technicolor, out of the past and into the present. I think it was my first inkling of how sheltered I'd been at Wyldcliffe Heights. It wasn't just the outside world my father had kept me from; he'd kept me in a sepia-toned version of the world, a past that had faded away long ago. Imagine my surprise to find myself sitting next to boys in torn flannel shirts and girls wearing short dresses and tights with heavy work boots like the ones Old Syms wore. Both the boys and girls sported tattoos and pierced eyebrows and noses and earphones from which strange tinny music leaked. I was worried I had no place to go, no plans, no friends in the city, but then I remembered the Josephine. I'd heard the girls talk about it as somewhere they could go when they left Wyldcliffe Heights and needed an inexpensive place in Manhattan while they were looking for work. Nanny told me it had been founded by my grandmother as a settlement house and had then become a women's hotel. I pictured the one Kitty Foyle lived in. When I got off the train in Pennsylvania Station, I found my way to a taxi stand and told the driver I was going to the Josephine Hotel, confident that he would know it. He didn't, but he guessed that it would be on Josephine Street in the West Village and so he took me there, dropping me off on a deserted, foggy street corner with half of my little savings already depleted by train and taxi fares.

The streets smelled like offal and blood, which I learned later was because of the proximity of the meatpacking district, but at the time it made me think that I'd carried the taint of Red Bess with me. I didn't know where on Josephine Street the hotel was, but I followed the sound of foghorns toward the river. Maybe I would come out of the fog to find myself back at Wyldcliffe Heights, still wandering the labyrinth of the Ramble. But then I heard laughter and running feet and a girl emerged out of the fog. There were two men with her, too, but I barely noticed them.

If the train had made me feel as if I were from an earlier time, this girl made me feel as if I'd slipped backward in time. She was wearing a sleeveless cocktail dress made of some iridescent fabric that shimmered like an oil slick under the streetlamp, beneath a silvery fur coat draped over her bare shoulders, its hem hanging down over her torn fishnet stockings, which were all that she wore on her feet. A pair of stilettos dangled from her hand. Her eyes were rimmed with so much kohl she looked like a raccoon. A diamond stud winked from her left nostril. She was so much an apparition that I stared at her with no thought that she was looking back at me.

"I adore that bag, darling," she drawled. "You look like Thoroughly Modern Millie running away from home."

"I am running away from home," I said, startled into truth. "Do you know if the Josephine Hotel is down this way?"

"We're on our way there now to hear some third-rate band Casey here is all het up about." She jerked her thumb back toward the slighter and blonder of the two men. "I know the manager. I'll get you the inside rate if you tell me where you got that bag."

She draped her arm over my shoulder, enveloping me in a warm fug of cigarette smoke, sweat, and tea rose perfume. "I'm Jayne, by the way, Jayne with a y, and these are Casey and Gunn." She pointed to the two men behind her like they were an afterthought. I barely took them in. Before I could tell her my name she leaned in and touched the locket that hung loosely from a violet ribbon around my neck. "I love your violet locket," she said, burying her nose in my neck as if we had known each other all our lives. "You even smell like violets," she whispered, her breath tickling my throat. "Tell me that's your name!"

And because I felt like I'd become someone entirely new, I said yes, Violet was my name.

CHAPTER FOURTEEN

"This Jayne—" I begin.

"Is different from the one in *The Secret of Wyldcliffe Heights*?"

I nod and then realize she can't see me. She must not need to because she goes on. "The Jayne in the book is rather . . ." She searches for a word. "Not meek exactly but a bit self-effacing."

"Yes," I agree, "but in that way that makes you like her and think well of her. Almost . . ." I pause, embarrassed by the thought that has come to mind.

"What?" she prods.

"She's a little . . . no offense . . . what people call 'virtue signaling' today."

Veronica barks a short gruff laugh. "Yes, that's it exactly. She makes sure you see her good side. And she would, wouldn't she? The story's from her point of view and she's the young innocent girl arriving at the corrupt old house. She's Emily St. Aubert and Jane Eyre and the second Mrs. de Winter—although I've never been sure the last was *entirely* innocent. But how do you think Jane looks to Bertha or Emily to Madame Montoni or the second Mrs. de Winter to Mrs. Danvers?"

"Like an intruder," I say, immediately wondering if that's how I seem to Laeticia. "So now that we're seeing Jayne from your—

I mean, from Violet's point of view—we see her differently. Violet's different, too. She's not . . ." I pause, embarrassed by my thought.

"Not mad?" Veronica asks.

"No. At least not . . . *yet*. I can see how growing up as she did she might struggle with mental illness."

"Yes, this house would be enough to drive anyone quite mad . . ." She pauses as the clock begins to chime and turns her face toward the window as if her blind eyes are watching Violet in her Peck & Peck coat fleeing with her carpetbag toward the Ramble, the shadow of the tower marking her progress. When the clock has finished chiming twelve times she says, "I suppose it's time to break for lunch . . . unless . . . you would like to go on?"

"Yes," I say before thinking that she might be hungry or tired. But if she is she doesn't say. She picks up the story without hesitation, with no "let me see where I was," as if it is always playing in her head.

When we got to the Josephine we found a line snaking around the corner, everyone dressed in outfits so outrageous—long cloaks and spiky hair, studded collars, white makeup with bloodred lipstick—that I thought we must have arrived for a costume party. "Do all these people want a room here?" I asked, fearful that I'd have no place to stay.

Jayne laughed. "No, silly, it's for the show. Come on, I know the bouncer."

We trailed behind Jayne as she sauntered boldly to the front of the line and wrapped herself around the bare chest of a brawny man in a leather vest and heavy chains. The one she called Gunn, who also wore leather and chains like they were all part of the same club, joined them. Casey hung back with me. He was less scary-looking than Gunn, his shiny too-short trousers, starched button-

down shirt, and paisley tie reminding me of my father's accountant. "Watch this," he said. "I give Leatherface there thirty seconds before he falls for Jayne's charms and Gunn's coke." He began humming the Jeopardy! theme under his breath.

"Who could blame him?" I said. "Jayne's so beautiful."

He gave me a long, considering look while lighting a cigarette. "You didn't even take thirty seconds before you tumbled for her, Violet. Be careful. Jayne loves to snare innocent naïfs into her web and raise them up in her image—especially ones who look a little like her. She's grown tired of her last one and is ready for a new recruit. You fit the bill perfectly."

"You think I look like her?" I asked, thrilled and a little wary he was making fun of me.

He squinted at me through the smoke of the cigarette that hung from his lower lip and reached out his hand to trace the line of my neck from earlobe to clavicle. Then he tugged the violet ribbon until it was tight around my throat. "You've got the same lovely long swan's neck," he said. "The rest will come."

I wanted to ask what he meant, but Jayne was beckoning us to join her at the front of the line where the bouncer, rubbing his nose from whatever Gunn had given him, was unhooking the velvet rope to let us through. I hurried ahead of Casey, pulling the collar of my coat tighter around my neck—my lovely long swan's neck—to banish the chill that had settled there.

We went up a flight of steps and into a lobby with art deco pillars and a high tiled ceiling. There was a stuffed peacock over the registration desk, its tail feathers drooping, and faded velvet couches where girls in vintage dresses and boys in leather pants sprawled. On second look I realized that some of the "girls" weren't girls and it was hard to tell what gender the leather-clad set belonged to, if any *at all. What I did notice was that none of them looked like me with my Peck & Peck wool coat and carpetbag.*

"Shouldn't I see about getting a room first before going—" I gestured toward the open double doors. Jayne had called it the ballroom, but the loud discordant cacophony that poured out didn't sound like ballroom music.

"Good idea," Jayne said, "that way we can primp a bit. This warm-up band is so Siouxsie-and-the-Wannabees. You boys go ahead," she told Casey and Gunn. "Vi and I are going to"—she reached into Gunn's vest pocket and extracted a tiny vial—"powder our noses."

She led me to the registration desk and tapped her black fingernails on the bronze domed bell. A man in a seersucker suit, bow tie, and a brass name tag that read Lars looked up with a bored expression.

"Yes?"

"My friend wants to check in. Is Sven here?"

"Sven's in Sweden," Lars replied. "And we're full. Your friend"—he gave me a withering look—"should have called ahead."

"Oh!" I gulped like the country rube I was. "I had no idea. I've heard about the Josephine from the girls at Wyldcliffe Heights for years. They made it sound like there was always a room."

"Wyldcliffe Heights?" he repeated, lifting a pair of gold-rimmed glasses from a chain around his neck to peer at me. "You don't look like a Wyldcliffe Girl."

My cheeks burned because he thought I was an inmate of Wyldcliffe Heights. "I'm not exactly . . . you see, I grew up there . . ." In my confusion I looked up and noticed a framed photograph of Josephine Hale—a copy of the one that hung in our library. I pointed to it and blurted out, "That's my grandmother."

Lars started to smile but Casey, who had slid in beside me, cocked his finger under my chin, lifting it a quarter inch. "Can't you see the resemblance, man? She's the spitting image—and look, she's even wearing the same necklace."

I noticed then that the locket I'd found in the carpetbag was the same as the one in the portrait, only Josephine wore the broad violet ribbon tight around her throat like a choker. Jayne peered closer and then looked back at the photograph. "Of course it's the same," she said as if she had discovered it. "This is Violet Hale."

I began to tell her that wasn't really my name, but then I realized it was better if they thought it was. Besides, Jayne was already plowing ahead, her black-tipped fingernails digging into my arm proprietarily. "You can't very well turn away the granddaughter of Josephine Hale, founder of the Josephine. And think of the publicity for the hotel! Sven will be furious when he gets back and learns you missed such an opportunity."

"Even if I wanted to there aren't any rooms," he said, holding up both his hands. "Except for the tower suite. Do you want the tower suite, Miss Hale? It's a hundred dollars a night."

"I-I-can't—" I began.

"Turn that down," Casey said, slapping a credit card down on the desk. "As Miss Hale's business manager, I'll take care of that."

"I can't let you—" I tried to object, but Lars was already sliding Casey's card through a credit card reader and Jayne, clearly pleased at Casey's offer, was handing my bag to Gunn and telling him to carry it up to the suite. Everything was happening so fast around me as if it didn't concern me at all. The only one meeting my eye was Josephine Hale, whose cool gaze seemed to suggest that nothing good ever happened in a tower.

IT WASN'T LIKE the tower at Wyldcliffe Heights at all, though. It was a big circular room with tall arched windows all the way around with views of the river and New York Harbor. There were a couple of mattresses on the floor, antique mirrors on the walls, trash everywhere, and a crystal chandelier festooned with party streamers hanging from the high domed ceiling.

"The drag queens who had it before threw a big going-away party and we haven't had a chance to clean up," Lars explained.

"It's perfect as is," Jayne declared, standing on tiptoe to touch one of the chandelier teardrops and setting the whole thing tinkling. "I don't know why I never thought of staying here before."

"Casey never offered to pay before," Gunn said, slouching in one of the window seats to look out at the view.

Casey shrugged. "As long as Violet needs a place to stay, why not? I don't suppose you'll mind sharing with us, will you, Vi?"

"Of course not!" I exclaimed, amazed I'd not only found a place to stay but ready-made friends.

"What do you think, Gunn?" Jayne asked. "The light will be amazing during the day. You can paint—"

"And I can film with my new camcorder," Casey remarked, extracting a bulky camera from his bag and pointing it at Jayne.

Jayne immediately preened and then grabbed my hand to twirl me around. I could see our reflections in the antique mirrors and windows spinning with us. "We'll be your muses."

"As long as you pay the rent the first of the month you can have orgies and paint the walls," Lars said, tossing the key onto one of the mattresses. "This place has seen it all. You know it's where that famous murder took place in the twenties."

Jayne stopped mid-swirl and opened her mouth in a round O. I thought she'd say we couldn't stay, but instead her voice sounded excited. "A famous murder? Do tell!"

Lars shrugged as if famous murders were all part of a day's work at the Josephine. "During the twenties this was a flophouse. Your ancestor"—he turned toward me—"tried to make it into something more respectable. They took in girls off the street and offered them a place to sleep and get a good meal—and to keep them safe from the Violet Strangler."

"The Violet Strangler?" we all echoed.

"A killer who stalked the waterfront and strangled prostitutes with a violet scarf. One night a girl named Bess Molloy and a few other girls were sleeping in here and she woke up to see a man bent over one of the girls, strangling her with a violet scarf. She jumped up and attacked the man with a pair of scissors. He put up his hand to stop her and the scissors went clean through his hand." Lars held up his hand to demonstrate and I felt Jayne squeeze my hand so hard I could feel the blades piercing my palm. "But he kept his cool and pummeled Bess with the handle of the scissors, knocking her unconscious. When she came to, she was lying in a pool of blood and all the girls in the room had been murdered, their throats cut, and her scissors in her hand. When a maid came in to clean, she ran screaming for the police. Bess told her story but no one believed her, especially because she couldn't describe the murderer, whose face, she claimed, was covered by a sheer violet scarf. The press nicknamed her Red Bess and started calling for her hanging. Josephine Hale spoke up for her at the trial and said she believed her, but a psychiatrist testified that she was mentally unsound. The judge convicted Bess but he spared her life and remanded her to a women's asylum upstate. Within the year, Red Bess murdered Josephine's husband and lit the place on fire," Lars finished in a singsong voice as if the gory story were a nursery rhyme.

"Are you sure you want to stay here, Violet?"

I wasn't at all sure. Everything was moving so fast. I'd come to the Josephine to escape Wyldcliffe Heights, but now it felt like the legacy of Red Bess had followed me here. But then Jayne squeezed my hand and looked at me, her eyes shining. "I can feel them here—Red Bess and Josephine. We could tell their story, write songs about them and Gunn can paint them and Casey the Chronicler will film us." She smiled sweetly at him. "Maybe you'll catch some ghosts on film."

He smiled back, his eyes flashing from Jayne to me. "I can just about see them now."

I felt the ghost of his fingertips on my throat again—or maybe it was just the cold air coming in through the windows that felt as if a hand had stroked my neck and tightened my grandmother's ribbon around my throat.

JAYNE SENT "THE boys" out for "provisions" and set about getting me ready for the ballroom. I thought she'd be disappointed by what she found in my carpetbag but instead she oohed and ahhed over the Peter Pan–collar blouses and plaid skirts.

"We just need to make a few alterations," she said, dumping her bag out onto the floor. She used a pair of nail scissors to hack six inches off my skirt, leaving a ragged, uneven hem. She ripped the sleeves off a blouse and tied the tails around my waist, unbuttoning it low enough to show my bra. She held me at arm's length and squinted at the effect. "Almost. Take off your bra."

I turned bright red but obeyed, removing the plain white cotton Maidenform bra and folding it neatly on one of the stained mattresses. "Here," Jayne said, sliding her own bra off from under her dress and handing it to me. "I think our tits are roughly the same size."

Her bra was black and satiny and still warm from her body. My hands were shaking so much I couldn't do up the hooks, so she helped me. Then she slid the torn blouse back on and tied it at my waist without buttoning any of the buttons. "Perfect!" she said. "Very Lolita. Now let's do your makeup."

She smoothed chalk-white foundation on my skin and ringed my eyes with kohl and mascara. She sorted through a half dozen lipsticks and picked out one called Madder Violet. "We'll get some purple nail polish to match tomorrow," she said, painting my lips. "And some purple hair dye. From now on we'll only wear black and purple. Those will be our signature colors. All the goth bands will love you. I bet they bring us up onstage to sing with them—Nosferatu invited me up last week and the lead singer dedicated a song to me."

"I can't sing—" I began, thinking that even if I could I'd be terrified to go up on a stage.

"Can you stomp your feet?" she asked. "Can you scream bloody murder and shout your heart out at everyone who's ever lied to you and held you back?"

I thought of my father lying to me about my mother and committing me without my knowledge. I thought about the things he'd said about me in his notebooks and felt a white-hot anger rise in me. "Yes," I told Jayne. "I think I can do that."

"Good," she said, pulling me to my feet and dragging me in front of one of the antique mirrors. She made a few adjustments and then ran her fingers along the embroidered satin of the ribbon at my throat. "I love this," she said. "Tomorrow I'll look for one like it in the thrift shops."

"I have another!" I said, excited to have something to offer her after what she'd given me. I dug in the carpetbag and extracted the second ribbon I'd found with the locket. "It doesn't have a locket but it's still pretty," I said, handing her the embroidered satin ribbon.

She ran her fingers along it as if I'd given her something precious, then held it up next to mine. "They both have the same design stitched into them. A heart with two initials—I think I see a J," she said, her eyes lighting up.

"For Jayne," I said, although I knew it was really for Josephine.

She gave me a radiant smile and spun around so her back was to me. "Tie it on," she said, handing me the ribbon and lifting her dark hair off her neck. As I tied the ribbon I noticed that the roots of her hair were a dull brown. It made me feel more comfortable with her; she wasn't perfect, she had to work to create an impression of someone so effortlessly carefree. She would help me to be a different person, too.

"Tighter," she said after I'd tied a loose bow.

I pulled the ribbon tighter, the satin cutting into my fingers as I tied the knot.

"There!" she said, turning and facing the mirror with her face pressed against mine until our cheeks touched. With the pale makeup, enormous kohl-rimmed eyes, and violet-painted lips, we looked like two china dolls from the same mold—or rather, I thought as she moved her face an inch closer to the mirror and my own face receded into the shadows, a pale reflection of hers: she was the original and I was the copy. She turned and tugged the back of the ribbon tighter around my throat. Against my dead white skin, it looked like a slash of blood. As if my throat—

CHAPTER FIFTEEN

Veronica stops in the middle of the sentence.

As if my throat—

Maybe she's giving me time to catch up, although she hasn't done that before. I look up, pen poised—

And see that Veronica's face has gone paper white and her hand is at her throat, fingers scrabbling as if trying to tear something away—

Because she can't breathe.

I jump up, the pen and pad clattering to the floor, and pull her fingers away to see what she's pulling at, but there's nothing around her throat. I can hear a thin, reedy whistle coming from her mouth. Her twisted fingers grab at my hands. Her lips are flecked with spit and they're turning blue.

"Are you choking?" I shout into her face, wondering if she'd been sucking on a lozenge and swallowed it. "Should I do the Heimlich?"

I know how. Sister Bernadette made sure we were well trained in first aid. But the thought of performing the maneuver on my employer terrifies me. Her bones are so fragile I will probably break a rib. Still, it's better than her suffocating. I move behind her and wrap my arms around her torso, knotting my hands beneath her sternum. I am just about to heave up when Laeticia comes running into the library yelling at me to stop.

"Get off of her, you fool, she needs her inhaler."

I step back and watch as Laeticia fits a plastic tube into Veronica's mouth and pumps it once, twice, a third time, each time releasing a hiss of air. Then she kneels in front of her employer and cups her hands in both of hers. "Breathe," she says. "Just one breath in—" She demonstrates by taking in a deep breath and I find myself doing the same. "And out." She blows out the air in a long, steady rush that sounds to me like wind moving through dry reeds.

"She was telling the story," I say. "And then suddenly she just stopped in the middle of a sentence. What happened? Is she going to be all right?"

Laeticia looks over her shoulder at me as if she'd forgotten I was still here. "She had an asthma attack," she says slowly, as if talking to a child. "Her lungs were damaged in the fire and she has advanced COPD. She shouldn't have gone on so long—you were supposed to break for lunch an hour ago."

I remember Veronica asking if I wanted to stop and me urging her to go on. "I didn't know. No one told me she had asthma or COPD."

Laeticia clucks her tongue as if it should have been obvious. "I told you not to wear her out—"

"It's fine, Letty, leave the girl alone." Veronica's voice is a painful rasp, like a rusted saw scraping across barbed mesh. "It wasn't her fault."

Laeticia tsks again. "I suppose it was mine for not coming in and telling you it was time. I won't make the same mistake again," she says, looking at me as if I am the mistake, the intruder who should never have been let in the house. "Surely you can see that's enough for today?"

"I-I have to type up today's dictation," I say, looking around for my pad and pen.

"That can wait—" Laeticia begins but Veronica interrupts her by laying her hand on her arm, and although her voice is still a rasp it's steady and commanding.

"No, it can't, Lettie. We don't know how much time I have." And then, looking up at me, her eyes watery: "Go ahead, Miss Corey, before you lose the thread."

I SIT DOWN at the typewriter but my hands are shaking too hard to type. What had Veronica meant that she didn't know how much time she had? Was her COPD that bad? Was she dying? Was she going to be able to finish the book? Finally, I force myself to type up the pages. I don't think about the unfinished last line until I get to it.

As if my throat—

I could leave it there and ask her tomorrow how she would like to finish it. I imagine how I will phrase the question.

Before you stopped breathing—

When you started choking—

I wonder if it was a coincidence that she choked on that particular line. Had the memory of Jayne pulling that ribbon tightly around her throat caused her asthma attack? I'd felt my own throat constrict when she described the ribbon cutting into her skin. I look back at the last line. The obvious way to finish it is: *As if my throat had been slit.* But somehow that doesn't seem right. It's too . . . *passive.*

As if someone had slit my throat?

No, too vague.

As if Red Bess had slit my throat?

No, it changed how Veronica had begun the sentence, which seems like too much intervention on my part.

I close my eyes, fingers hovering over the keyboard, and picture the moment as Veronica described it. Two girls standing in front of a mirror, their faces pale as death, one in light, the other receding into shadow, the dark ribbon at her throat merging with the dark as if it were the dark that had parted her head from her body—

My eyes still closed I begin to type.

As if my throat had been slit by the dark itself.

I stare at the line, as shocked by the image as if someone else had written it. Where had that come from? And then I realize where it came from. I've seen this image before.

I GO STRAIGHT upstairs, grateful that Laeticia is nowhere in sight until I guiltily realize that she's probably still taking care of Veronica after her asthma attack. I wonder how often she has them and how serious the damage to her lungs is. Will she be able to go on dictating the book to me? How much time *does* she have left? What will happen to the sequel if she's not able to go on? What will happen to me?

In my room I lock my door before unzipping my backpack. I'd slipped the photograph I'd taken from the Josephine into the padded laptop sleeve to keep it from getting bent. I slide it out and lay it on the desk to look at it in the light. The women's pale faces seem to float up out of the dark stage, cut off from their bodies by the dark ribbons tied at their necks. I look closer. Yes, both are wearing chokers—black chokers, I'd thought, but they could be purple. The photograph is eerily like the image Veronica described of Jayne and Violet pressing their faces together in front of the mirror, except the woman who has pushed her face forward into the light here is Veronica. All that is visible of the other woman is the bare outline of cheekbone and jaw, the black pit of eye, and a dark slash at her throat. It must be the woman Veronica calls Jayne in the book, but somehow she's no longer the one forcing herself forward into the light and Veronica is no longer the shrinking violet. At some point Violet must have gotten tired of being in Jayne's shadow and pushed herself forward. Just as Veronica is pushing her own story into the light now by telling the story from Violet's point of view—*from the point of view of the madwoman in the attic.* After all, she's the one left to tell the story because Jayne's not here.

Why not? Where is Jayne? *Who* is Jayne?

I stare at the picture as if the force of my will can penetrate the darkness and bring the second girl out of the shadows and into the light. Since I first saw the picture there has been something about it that draws me, something familiar about the woman in the shadows, something Veronica's description of the two girls in the mirror recalled. Something about the ribbons.

I look closer at the ribbon at Veronica's throat. The light catches a glint of metallic thread and the suggestion of a pattern. Violets? Like the ribbon Violet finds in the carpetbag.

Like the one in my copy of *The Secret of Wyldcliffe Heights.*

I grab the book on my nightstand and open it to the page marked by the scrap of ribbon. Yes, it has a pattern of violets. Lots of fans used purple ribbons as bookmarks—like my mother's copy, which has a thin violet ribbon bookmark attached to the binding as well as the piece of ribbon she kept inside the book. I'd assumed my mother had been one of those fans who pressed dead violets into their copies and tied purple ribbons around their throats and wrists. It doesn't mean it's the same ribbon.

I stroke the torn piece of ribbon, tracing the violet pattern with my fingertips, and remember the ribbon in the rolltop desk. *It's just a coincidence,* I tell myself as I walk up the attic stairs clutching the ribbon in one hand and the photograph in the other. Even if the ribbon my mother kept in her book looks like the ribbon Veronica described and the one in the desk drawer, that doesn't mean anything. I already know that my mother was here at Wyldcliffe Heights. She got my name from the children's cemetery. It's not even that surprising. My mother was . . . well, "troubled" would be putting it nicely. She was "volatile," a word that Sister Bernadette told us came from the Middle English for "a creature that flies." That described my mother to a tee. In all my memories of her she is flitting away from me, looking over her shoulder, black hair shimmering blue like a crow's wing, the lilt of her laugh soaring my heart into flight. When she crashed she would bury herself under the blankets with her copy of *The Secret of Wyldcliffe Heights,* reading it over and over again. When I asked her why, she would say it was *her* story, it had been taken from her and she had to figure out how to get it back.

Dr. Husack told me she was probably bipolar with psychotic symptoms. He said that people with psychotic symptoms sometimes identified so deeply with historical or fictional characters that they came to believe they were those characters. My mother had just chosen a modern gothic heroine, one who happened to have the same name as her (albeit with an added y) instead of Napoleon or Cleopatra.

I sit at the desk and open the little drawers, looking for the one with the ribbon. The glass marbles rattle, the dried violets release their dusty perfume. I am beginning to wonder if I imagined the ribbon until I find it in the last drawer I open. I lay it on the desk beside the one from my mother's book. The design of violets edged in gold is the same, only the one that's been used as a bookmark has lost most of its gold threads and its ends are more ragged. I finger the end of the bookmark where the embroidery has been picked away—I've always assumed by my mother, who in her manic stages would shred her cuticles and the hems of her sweaters until they unraveled. I look closer now at the pattern of needle marks left behind and notice for the first time that it's not a violet; it's a heart—or rather, half a heart with an initial J inscribed inside.

Like the ribbon Veronica gave Jayne.

I pick up the ribbon from the drawer and hold it up to the window. The gold thread glints in the sunlight. The violets seem to glow. I run my fingers along them, looking for a heart. I find it at the end of the ribbon, another half heart, this one with the initial J inside. And then, my hands shaking, I place both ribbons down on the desk, end to end, the two half hearts touching and making a whole.

My mother's ribbon is the one Violet—*Veronica*—gave to Jayne. Does that mean my mother is Jayne?

CHAPTER SIXTEEN

For the rest of the night the question—*Was my mother Jayne?*—thumps through my head. Eventually I drift off to a restless sleep but am awoken by a *whump-whoosh* that at first I take for foghorns on the river until I realize the sound is coming from inside the house. I creep out onto the landing and stand at the banister listening to a steady, rhythmic *whump-whoosh*. It sounds as if the river has made its way into the house. Even the air feels damp, as if fog is rising inside the stairwell. I inch down the stairs, the *whump-whoosh* getting louder. On the ground floor I realize that the sound is coming from the west wing, which Laeticia had said was off-limits. I move forward anyway, drawn to the sound as if it is the beating heart of the house and finding it would tell me all I need to know—especially, *what happened to my mother here to turn her into the broken woman I knew.*

The door to the west wing is heavy oak that looks as if it were built to withstand an invasion, but when I turn the brass knob I find that it's unlocked and that the well-oiled hinges don't make a sound. It opens onto a long room, empty except for four metal tables. There are two doors at the far end, one closed and one propped open by a cinder block. The *whump-whoosh* sound is coming from beyond the open door. I cross the room, my stocking feet sliding on the scarred linoleum. There are no rich carpets or wood paneling in this part of the house, and the air has the familiar smell of disinfectant and mold I recall from the institutions of my youth. I feel as if I'm going back into that past, as if the *whump-whoosh* is the sound of a pump pulling me back in time. The closed door is wooden with a brass slot with a card in it. The letters printed on it are faint so I have to move closer to read them.

Dr. Robert Sinclair, MD
Admittance by Appointment Only
Please Do Not Disturb

This, then, is the door to Dr. Sinclair's tower office, the inner sanctum where he conducted his private sessions with his patients. There's a burned smell emanating from behind it that's even worse than the damp medicinal air coming from the open door. That door leads to a long corridor with four closed doors on either side, each one with a little brass frame into which a card could be slid, but none of them have cards. The empty slots regard me blankly, like blind eyes, as I go by, and I can't help feeling as if the Wyldcliffe girls are still here, cowering behind their doors, still waiting for their release. Maybe that was the sound I heard—the heartbeat of all the captive inmates of Wyldcliffe Heights.

I follow the sound to the door at the end of the hall and press my cheek against it. Below the *whump-whoosh* is a softer murmur of a whispering voice, but I can't make out the words. I kneel down and press my eye to the old-fashioned keyhole. Through a cloud of mist, I make out a figure bending over a narrow iron cot, adjusting some kind of mask over the face of someone lying there. It looks like a scene out of *Frankenstein,* a nightmarish operation from the days when Wyldcliffe Heights was a psychiatric hospital or a barbaric punishment from when it was a women's training school.

"Just breathe," the standing figure murmurs, "and let Letty worry about the rest."

I flinch away, embarrassed that I'm spying on such an intimate scene. It must be some kind of nebulizer for Veronica's lungs—there'd been a girl at Woodbridge who used one when she had asthma attacks. I steal back down the long narrow hallway, past the blank cardholders, up the circling stairs to my room, where I fall into a deep sleep.

I dream I'm standing on the edge of the cliff looking back at the tower, which has become a lighthouse, its beacon rotating to the *whump-whoosh* of the machine at the heart of Wyldcliffe Heights. The sound vibrates in the ground beneath my feet, the soft soil pushing against my soles as if something is trying to get out. And then I see them, rising up from the graves, the ghosts of all the girls of Wyldcliffe Heights thronging around me, pulling me down into their graves—

I awake with my hands wrapped around the wooden post of my bed, as if trying to keep from being pulled underground.

When I open my door I find a tray with a note pinned beneath a mug. *Miss St. Clair does not feel well enough to work this morning. She will notify you when she has need of your services.*

Practically a dismissal. The breakfast—lukewarm coffee and watery oatmeal thin as gruel—reeks of disapproval. *Or maybe the woman is too busy taking care of her charge to make you breakfast,* a reproving voice that sounds like Roberta Jenkins suggests. Either way, I'm guiltily relieved that I don't have to see Veronica this morning. I still haven't figured out what I should do. Should I ask her who Jayne really was? Should I ask her straight out if Jayne is my mother? Did she know that I'm her daughter? Is that why she'd agreed to hire me? But then, why not just tell me that from the beginning?

The questions spin in my overtired mind until I'm dizzy. I have to get out of the house. I dress in jeans and a long-sleeved T-shirt and sweatshirt and pad quietly down the stairs in my stocking feet. The house is hushed as if holding its breath along with its mistress. Or as if in mourning.

Surely I'd know if Veronica had died in the night, I think, lacing up my sneakers in the mudroom.

I walk outside and break into a jog to shake the lingering miasma of Wyldcliffe Heights from my head. Real fog is drifting across the lawn, clumping on the edges of the woods like curdled milk—like the ghosts in my dream. As it rises, though, it burns off in the hazy sunlight that greets me on the other side of the gates. The rusty leaves of the sycamores smolder overhead; the air smells like apples. By the time I reach the outskirts of the village the day has brightened.

I pass up the temptation of coffee at Bread for the Masses to check the post office first. It's only been three days since I emailed my post office box number to Gloria so it's probably too soon to expect my laptop to have arrived, but I find a package slip in my box. I feel a little jolt of excitement and can't help grinning when the clerk slides the big shiny box across the counter.

"Wow! I didn't think this would get here so soon!" I say like a kid receiving their first Christmas present.

"Overnight express," the clerk tells me. "Someone paid a lot to get it to you fast."

I feel absurdly and uncharacteristically happy lugging the box out of the post office until I stop on the sidewalk and remember that I can't show up at Wyldcliffe Heights with a box sporting a big Apple logo after all the restrictions against social media and digital devices I agreed to. I have to unpack it before I get back. I look longingly at Bread for the Masses, but it's too crowded and public. Then I look toward the library. The little local-history alcove is private enough and there's Wi-Fi—but Martha Conway is friends with Peter Syms and will no doubt report back that I've acquired a laptop.

The quaint Hallmark Channel town suddenly feels cloyingly claustrophobic.

Then I remember Martha saying, "I'm here every day but Tuesday," and I'm grateful for her overeager sharing.

Sure enough, there's an elderly woman at the desk too busy checking out a father with two rambunctious preschoolers to notice me slide by into the local history alcove. I use my penknife to slice open the packing tape, trying to make a minimum of noise as I unwrap the sleek silver machine inside. When Gloria said Kurtis Chadwick was sending me a laptop, I'd imagined some used, out-of-date office castoff, not a brand-new MacBook Pro. At least I think it's brand-new. I notice the box has been opened and there is a letter inside from Gloria.

Mr. Chadwick asked Hadley to make sure this had all the software you need. He's also included an iPhone because Atticus pointed out that you didn't have one—

I feel a hot flash of shame at the thought of everyone discussing my deficiencies that almost spoils my delight in the sleek silver laptop and the slim shiny iPhone. But when I open the brushed chrome top of the laptop and the air fills with a deep resonate chime, the shame is washed away in delight. Hadley must have been green with envy that Mr. Chadwick was sending me a brand-new laptop and phone.

Once I've connected to the library's Wi-Fi, I log into my account and open a new email from Kurtis Chadwick.

Salutations! he writes. *I hope that you are reading this on your new laptop. Gloria tells me it's the top of the line. I wanted to make sure you had the best equipment to record the manuscript. We're sending you a phone too, which Atticus tells me you can use to scan the manuscript—just like James Bond!—and then download it onto the laptop so you can make changes. All the latest technology! Knowing Veronica, she has you using a quill pen. And knowing her, she doesn't want anyone to see her work-in-progress until it's completed. I've worked with a lot of temperamental writers over the years and what I've found is that you want to give them enough rope so that they feel free but not enough to hang themselves. Veronica, while a brilliant writer, has a tendency to go down certain unfortunate rabbit holes and needs a steadying hand. I have no doubt, though, that between you and me we'll be able to pull her out. When she wrote* The Secret of Wyldcliffe Heights, *she confided to me—as I now confide to you, trusting you will keep it entre nous—that she and "Jayne" had written the book together. At the time I thought she was speaking metaphorically, that she was one of those authors who say their "characters ran away*

*from them" or that they heard their character's voice dictating
the story to them. But over the years I've come to suspect that
she meant that the woman on whom the character Jayne was
based—one of the real inmates of Wyldcliffe Heights, in other
words—was in fact her cowriter and that is why she has been
unable to write a second book on her own. It is my dearest
hope that with you there to take down her words she will be
able to, that you will be her "Jayne." I eagerly await the fruit
of your labors.*

-KC

I read the email twice, parsing Kurtis Chadwick's florid
prose to make out the "deep subtext," as Atticus might put it.
Was he suggesting that Veronica St. Clair hadn't written *The
Secret of Wyldcliffe Heights* by herself? Is he suggesting she
might need more than an amanuensis? That she might need a
ghostwriter? Does he know who the original Jayne was and what
happened to her? Does he know that she might have been my
mother?

I dismiss the last possibility. There's no way he could suspect
that my mother was the real Jayne; if he did, he'd have said
something. But there is a chance that he knew the original
Jayne. I remember Atticus telling me that Kurtis Chadwick had
discovered *The Secret of Wyldcliffe Heights* and he'd personally
brought the manuscript back from Veronica.

I suddenly regret leaving things so badly with Atticus. What if
he knows more about the story behind the story? What if—I hate
to admit it—Hadley has learned something useful in researching
her true crime book?

You cut people off before they can abandon you, Dr. Husack told me once.

No duh, I'd responded, *who in their right mind wouldn't?*

I drum my fingers on the keyboard of my new laptop, trying to think of a way to mend fences enough to ask Atticus what he knows about the person who inspired Jayne's character. There's really no way, I conclude, without coming off sounding like a jerk. But then, that never seemed to stop anyone else, Atticus included. I read my last email to him, wincing at my petulance. Sighing, I hit "reply" and change the subject line from *Sorry, not sorry* back to *Sorry.*

*I'm sorry I was a jerk. I really could use some help up here. If you're not too pissed off at me, could you tell me what you know about the girl who was supposed to be the origin of Jayne? Have you ever heard who she was? Or what happened to her? Does—*I grit my teeth and keep typing—*Hadley know anything?*

Apologetically,
Agnes

I hit "send" without much hope of getting a civil reply. He'll probably screencap it to Hadley and they'll have a good laugh over it at the White Horse. I spend the next half hour exploring my new laptop and iPhone, setting up preferences and downloading apps, until I'm interrupted by a ping and see it's an email notification from Atticus. I brace myself and open it.

I guess I was a jerk, too. Let's say we're even. I'm glad you asked about Jayne.

Hadley has a theory that Jayne was based on a patient at Wyldcliffe Heights named Jane Rosen and that she's the one who died in the fire.

CHAPTER SEVENTEEN

I write to Atticus thanking him and asking if he could find out if Hadley knows who Jane Rosen was and how she knows that she's the one who died in the fire. *Because that would mean my mother wasn't Jayne,* I think but don't add. Then I surf the web looking for anything I can find out about the Wyldcliffe Heights fire. I get half a dozen news stories and open one from the *Poughkeepsie Journal.*

A fire broke out Monday night at the Wyldcliffe Heights Psychiatric Treatment Center. The Wyldcliffe fire department was able to confine the damage to the tower, where Dr. Robert Sinclair, resident physician, was treating a patient. Authorities believe the patient, whose name has been withheld until her family can be notified, may have started the fire and that in attempting to rescue her from self-harm, he and the patient were trapped in the tower and overcome with smoke inhalation. Dr. Sinclair's daughter, Veronica Sinclair, was also injured in the blaze. In the aftermath of the fire several patients escaped. Authorities are still searching for them.

I read the article over and then click on several more, looking for the name of the patient who died, to no avail. I spend an hour or so searching the shelves in the history alcove, sorry, after all, that it's Martha Conway's day off. In the end I conclude that the only one who has the answers is Veronica St. Clair. *If she's well enough to go on tomorrow.*

I slide my laptop into my backpack's padded sleeve, relishing the sleek feel of its chrome case, and tuck my new iPhone in my pocket. Tonight I'll sneak into the library, scan the pages Veronica has dictated to me so far, and type them in my room. Then I'll be able to send them to Kurtis to repay his trust in me. When he sees what I've gotten so far he'll know there's a book here that will save Gatehouse and he'll have to offer me a permanent position. What's more, I'll have the story for myself, safe inside the laptop like a photograph in a locket. Even if my mother wasn't Jayne, I see why she called *The Secret of Wyldcliffe Heights* her story. It's beginning to feel like mine.

BEFORE I HEAD back to Wyldcliffe Heights I stop at the gas station to buy a memory stick to back up the file and a charger for my new phone. I also grab two bottles of some fancy local IPA and a few bags of chips. Something greasy and spicy to counteract all Laeticia's wholesome nursery food. I need, I realize, to feel like myself before Wyldcliffe Heights absorbs me into its spongy web.

I have to ring at the gate three times before a male voice speaks through the intercom and buzzes me through. *Where's Laeticia?* I wonder, approaching the dark house.

I find Peter Syms lounging in the kitchen, his muddy boots up on a chair, scrolling through a cell phone. "Letty said to help yourself to leftovers," he says without looking up.

"Where is she?" I ask, affronted on her behalf for the rules he is breaking. "Is Veronica all right?"

He shrugs. "Letty wasn't satisfied with her progress after that attack. She had me take her to Vassar Brothers Medical Center and then sent me back to keep an eye on you." He looks up from his phone. "I saw you coming out of the post office with a big box. Someone sent you a care package? Anything fun you'd like to share?"

For answer I take out the two beers and the chips and pass him a bottle and a bag of extra-spicy Doritos. "Wow, this really is a small town," I say. "Do you all have a lottery in the spring and sacrifice the newcomer in a bonfire?"

"Why wait for spring?" he asks, popping the cap off his bottle and taking a long swig. "As soon as the river freezes, we invite all the new city people to a winter festival and send them downriver on an ice floe."

"Nice," I say, taking a sip of the sour, hoppy IPA. "I'll remember to stay onshore. I guess 'your people' have been here a long time."

"Twelve generations," he says, wincing, but whether at the ale or that I've called out his xenophobia I'm not sure. "On the Syms side at least. The other half came up to work on the reservoir across the river a hundred years ago. So yeah, I suppose we were the newcomers once, but I don't think the McLeods came with Labradoodles or MINI Coopers."

"So, it's the rich you object to," I say, "or at least the new-money kind. You seem pretty comfortable with the amenities of the old." I look pointedly at his muddy boots resting on the kitchen chair.

"My dad kept this place running through some rough times," he says, as if that gives him the right to muddy the furniture.

"You mean after the fire killed Dr. Sinclair and blinded Veronica?"

"Yeah—and all that stuff came out about the doc's methods and the treatment center was closed. There were lawsuits and the income from the hospital was gone. Veronica would have had to sell up if my dad and Letty hadn't kept the place going until her book was published and started making money."

"Why did it take so long?" I ask. "Hadn't she already written it?"

"Your publisher had to have it typed up from her handwritten notebooks. She couldn't type it when her father was alive."

"Why not? Was he some crazy tyrant? Why wouldn't he want his daughter writing a book?"

"My father said that Dr. Sinclair wouldn't have wanted all that stuff about Red Bess in it. He said all the talk about Red Bess was giving Veronica nightmares and affecting the other girls." He leans across the table and lowers his voice as if there was someone in the house who could hear us. "My father said it was like a hysteria with the girls. He'd find them sleepwalking around the house and grounds chanting 'Red Bess, Red Bess is here' and then they would clutch at their throats like they were being strangled. He said it scared the hell out of him. It was one of those girls who started the fire."

"The patient who died," I say, "did your father say anything about her?"

"Only that she was the one who started the Red Bess mania by claiming that she was her reincarnation."

"Do you remember her name?"

"Jane," he says. "Jane Rosen."

"Are you sure your father said she was the one who claimed she was Red Bess in another life?"

He nods. "Yeah, my dad talked about it all the time. He said he remembered her because she was very pretty and had a flair for the dramatic."

"And he's sure—" I begin to ask, but Peter's phone rings. We both look down and see the name on the screen is Letty. He picks it up right away and listens, nodding. "Yeah, I can be there in half an hour . . ." He pauses, pulling the label off the bottle as he listens. "You want me to go there first? Yeah, I know where it is."

"Is Veronica okay?" I ask when he hangs up.

"They're releasing her so I guess so. Laeticia wants me to pick up a prescription on the way. I'll be gone about an hour. Will you be all right here alone?"

"Of course," I say. "Did you think your stories about Red Bess have scared me off?"

He shrugs as he puts on his jacket and takes out a set of car keys. "Nah, I can tell you're made of tougher stuff. It's just . . ."

"What?" I demand when his voice trails off.

"You've been taking down that new book from Veronica."

"I'm transcribing it, yes," I say primly. He's made me sound like a secretary, which I suppose I am, only already what I'm doing with Veronica feels like more than that, as Kurtis had suggested in his email.

"Yeah, well, Dr. Sinclair thought that telling the story of Red Bess drove that girl crazy. He told my father that he sometimes wondered if the girls had it right, that telling the story of Red Bess had brought her back. I thought—"

"That I might be afraid that Veronica dictating her book was going to bring back the murderous spirit of Red Bess?" I ask, lifting my eyebrow and then my bottle. "Then let's hope Bess likes overpriced IPA and spicy chips. Because that's all she's going to get out of me."

As soon as Peter leaves, I pick up my backpack and walk to the sidelight by the front door to watch the lights of his car disappear down the drive. Then I hurry to the library. I have an hour to scan the pages, which should be plenty, but the door is locked. I'd been hoping Laeticia had forgotten in the stress of taking care of Veronica but of course she hasn't. I hadn't locked the French doors from the library the last time I went out of them, though, so hopefully Laeticia hadn't noticed and locked them since. I should be able to get through there.

I follow a narrow path around the side of the house through a dense thicket of giant rhododendrons, their knotted branches woven tightly together like a wicker basket. A movement near the edge of the woods draws my attention, but when I look there's nothing there. It's just my nerves. Approaching the library, I catch my reflection in the dark glass of the French doors and I'm startled by how pale and frightened I look. I've become that girl on the gothic romance covers.

Only I'm not fleeing the castle, I remind myself. *I'm storming it.*

The door sticks but yields finally, and I slip into the dark space behind the green couch. I cross the long room quickly, peering into the shadowed recesses between shelves, the white marble busts of ancient philosophers and writers peering out like censorious ghosts. The pages are where I left them, pinned by the round gray stone, but now two more have joined it. Laeticia must have come in and added them. Does she think a typhoon is going to blow through the house and snatch them up? I take out my new phone, find the camera, and take a picture of the page. When I look at it on my screen, though, I wonder if I'll be able to make out the words. Hadley probably knows some fancy way of transferring the words to the page but I don't.

I do know how to type fast, though. I take out my laptop and place it on the desk, pushing the typewriter back to make room.

The moonlight coming in through the window is strong enough to read the pages so I don't have to turn on any lights. When I glance up, though, I see from my reflection in the window that I am lit up by the light of the computer screen. Anyone on the lawn could see me. Should I move somewhere else? But that will waste time and, after all, who's out there to see me?

I type quickly, barely glancing at the screen, my eyes glued to the pages, grateful for Sister Bernadette's insistence we learn touch typing, and delighting in the muted patter of the keyboard after the loud clatter of the typewriter. When I'm done, I read it over, cross-checking against the typed pages for typos. When I get to the part where Jayne and Violet primp in front of the mirror, I can't help sliding the photograph out of my backpack and studying it again.

You look alike, Casey had told Veronica, and they do, I think as I study the picture. It was hard to tell now, with the scarring and green glasses, if Veronica looks like my mother. Everyone always said I looked like my mother . . . do *I* look like the girl in the picture?

I look up at my own reflection in the window and hold the photo up next to my face, moving it until the half face in the photo meets the midpoint of my face and forms one face—half lit, half in shadow—like a carnival mask. The sight is suddenly unnerving, as if my face has been replaced by someone else's. I fling the photo away so fast it slides to the floor and another face stares back at me from the window that *still* doesn't look like my own, as if I'll never be able to tear away the mask. The face that looks back from the window looks as terrified by that possibility as I am. I lean closer—

Then I hear a car on the drive. I wheel around and see the

beam of headlights illuminate the glass fanlight over the atrium
door. I turn back to the window and find that woman in the window is gone, as if she had the good sense to flee while I am still
stupidly becalmed in my chair. Then I shake off the spell of tor-
por, shut the laptop, grab my backpack, and sprint toward the
French doors. My hand is on the latch when I remember the photograph I flung to the floor. I can't leave it there.

I have time, I tell myself, creeping back to the desk. *There's no
reason to think they'll come in here as long as I'm quiet.* I can't use
a light, though, so I sink to my knees and feel along the floor. I
come across not the photograph but something hard and metal.
A coin I dropped? A bottle cap that fell out of my backpack? Just
in case it's something incriminating I stuff it in my pocket as I
hear the front door opening and voices in the atrium. I sweep my
hands over the floor frantically and find the photograph next. I
grab it and hurry, half crouching, to the French doors. My hand
is on the latch again when I hear a key rattling in the library door.
Too late to flee. I crouch behind the couch and hold my breath.

"We can look for it in the morning," Laeticia is saying as she
comes into the room. "You should be in bed."

"I'll rest better knowing it's safe," Veronica replies, her voice
weakened since I heard it last. "It must have fallen when I had my
spell."

"You mean when you wore yourself to exhaustion?" Letty snaps.
"Sit down and I'll look for it. You can't go on like this. You'll—"

"Kill myself?" Veronica finishes for her. "You know that isn't
what will kill me."

"You don't know that. The doctor said they can't say—"

"Won't say. They're afraid of getting sued. My lungs are giving
out, Letty. It's a miracle they survived the fire. But now I know

why I was spared. I still have breath enough to give a reckoning before I die. To set things straight."

"Isn't that done already? The story's been told."

"Only half of it," Veronica replies. "*She* has to know the other half."

"But what if it brings her back?"

"That's what I'm counting on . . . Have you found it?"

"No, I haven't. Maybe you lost it in your room. Let me take you there. If you're really bound on continuing, you'll need your rest."

Veronica sighs. When she speaks again her voice is husky. "Do you think she hates me?"

Laeticia doesn't answer. I gather from the sound of heavy breathing and creaking of floorboards that she's crawling around the floor looking for the lost object. I feel in my pocket for the hard, round object I picked up, wondering if it's what she's looking for. Will they ever leave if they don't find it? After a few more minutes Laeticia lets out a long sigh.

"I wish I could tell you that she didn't."

"It's all right," Veronica says, her voice soft and more in control now. "The more she hates me the more likely she is to come. You can stop looking, Letty, the damned thing will turn up. It always does—and she will, too. I have to tell the other half of the story before she comes back."

I hear Laeticia get to her feet, grunting with the effort, and then I hear them making their way to the door. I wait until they close the door behind them, and then a few minutes more to give them time in case they change their minds and come back. While I wait, I go over in my head what they were talking about. Veronica must be sicker than she let on. She needs to tell *the other half* of the story—*Violet's* story. But why? And what did she mean by a *reckoning*? And who was Laeticia afraid the story would bring back?

Red Bess?

Or Jayne?

I think of the face I'd seen in the window, my own features contorted by fear, or—

For a moment I thought it was my mother.

THE FIRST THING I do when I get to my room is to back up the file I've typed. I put the memory stick in my pocket for safekeeping, where it rubs against the metal thing. Taking it out I see it's a brass locket, engraved with a worn design that might have once been a violet, like the locket Veronica described in the story that she took with her the night she ran away. Josephine Hale's locket. I try to open it but the hinge is rusted shut. I take out my penknife and wedge its point between the two halves. It springs open so suddenly that the knife nicks my thumb and a drop of blood falls on the desiccated violet inside. I wipe the blood and violet dust away from the photo to reveal a woman in a white lace-collared blouse with dark hair piled high on her head. Her face is blurry, as if it had been caught in motion, but still I recognize it from the photograph I found in the attic. It's Bess Molloy. Josephine Hale had kept the portrait of the woman who slit her husband's throat tied around her own throat.

CHAPTER EIGHTEEN

When I enter the library the next morning, I'm relieved to find Veronica seated on the couch. All night I'd been afraid that she might be too sick to go on and that I'd have to leave Wyldcliffe before uncovering its mysteries. Is Jayne my mother? Why did Josephine wear a picture of her husband's murderer in her locket? Who started the fire in the tower?

As I get closer, I notice there are two plastic tubes strung along her cheeks beneath her dark glasses.

"You needn't be afraid, Ms. Corey," she says, hearing, I suppose, my hesitation. "I'm not on death's door. It's just a little oxygen the doctor prescribed to make it easier for me to breathe."

I notice now that there's a canister tucked by her feet. I pick up my notebook and start to sit on the chair, but she pats the cushion next to her on the couch. "I believe it will be easier if you sit closer so I don't have to strain my voice."

"Of course," I say, walking around the low table to sit on the couch. Its cushions are softer than I remember, and I have to sit very straight on the edge to keep myself from sinking. "I'm glad to see you're feeling well enough to go on."

She waves her hand in the air, the fingers like a pale moth stirred from the upholstery. "As the Romans say, *dum spiro, spero*."

"'While I breathe, I hope,'" I say automatically, trained by Sister Bernadette to translate Latin on command.

A smile flickers across Veronica's face, as pale and fleeting as the moth I'd imagined a moment ago. "Well, then, let's not waste any more of those breaths . . ."

I LEARNED THAT *first night at the Josephine that Jayne had the power to shape anyone to her will. Just as she had mesmerized me, she cast her spell over everyone in her orbit. When she swept into the ballroom heads turned and the gyrating bodies on the dance floor cleared a path for her—and for me, too, as long as I stayed close. She clasped both my hands and spun me around. When she released me Casey was there to catch me and Gunn moved into my spot with Jayne, but I still felt the magnetic pull of her, binding us all together. We danced—or what people called dancing then, which was more a wild thrashing to the thumping beat—our bodies colliding like atoms in a cosmic pinball game. Later we collapsed into the big velvet couches that ringed the room and drank cold clear shots that Casey appeared with and snorted assorted powders Gunn provided. And then, somehow, Jayne was heading up onstage and pulling me with her and we were both singing into one mic, our voices so in sync I could feel her heart pounding in time to mine. Afterward, Jayne invited the band up to "our" tower room and then we were all up on the roof watching the sparkling lights of the boats moving on the river, north toward the Maxwell House coffee cup dripping its red light into the water. I felt like the river had brought me here and that this was where I was always meant to be.*

Or maybe that didn't all happen on the first night. The nights bled together into one long river of light that swept us out to sea and then dragged us back in with the tide, leaving us spent and half drowned. The tower room at the Josephine took on the appearance of an underwater cavern as painted by Gustave Doré. Gunn, who had dropped out of art school, painted the walls with figures from myth and history—Salome, the Valkyries, Scheherazade, Medusa—all with Jayne's face. Purple and green scarves, scavenged from the city's thrift shops, hung from the ceiling like seaweed. We wore violet ribbons around our throats and rimmed our eyes with violet kohl. I woke up one morning with a violet tattoo on my arm seeping ink-stained blood, as if I'd begun to bleed the color of crushed violets. In the late afternoon, when we awoke, the sun setting across the river would catch the crystal chandelier and spin rainbows around the room, and as dusk settled the red light from the Maxwell House coffee cup tinted the room crimson. Casey, who disappeared early before we were up because he had a job he had to show up for, would appear in the evening with provisions—loaves of bread and salami and cheese from Little Italy, bottles of wine and vodka—and drugs. Pot and cocaine at first, and then crystal meth and hashish, and finally, heroin, because Jayne said we should try everything at least once.

Only once you tried it, you wanted it again. And again. It made me unafraid, even of singing onstage, although I always tried to stay in Jayne's shadow. The goth bands that played at the Josephine—Skeletal Family, Nosferatu, the March Violets—liked our looks and the drugs Casey always had on hand. I noticed some of the punk rockers wearing the same violet tattoos on their arms and violet ribbons tied around their necks, and the groupies on the dance floor were wearing them, too. It was like pieces of us had broken off and multiplied.

Pieces of Jayne, that is; we were all just her shadows.

Casey was always filming her. Gunn seemed to have no purpose but to paint and protect her. Once, some punk pushed her on the dance floor, and Gunn punched him so hard he broke his jaw and got arrested. While Jayne sweet-talked the manager of the Josephine not to throw us out, I went with Casey to the police station to bail him out. Casey told me on the way that Gunn had anger issues and a record for assault. We had to keep an eye on him to prevent him from losing his temper and winding up in prison for years. At the police station Casey spoke in a soft voice to the desk sergeant. I heard him mention his father and some judge who was his uncle and a DA who was a cousin.

Jayne had sometimes teased Casey by calling him "poor little rich boy" and "trust fund baby" and, of course, he was the one who always had money. I'd never really thought before about what that meant, that he had power as well as money.

I watched as money was slid across the desk. "Bail plus," Casey called it, and we collected Gunn, who looked like he had shrunk two inches during the two hours he had spent in a cell. Out on the street he started to shake, his limbs as jangly as a rag doll's. Casey pulled out a silver flask and palmed him some pills to take with it to calm the hell down. Casey always stayed in control, he was the one to figure things out, always watching Gunn—and all of us—a little off to the side, behind the lens of his camera. And even though he bought the drugs, I'd noticed he didn't take them. He hardly even drank. "Someone's got to keep a level head," he told me when I mentioned it.

I wondered, too, if Jayne knew what a powder keg Gunn was and what his obsession with her might cost him—and all of us. At least Casey was keeping an eye on him.

I started to also. I even tried to cut down on the booze and drugs. To keep a level head for Jayne's sake. I'd begun to see that beneath the makeup and spangles and bravado she was fragile. She wouldn't talk much about where she was from—just some shitty town, *was all she would say*, sometimes adding that her dad had left and her stepfather was a jerk. Blah, blah, blah, poor me.

"Her stepfather wanted to have her committed to a mental hospital," Casey told me, "because she told her mother that he'd groped her."

When I told her that my father had treated me like a patient instead of a daughter, she hugged me and said, "That's what they do to strong women. They call us crazy and lock us up. Just like what they did to Bess Molloy."

Casey, though he kept an eye on all of us, liked to invite girls up to the tower to party.

I was jealous at first. I'd thought Casey was interested in me, and while I wasn't all that attracted to him (I always remembered that chill I'd felt when he touched my throat that first night) I thought Jayne might want us to be together so we'd be a matching pair to her and Gunn. But whenever Casey tried to get me alone, Jayne would slide in between us. She even told me once that it would be better if I didn't get involved with Casey, that it would complicate things. Casey goes through girls like chewing gum, *she confided.* We don't want him—and his money—flaking off when he moves on to the next flavor-of-the-month.

I could tell there was something she wasn't telling me but I guessed it was because she didn't think I was sophisticated enough for Casey and didn't want to hurt my feelings. So I watched Casey slink off with a new girl most every night—doe-eyed goth girls in short skirts and torn stockings with a taste for expensive alcohol and drugs. Most only lasted a night or two, but there was one, a fox-faced girl with hair dyed the color of maraschino cherries, who draped herself around him like a boa and hung on longer. She introduced herself as "Anaïs with an umlaut," and Jayne called her "umlaut" from then on. Still,

Jayne let her up to the tower because Anaïs always had good drugs and—I suspected—because of the way Anaïs fawned over her. She was always asking Jayne where she got her clothes and makeup, and after Jayne told her the story of Red Bess she kept asking her questions about her as if Jayne were the expert. One night we'd smoked some hash Casey brought that he said was "really special." After a couple of hits I got the feeling it was laced with something because I felt higher than I'd been before, even the couple of times I'd tried heroin. Anaïs kept picking up an antique mirror and catching the light to throw reflections around the room that made me feel dizzy. When I told her to stop it she held the mirror up to me and said, "What are you afraid of, Violet? That you'll see Red Bess in the mirror?"

"That's Bloody Mary," Jayne said, giggling. She must have been really high, too, because she never giggled. "And you have to say her name three times to make her appear."

"I bet it would work the same," Anaïs said, batting her fake eyelashes. "If we summon Red Bess we can ask what really happened the night of the slaughter."

"I think it's a bad idea," Gunn said.

"So do I," I said, remembering the way the girls would whisper about Red Bess at Wyldcliffe Heights.

"I think it sounds amusing," Casey said, sliding his arm around Anaïs and trailing his fingers along her throat beneath the cheap plastic choker she wore in imitation of our ribbon ones. "I could film you doing it. It would make a great video."

"Why not?" Jayne said, shrugging her shoulders as if she was just going along with the idea for fun. But I could see by the glint in her eyes that she liked the idea.

We turned off all the lights until the room was lit only by the red glow of the Maxwell House sign across the river. We sat in a circle with the mirror in the center. Jayne laughed and said this was like the sleepover parties she used to go to, and Casey, his video camera pressed to his face, said all the girls he knew at boarding school wanted to play spin the bottle at sleepovers. Gunn sneered and said the kids in his neighborhood made Molotov cocktails out of used bottles. Even Gunn, who was clearly angry at Anaïs for starting this, was more a part of the group than I was. I felt left out, so I told a story about sneaking into the west wing and finding the girls playing cards.

"They weren't allowed but I didn't tell," I said.

When Anaïs snickered, Jayne came to my rescue. "Violet has the strongest connection to Red Bess. She even has a locket that belonged to her."

"Well, it belonged to my grandmother, Josephine Hale—" I began.

"Haven't you noticed?" Jayne asked, looking disappointed with me. "The photo inside is of Bess."

I'd tried to open the locket once but it was stuck. I wondered how—and when—Jayne had managed it. It made me feel like the locket belonged more to her than to me. I took it off and handed it to her and she laid it in the middle of the circle. Then she held up the hand mirror and the candle and said "Red Bess" three times. She passed the mirror around in the circle and everyone took a turn, even Casey, holding the camera in one hand to film himself doing it. When it came to Anaïs she whispered the words in a husky voice like she was in a horror movie.

"I see something!" she cried.

Jayne squeezed next to her to look in the mirror, their faces touching. I felt a pang of jealousy and remembered what Casey had said that first night—Jayne loves to snare innocent naïfs into her web and raise them up in her image, especially ones who look a little like her. She's grown tired of her last one and is ready for a new recruit. *At the time I'd been so flattered that he thought I looked like Jayne that I hadn't thought about what would happen when Jayne grew tired of me. Would Anaïs be her new recruit? They didn't really look alike except for the purple-red hair dye that might have come out of the same bottle, but that was just Anaïs copying Jayne, which Jayne was sure to see and despise. Only, as the two looked into the mirror, it seemed to me that they shared a complicit smile.*

When the mirror was passed to me, I held it up and looked at my face dispassionately. I'd grown thinner in the months I'd been in the city, my cheeks hollowed out, my eyes rimmed not just with kohl but also with dark circles from sleepless nights. I looked like the girls in the west wing, the ones who screamed at night and had to be confined in straitjackets and padded rooms. My father was right, I found myself thinking, Wyldcliffe Heights was where I belonged.

"Are you too afraid to say her name?" Anaïs teased, reaching her hand out for the mirror.

"Red Bess," I said, spitting the words into the mirror.

The face in the mirror seemed to grow paler against the red candlelight. If I squinted a little, I saw my grandmother's face as she looked in her portrait.

"Red Bess," I said again, imagining my grandmother calling for the woman she had trusted, only to have her turn on her and kill her husband. The air in the room felt warmer and redder, as if a fire raged somewhere close.

"Red Bess!" The name came out of me this time as if pulled from my throat like a crimson scarf in a magic trick. It was the face in the mirror who spoke, not me. The air around me turned red and washed over me like the tide retreating, leaving me ice cold and drowned at the bottom of the river. But not alone. She was with me. She *was in me. Red Bess. I'd called her and she'd come for me. She'd come into me. Because I was just like her. When I looked into the mirror I saw her—and she saw me.*

Let go, *I heard her say as a red mist washed over me,* I've got you.

WHEN I OPENED *my eyes, it was daylight. I was lying on one of the mattresses on the floor, Jayne's fur coat over me, a red scarf twisted around one of my hands. When I moved, the room spun, the sunlight sending prisms skidding in a circle. The floor was littered with piles of blankets, coats, scarves, and shawls—some of which, I realized, concealed bodies. I saw Gunn sprawled out under an old army surplus sleeping bag, his mouth open, and Jayne, curled up by his side in a Persian rug like the one Cleopatra had wrapped herself in to present to Marc Antony. I sat up and looked around for Casey but instead I spotted a cascade of purple-red hair spilling out from beneath Jayne's red cloak. Had Jayne given it to Anaïs? The red was too bright to look at but when I closed my eyes it vibrated beneath my eyelids and I remembered the red mist that had washed over me last night and the feeling that I was not alone. What had happened? Had I passed out? Had I said—or done—anything embarrassing before I did?*

I looked down at my hand and saw that the scarf tied around it wasn't red—it was bloodstained. Had I cut myself? Is that why I'd dreamed of blood? My eye was drawn back to the red cloak. I grabbed a corner of it, and pulled—

A white face appeared, like a rabbit pulled out of a hat, its blue eyes staring blindly at the ceiling.

I screamed and pushed myself away, scrabbling backward on the floor until I hit a wall of hard flesh. Gunn's arms wrapped around me and his hands gripped my arms. "What's wrong?" he demanded.

Jayne was struggling awake, pushing her hair out of her eyes, but she saw the girl's face before Gunn did. "Shut up!" she snapped at both of us.

I closed my mouth, used to doing what Jayne said, as she crawled over to Anaïs. She pulled the cloak further down to uncover the girl's mouth and bent over it, listening. "Get me a mirror," she said.

The hand mirror we passed around last night was lying on the floor. I hated to touch it but I picked it up, noticing it had broken and a shard was missing, and passed it to Jayne. She held it up in front of the girl's face. In my shock and confusion, I thought she was performing some ritual to call back the girl's soul. Maybe if we said her name three times like we'd said Red Bess's last night—

"She's not breathing," Jayne said, putting down the mirror, which, I realized, she'd been only using to check for a mist of breath. She pulled the cloak down further and a hypodermic needle clattered to the floor. A purple ribbon was tied around her bicep. It looked horribly like my *ribbon and when I touched my throat I found that my locket and choker were missing.*

"What the hell," Gunn said. "Did she OD? How much smack did Casey give her—" He stood up and started kicking the piles of blankets and clothes on the floor. Something heavy thunked to the floor. Jayne picked it up. It was Casey's video camera. "Where the hell is Casey? He's the one who brought the smack—"

"Shut up, Gunn," Jayne said, picking up the camera, "and let me think."

"I have a record, Jay, I'll do time if I'm found here with a dead body. The cops will think I brought the drugs."

"We'll tell them you didn't," I said. "We'll tell them Casey—"

"No," Jayne said. "We can't tell them it was Casey."

"Why the hell not?" Gunn asked, his panic turning to anger. "Why are you protecting him?"

"I'm not," Jayne said, "I'm protecting us. Guys like Casey, they never end up paying for what they do. He'll get a fancy lawyer and twist it so we all end up going to jail—"

Gunn slammed his fist into the wall so hard the plaster shattered and the chandelier swayed above us like it was going to come crashing down. I jumped but Jayne got up calmly and took both his hands in hers. She leaned in and whispered something in his ear. When she was done he looked down at his hands and nodded. She had pressed something into his hands. Money, I guessed.

"Go down the fire stairs and out through the alley," Jayne said. "Find someplace to stay for a few days and lay low. Violet and I will take care of this." She looked at me. "Right, Violet?"

"How?" I asked. "What are we going to do with her?" I stared at Anaïs. Why did she have to come last night with her stupid game?

"We'll go to the police. We'll say she brought the heroin—we'll leave Casey and Gunn out of it—and that you and I passed out because we'd never tried it before and she was dead when we woke up."

"What about the thing with the mirror that happened with Violet?" Gunn asked, looking first at Jayne and then pointing at me. "They'll see the cuts on her."

I looked down at my hand and saw that my fingertips were stained red. "What did I do?" I asked.

"Oh man," Gunn said, "she doesn't even remember."

"Oh honey," Jayne said, "it was all my fault for letting that stupid girl play that game. I should have known it would upset you. When you looked into the mirror you screamed and said you saw Red Bess.

Then you broke the mirror and lunged for Anaïs with a piece of it, you slashed at her—"

Jayne pulled the cloak off of Anaïs, revealing bloody scratches on her hands and forearms, as if she'd been trying to ward someone off. I stared down at my hand, willing the memory back, but all I saw was the red mist that had spread over everything.

"It doesn't matter," Jayne said. "It's the heroin that killed her—"

"And Casey gave her that," Gunn said.

"But we won't say that," she said, glaring at Gunn. "Now, go!"

Gunn looked like he wanted to say something else but then he looked at Anaïs again and shook his head. "I hope you know what the hell you're doing, Jayne." And then he left without looking at either of us again.

CHAPTER NINETEEN

W hy was Jayne protecting Casey?" I ask.

I expect Veronica to chide me again for mixing fact with fiction, but instead she considers the question carefully before answering. "I think Jayne was protecting him because she thought she needed him."

"For what?" I ask.

"His money, his position . . . you'll see . . ." She stops and reaches out a hand toward me. I think she means to take hold of my hand but instead she brushes the pad in my lap. "You might as well take the rest of this down," she says. I'm surprised but I do as she says. As soon as she hears me open my notebook, she goes on, her voice calmer and somehow no longer her own. Her authorial voice, I suppose.

JAYNE TOLD ME to shower and scrub my nails. When I came out, she made me dress in my old clothes that I'd brought from Wyldcliffe Heights—a wool skirt and cotton blouse from Bonwit Teller's and the Peck & Peck coat. "We went to bed early," she told me, as she braided my hair like a schoolgirl's. "There were a lot of people in the tower, so you and I went to sleep in one of the empty rooms down the hall. We found Anaïs here in the morning and called the police *right away. Don't mention Gunn or Casey. Just say there were a lot of strangers and that Anaïs brought the drugs."*

We waited for the police downstairs in the lobby. One detective, a middle-aged man in a shabby suit who introduced himself as Detective Larsen, interviewed us while another went upstairs with two uniformed officers. Jayne sat next to me and held my hand as she described finding Anaïs, sniffing back tears and dabbing her eyes with one of her thrift shop violet-embroidered handkerchiefs. She handed me one, as if I were crying, too, or maybe to suggest that I ought to be, but the spots on it reminded me of the bloodstained scarf—what had she done with it? I wondered—and I couldn't cry. I felt like something had dried up inside me.

"How'd you cut your hand?" the detective asked me.

"I broke a mirror," Jayne said for me. "Violet picked up the pieces. I guess I'm in for seven years' bad luck."

"Let's hope it's not seven to ten," Detective Larsen said. "You've got form, kid. This isn't the first time you've woken up next to a dead body."

Jayne sniffed and dabbed her eyes with the violet hankie. "My stepfather fell down the stairs and broke his neck," she said. "It was an accident. I ended up in JD because there were drugs in the house— his drugs—"

"Let's go down to the station and talk about it," the detective said, like it was a suggestion. "You, too, Miss Sinclair," he said to me. "Your father is on the way."

I startled when I learned they'd called my father. How had they gotten his name so quickly? I'd never used my real name at the Josephine. I looked at Jayne as they led her away, and she reached out and squeezed my hand. When I opened it, I saw she'd left me the violet hankie. Tied to one corner was Josephine's locket, which

I'd taken off last night, and my violet ribbon. Which I'd seen tied around Anaïs's arm. Why had Jayne taken it back and given it to me?

"Don't worry," she mouthed. "They won't keep us apart."

But they took us in separate squad cars to the station and put me in a room by myself and left me there for what felt like hours. While I sat there, I decided I would confess. I would tell them that I gave Anaïs the drugs because I was jealous of her. They would let Jayne go and I would go to jail. It would be better than going back to Wyldcliffe Heights, and Jayne would know that I had done it for her. When the door finally opened, I had my confession planned out, but it wasn't the detective standing in the door—it was my father.

"Darling!" he said, his voice loud and theatrical. "Thank God! I've been going mad looking for you."

He held out his arms as if to embrace me, something he had never done in my life, but before he'd taken another step, Detective Larsen appeared in the doorway. Of course, he'd been there all along, the audience to my father's performance.

"I have a few more questions for your daughter."

"Is that really necessary?" he asked. "The guilty party has confessed."

Had they caught Casey? I wondered but was too afraid to ask. Had he turned himself in? But that seemed unlikely. Maybe they'd caught Gunn and coerced him into a confession.

"Even so," the detective said, "I still have questions."

I looked from my father to the detective—my father slim and handsome in his tweed suit, the detective unshaven and seedy, a stain on his tie; of the two of them I was more afraid of my father. "I don't mind answering questions," I said.

"Not without a court-appointed psychiatrist present," my father growled, withdrawing from his suit jacket pocket a folded packet of

*papers that he snapped open. "My daughter has been certified men-
tally incompetent by the State of New York. She cannot be questioned without a doctor present—and if you do charge her, I can
guarantee you she won't stand trial; she'll be remanded to the care
of the Wyldcliffe Heights Psychiatric Treatment Center, which is
where I propose to take her now. So, Detective Larsen, do you want
to go through all that red tape for a routine overdose when someone
else has already confessed to providing the drugs?"*

*Detective Larsen looked from my father to me. I thought I saw
a hint of pity in his eyes, but maybe that was for himself. Then he
looked back at my father. "You didn't do too good a job keeping her
there last time," he said.*

"We've increased our security," my father said.

*A cold rage bubbled up inside me and a red mist blinded my eyes.
"I won't go back," I said, getting to my feet. But the detective had
already gone, leaving me to my father, my prison keeper.*

*"Sit down," he said, "or your friend will end up in prison until
she's forty."*

*"She? What do you mean—" I began, but then I guessed. It wasn't
Gunn or Casey who had confessed; it was Jayne.*

"Jayne didn't give Anaïs the drugs," I said.

*He sat down in the chair on the other side of the table and crossed
his leg over his knee. "Why don't you tell me what happened, then?"*

*And just as I always had, I poured out the whole story to him. I
told him everything. It was a relief, confessing to him as he nodded
sagely, his hands clasped over his tweed-trousered knee, the smell of
cherry pipe tobacco lulling me into a sense of security. When I finished, he asked me one question: "You really don't remember what
happened after you passed out?"*

I shook my head.

"Then you can't be sure it wasn't your friend who gave the girl the heroin. She has a record, you know, a long history of drug use, truancy, and shoplifting capped by an assault charge against her stepfather."

"A grown man? How can anyone believe that?" I asked.

"He had to have sixteen stitches from her slashing him with a razor blade. Then six months later he fell down the stairs and broke his neck."

I choked back my shock, picturing Jayne wielding a razor blade. What I saw was her pumping her fist on the dance floor crying, "I am Red Bess!"

"She must have been defending herself."

To my surprise, my father agreed. "Most likely. Which is why I'm going to petition to have her remanded to Wyldcliffe Heights . . . unless . . ." He opened his hands like a magician revealing a hidden coin at the end of a trick, only his hands were empty and what he was showing me was my lack of options. "Unless you want me to leave her to the mercy of the legal system. She was violating the terms of her parole just being in the same room with those drugs. She'll end up in prison if I don't intervene."

"Can I talk to her?" I asked.

He furrowed his brow and looked like he was going to say no, but he didn't. "For just a minute," he said. "And on our way out. Put your coat on—" He looked down at my hands, noticing the cuts on them. "Do you have gloves?"

I dug in my coat pockets and found the leather gloves I'd worn when I left Wyldcliffe Heights six months ago, only now it felt like it had been only hours. As I smoothed the kid leather over my scratched hands, I wondered how I ever thought I could get away. My father tucked my hand under his arm as we walked out of the interrogation room and down a long hallway to a desk where Detective Larsen stood talking to a uniformed officer.

"My daughter would like to say goodbye to her friend," he said.

The officer started to object but Detective Larsen said go ahead and took out a key to unlock a door. It was a long narrow cell with a built-in bench at the end where Jayne sat huddled in a tight ball, chin resting on her knees, hair falling over her face, looking younger and more vulnerable than I'd ever seen her.

When she looked up and saw it was me, she sprung up and wrapped her arms around me. "They're letting you go, aren't they?" she said, looking me up and down.

"My father is taking me back to Wyldcliffe Heights—oh, Jayne, why did you tell them you gave Anaïs the drugs?"

"It's better this way," she said. "They would have arrested both of us. This way we'll both go to Wyldcliffe Heights. Your father promised me."

"What? When?"

"This morning," she said, taking both of my hands in hers and looking me in the eyes. "When I called him."

"You called . . . but how . . ."

"I looked up the number. I told him what happened and he said that if I said I was the one who gave Anaïs the drugs he'd make sure that we both ended up in Wyldcliffe Heights. I knew it was the right thing to do"—she squeezed my hands and moved closer to me, lowering her voice—"because it's what you said last night when you lunged for Anaïs. You said, 'We have to go back to Wyldcliffe Heights because Red Bess is coming there for us.'"

"Did you believe her?" I ask when I see Veronica doesn't mean to go on. She's slumped down into the cushions, one hand curled around the armrest as if holding on to the edge of a cliff.

"I believe that she believed it," she rasps. "And that being together was all that mattered—"

"That's enough for today."

Laeticia is standing on the other side of the room, her hands braced on a wheelchair. I close my notebook and struggle out of the grasp of the couch and the story.

"I'll start typing," I say.

"That infernal sound will keep her from resting," Laeticia hisses as she helps Veronica into the chair and slings the oxygen canister over its handles.

If you'd just let me use my laptop, I think, *that wouldn't be a problem.*

"On . . . the contrary," Veronica says, her breath coming in gasps from the slight exertion of getting up, "I find . . . the sound . . . enormously comforting. All . . . those . . . words . . . all those . . . moments . . . let go . . . onto the page." She waves her pale hand and I picture all the words I've written beating against the cardboard covers of my notebook like moths battering themselves against a screen door.

When they're gone and I begin typing, though, the key strikes sound more like the drumbeat of an advancing army, like something is coming. When I get to that last line—*Red Bess is coming there for us*—I can actually hear footsteps behind me.

"Agnes."

I jump at the voice—the footsteps were real—but when I turn around, I find it's only Laeticia.

"I just wanted you to know that Peter is taking Miss St. Clair and me to a doctor's appointment. There are leftovers in the refrigerator—"

"Is she all right?" I ask.

"She would be if you weren't wearing her out with these sessions," she barks.

"This isn't *my* choice," I snap back.

"*You* wrote to her asking for a sequel."

"*Hundreds* of fans have written to her asking for a sequel!"

"And yet it was your letter that made her decide to go through with it. Think about that when you see her gasping for breath and remember—" She points down at the typed pages lying beside the typewriter. "Those stay here. She may change her mind about letting loose the things she's been telling you into the world after all." With that she turns and leaves. As she goes, I continue staring at the three stones lying on top of them. I remember adding two more stones to the pile, but one of these stones is a speckled pink that I don't recall seeing before. Someone has switched the stones, which means someone is reading the pages.

I can hear Laeticia, Peter, and Veronica going out of the atrium, Laeticia loudly admonishing Peter to be careful with the chair. Then I listen to the sound of the car going down the drive. When I can't hear it any more, I bolt out of the library, up the stairs to my room, and down again with my backpack and laptop. I type the pages again quickly, this time Laeticia's words accompanying the drumbeat in my head—

She may change her mind about letting loose the things she's been telling you into the world after all.

How easy it would be to burn these typed pages. Without an electronic backup they'd be gone forever. And it might not be Veronica's choice at all. It's likely Laeticia who's reading these pages at night—and rearranging the paperweight stones on them. And she might decide the world shouldn't see them.

I arrange the smooth river stones into a pattern that I'll remember, then back up the file on the memory stick, but it doesn't feel like enough. I check for a cell signal on my phone and then for a Wi-Fi signal, hoping Laeticia lied about there not being any or that there's a neighbor's signal close enough to use. But there's nothing. There are no nearby neighbors here at Wyldcliffe Heights. I'll have to walk into the village.

I borrow a rain jacket and rubber boots from the mudroom because it looks like rain. It's colder, too, the bright autumnal sunshine having ceded to a chill damp gray that presages winter even though it's not yet November. The wind whips the last leaves from the sycamores and flays the bare limbs white as naked flesh. I'm frozen by the time I reach the village. I decide to go to Bread for the Masses and use their Wi-Fi while warming up with a big pumpkin spice latte.

It's less crowded today, maybe because the weekenders are gone or the weather has driven the young mothers home. I order the latte and an apple cider donut and sit at the end of a communal table marked for laptop use, far enough from anyone who might see my screen—

Which is just being paranoid.

Even if it gets back to Laeticia that I was seen using a laptop, I signed an NDA, not a Luddite oath. And I didn't exactly say I wouldn't send copies of the manuscript to Kurtis Chadwick. He is my boss, after all, the one who I need for a job after this one ends.

I open my inbox and see an email from Atticus with the subject line *Jane Rosen*. I click on it with a feeling of excitement that quickly deflates to disappointment.

> *Hadley says Jane Rosen is definitely the name of the girl who died in the fire. Hadley was also able to get the arrest records for that night at the Josephine. The girl who died was Annemarie Moroni; the woman who was arrested for providing her with the heroin was Jane Rosen.*

Interesting, I type in answer to Atticus, *but please be careful what you tell Hadley. She isn't exactly great at keeping secrets.* I think of telling him that she'd called him a heartbreaker who went through assistants like Kleenex. But then he'd think I was being paranoid—or worse, jealous of Hadley.

I delete all references to Hadley and type: *Please be careful of who you tell. If Veronica finds out that someone is looking into what happened at the Josephine she'll think I've been talking about her book and then she might decide not to go ahead with it.*

I hesitate before hitting "send," itching to say something that will decrease Hadley in his estimation. Has she decided that Red Bess is *her* story to tell? Is she jealous that I'm up here working with Veronica St. Clair?

I go back to the email and add one more line: *Please tell Hadley to be careful where she's poking around and what she's posting on social media—especially about that girl who died at the Josephine. Veronica just got to that part in her book and there are some issues that might be sensitive.*

I pause again, thinking about the scene at the Josephine. There was something that seemed off about Jayne's behavior. What had she whispered to Gunn? What had she put in his hands? And why had she confessed to giving Anaïs the drugs? Was she hiding a bigger crime? Was Veronica suggesting that Jayne—*my mother?*—had something to hide? Or that she herself was the guilty one?

I think Veronica knows something about who really killed Annemarie, I add, *and if she thinks I'm leaking information to you and Hadley she might put a halt to the sequel.*

I hit "send" before I can change my mind. Then I open a new email to Kurtis Chadwick. *Here's what Veronica has dictated to me so far. She doesn't know I'm sending this to you but I think she does want the story out—she said as much today, that she felt relieved that the story was getting onto the page. And I am, too. To tell you the truth, Veronica doesn't seem well. I'm worried about her health and that if something happened to her—*I hesitate, looking guiltily around the café to make sure no one is close enough to see me badmouthing Laeticia—*I'm worried that the housekeeper might take it into her head to get rid of the pages. And, as I think you will agree when you read them, that would be a shame.*

Before I attach the pages I reread them. There is definitely something odd about how Jayne behaved after Anaïs's death. I wonder once again if Veronica means to make it seem that way. I linger, too, on Gunn's question: *Why are you protecting Casey?*

I'm not, she'd said, *I'm protecting us.*

Did she mean her and Violet? Or her and Gunn?

I attach the manuscript and hit "send." As the little paper airplane indicates my message has flown off into cyberspace, a notification dings on my new phone. I look down and see that someone's tagged me on Instagram. Which is odd because I barely use Instagram. Hadley insisted I open Twitter, Instagram, and TikTok accounts to follow our books and authors, but since I didn't have a smart phone until now I've hardly used any of the platforms. Who would tag me?

I click on the link and I'm directed to a moody filtered shot of a brick tower, a yellow light glowing from one of its windows. It takes me a moment to recognize the tower of the Josephine Hotel. Could Roberta Jenkins have tagged me? But that seems unlikely. Then I see the caption and I'm sure it wasn't Roberta.

A spirit awakens in the tower of the Josephine, it reads. *Red Bess lives!*

It's posted by someone calling themselves "Red Bess."

CHAPTER TWENTY

I drop the phone, and then close the laptop for good measure as if Red Bess might appear on the screen, and find Martha Conway sitting across from me.

"I thought you didn't have a laptop," she says.

"It's new," I say defensively, rattled by the Instagram post. Who could be posting as Red Bess? Is it a coincidence that I'd just asked Atticus to tell Hadley *not* to post? "From work . . . speaking of which, shouldn't you be in the library?"

"It's my lunch break," she replies, "and I needed to get out of there. We're always packed when the weather gets cold and gray like this . . . actually"—she takes a sip of her foamy drink that smells strongly of cinnamon, cloves, and cardamom—"there's been a lot of requests for local history materials about Wyldcliffe Heights. You're not the only one who's been researching the fire."

"Oh?" I say because she seems to expect me to say something. "Is that unusual?"

She frowns, and I notice there's a fleck of foam in the corner of her mouth. "Not really. The Red Bess story is popular around Halloween. It's our local ghost story and part of the Halloween parade, so there are always a few goth kids reading about it."

"Oh yeah?" I say, wondering suddenly if it's just a coincidence that Martha showed up right as I got the Red Bess post. I pass my phone over to her. "Could this be one of your patrons? Or maybe you, since you seem to be such a big fan of Red Bess?"

She picks up my phone and studies the screen. "It's a new account," she says as if I couldn't have figured that out for myself. "With only one post." She looks up. "Why would you think it was me? This was taken in New York City and I haven't been there in a while."

"You could have taken the picture anytime—" I begin but then I realize how paranoid I sound. I hardly know Martha; why would she be trying to taunt me?—unless she's really working with Laeticia. "And you do seem . . . well, a little obsessed with Red Bess."

She snorts but doesn't seem offended. "Who isn't in this town? Every year some crazies try to break into the grounds of Wyld-cliffe Heights. Last year some teenagers scaled the cliff and Letty had to chase them off with a shotgun."

I smile, picturing Hadley running away from a gun-toting Laeticia, and then sober. "Laeticia has a shotgun? She wouldn't actually shoot someone, would she?"

"If they threatened Veronica St. Clair she would. She's very, very loyal to her. You know it was Letty who saved her from the fire. And afterward Veronica defended her against the police."

"For what?"

Martha looks around the café and then leans closer to me. "She was accused of setting the fire," she whispers.

"But I thought it was the other girl . . . the one who died . . . Dr. Sinclair's patient . . . Jane Rosen."

"That's what Veronica told them, but first they thought it was poor Letty because of her history of arson."

"Letty has a history of arson?" I hiss back.

"Well, yeah, that's why she was at Wyldcliffe Heights. She'd been caught lighting fires. She was going to get sent to jail until Dr. Sinclair stepped in and testified that she was mentally un-stable and belonged at Wyldcliffe Heights."

I blink, trying to absorb all this new information. "Wait, are you saying that Letty was a patient at Wyldcliffe Heights?"

"Uh-huh. The family thought they were lucky Dr. Sinclair took her so she didn't have to go to jail, but Letty was never the same after she went there. After the fire the matron testified that Letty said under hypnotism that she'd been a witch in a previous life who'd been burned at the stake and that's why she kept setting fires."

"That's crazy," I say.

"Maybe, but it made everyone think she was the arsonist. Only Veronica defended her and said it was the other patient, the one who died, who had set the fire. And to prove she trusted Letty she hired her when no one else would. I mean, who's going to hire a housekeeper with a history of burning down houses?"

"No one," I say, thinking of Laeticia holding a match to the pilot light in the kitchen, the blue flames reflected in her face.

"You can imagine how loyal she is to Veronica. I've probably said too much. Would you do me a favor and not tell Letty I told you about the arson stuff? She's still touchy about it."

I promise, certain I won't be able to utter the word "fire" any-where near Laeticia from now on.

Martha smiles and holds out her hand. It takes me a second to realize she wants to shake. When I put my hand in hers, she squeezes it tight. "We've got a deal. I won't tell her about the lap-top and brand-new iPhone either."

It begins to rain on my way back to the house. Despite the rain jacket and boots I'm soaked through by the time I get back. I start up the stairs in my damp socks, intent on getting back to my room without running into Letty, but she appears on the first landing, arms crossed over her chest, blocking my way.

"There you are!" she says as if she's caught me sneaking in after my curfew. "I've been looking all over for you."

"I went into town," I say. "I thought we were done for the day."

"Veronica's been asking for you. She wants to go on."

"Now?" I ask, looking down at my soaked jeans and socks.

"Do you have anything else to do?" She looks suspiciously at my backpack. Has Martha broken her promise already and told her about the laptop?

"No . . . I just thought she was tired . . . and you didn't want me to wear her out."

"I don't, but she says she wants to get it all down while it's coming back to her. She says that you being here has dredged up the past." She sniffs and looks at my feet as if the past isn't all I'm dredging up and tracking onto her clean floors.

"Okay," I say, turning to head down the stairs.

"Not with that filthy bag dripping all over," she snaps. "Please leave it in your room and change into more suitable clothes. Miss St. Clair may be blind but that's no reason to be disrespectful."

"Got it," I spit back. "No backpack. Nicer clothes. Anything else?"

"Be quick about it. You've already made her wait."

I edge past her, biting back a cutting remark about how long Veronica has made her fans wait for her next book. *Must not anger the arsonist,* I say to myself as I head to my room. Laeticia only cares, I think as I walk up the stairs, because she's fanatically loyal to Veronica St. Clair. If Veronica lied for her, the hold she has on Laeticia might be more than loyalty; it might be fear that Veronica would someday reveal that she was the one who started the fire.

The first thing I do is take out my laptop and look for a place to hide it. I slide it between the mattress and box spring, my go-to hiding place at Woodbridge. Then I change into the wool skirt, button-down shirt, and warm tights, feeling like I'm back at Woodbridge putting on my uniform.

I head back downstairs and into the library, expecting to find Veronica slumped in the corner, tethered to her oxygen machine, an invalid gasping out her last breaths. Instead, she is seated in the center of the green couch, bolt upright, her hands clutching the knob of a cane, her green robe spread out around her like that of a priestess who holds all the secrets locked tight behind those blind eyes. Secrets some people might not want told. Maybe that's why Laeticia has been so hostile to me since I arrived. She's afraid of what Veronica might say about her.

I pause on the other side of the table, unsure if she wants me on the couch. In truth, I'm afraid of getting closer.

"You can sit there," she says, gesturing toward the chair placed directly in front of her. "I think that today my voice will carry."

And indeed, her voice is not only stronger than it was this morning; it's stronger than it's been since I arrived. *Maybe the doctor gave her some good drugs,* I think as I sit and open my notebook. Or she's channeling some other force that wants this story told.

I THOUGHT IT *would be terrible to return to Wyldcliffe Heights, but knowing Jayne would be there made it different. I would not be alone—the madwoman in the attic—I would be one of the girls. I* told my father on the drive up that I wanted to stay in the west wing and be treated like all the other girls.

"You're not afraid to be with the patients?" he asked. "Some of them have serious problems."

"Then they're like me," I told him. "I belong with them."

I expected him to argue but he surprised me by conceding. "Perhaps you're right. But remember, this means you'll be treated just the same as all my patients. I'll expect you to attend group therapy as well as your private sessions with me. I'm hopeful that we'll recover the time you lost from last night through hypnotherapy."

I didn't want to recover what had happened after I'd lunged at Anaïs, but I couldn't tell my father that. When the gate opened the first thing I noticed were the dogs—not the harmless old guard dogs our groundskeeper had coddled and spoiled but three muscular mastiffs in a pen by the gatehouse charging at a new wire fence.

"How do you like our new Cerberus?" my father asked. "I've named them Cerberus, Baskerville, and Garm. There won't be any more midnight escapes with these three patrolling the grounds."

My mouth went dry imagining their slavering jaws snapping at my heels.

The dogs weren't the only change. At the house, I looked for Mrs. Gorse but my father told me he had let her go. "She let you run away," he said. "I couldn't keep her on after that."

I felt a pang but steeled myself against it. I didn't need Mrs. Gorse; I had Jayne.

The matron was new as well, a solid-looking woman with a humorless gray face. She checked me off on her clipboard and said, "Room Five," as if that were my name now. I looked back for my father, but he had already turned away and gone back through the door to the atrium. As the heavy bolt slid into place, I felt my throat tighten and tasted metal. I turned and followed the matron down a long hallway. It was like entering a familiar place but through a mirror, where everything is reversed. I'd lived my whole life in the east wing, where the hallways were carpeted and paneled in dark wood and the ceilings were coffered and trimmed with decorative fruits and angels. Here the walls were bare plaster painted a diseased ocher, the floors were cracked linoleum, and everything smelled like disinfectant. And yet the layout was the same. I recognized the long room that was the library on the other side, only here it held four metal tables with attached benches, each one clamped to the floor, and the windows were barred.

"This is where you will eat and attend recreation hour," Matron informed me. The room smelled like boiled cabbage and stale body odor. Four girls sat at one table picking at something in front of them. I thought they might be eating but as we passed, I saw that they were working on jigsaw puzzles. The picture they were assembling was a landscape with woods, a river, and a mottled glowering sky. One of the girls looked up as I passed and regarded me with an expression as blank as the piece of gray sky she held in her hand.

"You'll be allowed to join the community activity only after you've been evaluated and cleared by Dr. Sinclair," she said, as if it would be a great privilege to sit in this dreary room and move pieces of cardboard around. I felt all the color and light of the last months draining out of me. Where was Jayne? What if my father had lied to get me to come with him peacefully? What if he wasn't able to get her charges dropped? I didn't think I could survive here without her.

We passed a door with my father's name on it. I realized it was the interior door to the tower. I had only ever entered through the outside door.

Matron led me into a narrow hallway past the tower door, recit-
ing as she went a list of rules. No eating in your room. No smoking
anywhere. No talking after lights-out. No trips to the bathroom
after lights-out. *There were four closed doors on either side of the*
hall. We stopped at the second to last on the right-hand side. This
was the pantry in the east wing. I half expected to see sacks of cof-
fee and flour, rows of canned vegetables and jars of summer fruits.
Instead, the room held two narrow metal beds, two small metal
cabinets, and one barred window. The light from the window was
so thin and watery, as if it had been strained by the bars, that it took
me a moment to realize there was a girl sitting on one of the beds,
her knees tucked up under her chin.

"Here's a new roommate for you, LeeAnn. Try to behave better to
this one or you'll be back in solitary."

LeeAnn raised her eyes without lifting her head from her knees
and glared at me. I realized I'd seen her from the window when I
watched the girls at their daily exercise. She always walked alone,
the other girls giving her a wide berth. I'd asked Mrs. Gorse why that
was, and she'd told me it was because she'd burned down a house.

"Is that really so much worse than what the others have done?"
I'd asked.

As the matron closed the door behind her, sliding the bolt home,
I remembered how Mrs. Gorse had answered.

"Her family was in it. They were all burned alive."

VERONICA MUST HEAR my gasp because she stops and turns toward me. "Is there something wrong?" she asks.

"No—" I'm dying to ask her if "LeeAnn" is Laeticia—and if it's
true her family was killed in the fire she set, a detail that Martha
Conway had left out—but then I'd be revealing that I'd talked to a

local about the house. "I just . . . that must have been scary, being put in a room with a stranger who had done something like that."

"It would have been," she says with a coy smile, reassuming her authorial distance. "Shall we go on?"

I think about Laeticia's warning not to tire Veronica. Is that what she's really worried about? Or is she afraid of what the sequel might reveal about *her* history? I glance toward the closed door, picturing Laeticia hovering on the other side, her ear pressed to the keyhole. *Too bad*, I think, picking up my pen. It's not just her story; it belongs to the rest of us.

LEEANN WAS SILENT *while I changed into the scratchy gray uniform and made my bed. Maybe her voice burned up in the fire, I thought meanly. Maybe I could ask my father to allow me to change roommates. But he'd said no special treatment. And what if it got back to LeeAnn that I'd asked? I didn't want to make her any angrier than she already appeared to be. When I was done changing and turned around, I saw she was staring at me.*

"You're his daughter," she spat out. "I've seen you in the window watching us."

"I'm not supposed to talk about my relationship with Dr. Sinclair," I said prissily.

"Are you here as his spy?" she asked.

"No!" I exclaimed, and then, I asked warily, "What are you afraid of him finding out? Don't you tell him everything in your therapy sessions?"

She smirked at that like I was the stupid one and began to answer but then we heard footsteps and voices in the hall. She bolted up from the bed and crouched at the door, her ear pressed to the keyhole. I stood next to her—and heard Jayne's voice.

"I get it, no eating and no smoking," she was saying. "But no talking? What if I talk in my sleep? And what if I need to use the bathroom? What if there's a fire—"

"THERE WILL BE NO FIRE," Matron roared. It sounded like they were right outside our door. I shoved LeeAnn aside and plastered my eye to the keyhole. I was just in time to see Jayne whirl around and crouch down to press her face to the keyhole. Her eye loomed large and rimmed with black and purple.

"Violet, is that you?"

"There will be no talking to other patients until—"

"I've been evaluated," Jayne mimicked. Then she winked at me. Was that kohl, I wondered, or a bruise?

"I can't wait," Jayne added as she followed the matron to the room next to ours. LeeAnn was already sitting on the floor by a heating vent—a wide rectangle about the size of a bread box covered with a brass grate. I sat down across from her and listened as the matron gave Jayne the same speech she'd given me. As soon as she left, we heard Jayne give out a loud, exaggerated sigh and then exclaim, "This wardrobe does absolutely nothing for my figure."

Dour LeeAnn giggled.

"Are there mice in the walls?" Jayne cried, her voice so loud in the grate I thought she had crept into it. I pressed my face to the floor and saw that the vent went straight through to the next room. I could see Jayne's bruised eye pressed against the grate on her side.

"What happened to your eye?" I asked.

"A parting gift from one of New York's finest," she said, "when I slapped his hand away from my thigh. Am I in solitary? Why didn't they put us together?"

"Your roommate is Dorothy," LeeAnn said. Apparently, she didn't hold Jayne in the same contempt she held me. "She's in the infirmary for force-feeding."

"Lovely," Jayne replied. "What's your name?"

"LeeAnn."

"Nice to meet you, LeeAnn. I hope you've been treating my friend Violet well."

LeeAnn gave me a nervous look, afraid I'd rat her out for her less than gracious welcome, but just hearing Jayne's voice had made me strong enough to be generous. "She's been fab," I enthused. "LeeAnn and I have been bonding over our shared memories of Wyldcliffe Heights."

"What a place!" Jayne said, her voice full of glee as if we were in Cinderella Castle in Disney World and not a mental institution. "It's like Thornfield in Jane Eyre. We're going to have so much fun. Wait, just give me a sec . . ."

Her voice faded away and I wondered what she could be doing in her tiny room. LeeAnn and I sat, silently poised like children waiting on the hearth for Santa Claus to come down the chimney. The drab room seemed to glow with a new light as if Jayne had already cast her spell over it. Suddenly the door flew open with a bang.

"DID I NOT MENTION THERE WILL BE NO SITTING ON THE FLOOR?" came a loud bellow from the doorway.

LeeAnn and I whirled around to find Jayne standing on the threshold, arms raised, displaying her bare tattooed belly above the waistband of her gray uniform, the shirt ends of the top tied under her visible black bra. She was holding a liquor flask in one hand and an unlit cigarette in the other. How had she smuggled them in? And how had she gotten past two locked doors? LeeAnn's face was lit up, and I knew that I'd never have any trouble from her—or anyone else—as long as Jayne was here. Jayne would provide enough trouble for all of us.

CHAPTER TWENTY-ONE

aeticia appears as soon as Veronica stops talking, as if she had been listening at the door for a pause. As I watch her help Veronica into the wheelchair and wheel her away, I think of how easy it would be for her to stop her mistress from telling anything more. A mistake in her medications. A pillow over her face. A slip on the hard bathroom tile. A lit match near those oxygen canisters.

I shake the images from my head and sit down to type. Martha said Laeticia was devoted to Veronica. She's not going to murder her. On the other hand, I don't think Letty would spare a tear at my demise. As I type up the new pages, I notice how hostile LeeAnn was to Veronica and then how quickly captivated she was by Jayne. If LeeAnn is Laeticia, she must have switched her allegiance to Veronica at some point. I can imagine how it might have happened. Girls like Jayne are exciting and fun to be with at first. They light up the room and make you want to follow them into their next crazy escapade no matter where it leads. Usually no place good. When they crash, they bring everyone close to them down with them.

I should know. I lived through the cycle with my mother dozens of times. In her manic state she would send me a postcard to convince me to run away with her. She always had a scheme—we were going to pick apples on a farm and live on cider and donuts; we were going to house-sit for a friend and sell honey from a roadside stand and—always—she was going to write a book that would make a fortune. She had an idea this time for a fail-safe bestseller. All she needed was a quiet place to focus. For a while she would seem to be working really hard. The stack of pages would grow beside her typewriter (she wouldn't touch a computer because she thought "the internet" would steal her ideas).

The first sign that something was amiss was when she would start to talk to herself as she typed. I'd tell myself she was reading her pages over to herself. But then I'd hear her arguing with herself—or, rather, the different voices in her head began arguing with each other. I'd find her crouched in the dark at night underneath her desk. *Look,* she would say, pointing to a scattering of pebbles arranged on top of the pages, *the pattern has been changed. Someone is coming in at night and stealing my book.* Eventually she would burn what she had written. *It's no good,* she would tell me. *They've stolen my story from me; I'll never get it back.*

Could Jayne be my mother? But if she was, what had happened to her to change her from the vibrant girl in Veronica's story into the fragile wreck that was my mother? What did they do to her here?

When I finish the new pages I add them to the stack beside the typewriter, adding one more stone in a pattern I memorize so I'll be able to know for sure if the stones are rearranged tomorrow. When I look up the window is dark and my own reflection looks back at me. *My* face, not my mother's. *I am not her,* I tell myself. *There's no certainty that you'll inherit your mother's mental illness,* Dr. Husack told me, *and even if you do your outcome doesn't have to be the same as hers because you won't live the same life that she did.*

And yet, here I am, in the place where she had been, following in her footsteps, taking on her old paranoid ways, arranging stones to catch an intruder and imagining the housekeeper is plotting to murder me.

I get up to leave the library, feeling weary. In the atrium the *whump-whoosh* of Veronica's nebulizer echoes in the hollow space like the heartbeat of the house. I pause, looking toward the door to the west wing recalling Violet's first day on the ward. She was in the third room on the hall and Jayne was in the last. I'd looked at the first three doors and seen that the name cards had been taken out, but had I looked at the fourth door? I can't remember. I find myself wondering if there might be a card with Jane Rosen's name on it—a small clue tying the Jayne in the book to the woman who died in the fire.

The door to the dormitory wing is still propped open with a cinder block. When I reach it, I hear a door opening at the end of the hall and Laeticia's voice. She's coming out of Veronica's room. There's no time to get across the recreation room and into the atrium and no place to hide except the tower. I open the tower door, step inside, and close it behind me.

It's like stepping into a crypt. Dark and cold and smelling like cremated bodies. I feel along the stone walls and find the steps leading up to where I can sense fresher air. I start toward the air, corkscrewing myself into the narrow, twisting stairs. The burned smell grows as I climb up and I imagine being trapped inside by a raging fire. I'm ready to turn back but then I hear something above me—a fluttering sound like pages being turned in a book or—

I picture manuscript pages flying loose in an empty room like snowflakes in a snow globe. All the secrets of Wyldcliffe Heights trapped in its tower. I envision the cover of the book, the single light from the tower looking out like an eye. Of course, this is where the mind of the house resides. I come around the last tight bend and step through a doorway, its door burned to ashes, into Dr. Sinclair's office. All the furniture and wood paneling and floorboards and roof beams have been gutted by the fire. The fluttering comes from a rag snagged in a broken window frame, flapping in the wind and shining white in the moonlight. It sounds like the last mad gibberish inside a ruined brain. I cross the empty room, my shoes crunching over broken glass and scorched wood, to make it stop. When I reach it, I see that it's a handkerchief embroidered with violets, like the ones Jayne used. Did she leave it here the night of the fire? When I free it from the window frame, though, I see the cloth is too pristine to have been here all those years and, as I lift it to my nose, I smell violets, the same perfume my mother always wore. I look down at the lawn and there, in the moonlight, stands a woman who looks exactly like my mother.

When I wake up the next morning the room is full of gray light and I can't see anything. The outside world has been swallowed by fog.

"Have you been sleepwalking?" Peter Syms asks me when I come down to the atrium.

"What? Why would you ask that?"

"I saw footprints on the back lawn this morning."

"It wasn't me," I say, thinking of my mother's haunted face looking up at me in the tower last night. Had it really been her? The moment after I saw her a cloud had passed over the moon and she had vanished. Was it possible I had imagined her?

He holds my gaze for a beat and then says, "Probably locals.

They get pretty excited about Halloween around here and dare each other to sneak onto the property. Whoever it was," he says, opening the library door for me, "they'd better be careful. I have instructions from Letty to shoot any trespassers."

I shudder as I cross the library to the green couch. I clear my throat to let Veronica know I'm here, but she doesn't even flinch. She's still as a marble statue, and for an awful moment I think she might be dead, her corpse propped up by Laeticia as some horrible joke at my expense. When she speaks, I nearly jump out of my skin.

"I know you're there, Miss Corey. I am collecting myself for the task."

"We ended with Jayne bursting in," I say, "and surprising you—I mean, Violet—and LeeAnn. She's quite the character, Jayne. I think I like her in this version even better than in *The Secret of Wyldcliffe Heights*."

"And what about Violet?" she asked. "Do you like her more or less in this version?"

"I feel sorry for her in this version—" I begin and then instantly regret my choice of words. "I mean . . . she's always in Jayne's shadow."

She tilts her head at me. "Yes, Jayne was a charmer," she says. "She knew how to light up a room. The only problem was that she often did it by setting something on fire."

IT WASN'T JUST *LeeAnn who fell for Jayne's charms. She cast her spell over all the girls—the drug addicts from the Bronx, the anorexic, self-harming college girls, the sex addicts and kleptomaniacs and firebugs. It was Jayne who realized we could not only talk through the vents but if we unscrewed the grates we could pass mes-*

sages and contraband from room to room. And it was Jayne who could pick the locks and gather us together in the middle of the night. We'd post one girl as lookout by the dormitory door to watch for the matron, but she rarely made night rounds even though she was supposed to.

"She's probably getting drunk in her room," Jayne said. "Can't you smell the whiskey on her?"

Jayne started out by telling the story of how she and I got there. She told them about my daring escape from Wyldcliffe Heights down the cliff, across the marsh, and onto an open railcar, never mind that I'd actually bought a ticket and rode next to a retired sanitation worker from Utica. She made me sound like the heroine of an adventure and our days at the Josephine like a picaresque novel peopled by punk rockers and Manhattan socialites. Her stories were so vivid that I could see us dancing at Limelight and the Roxy. She said we'd ended back here after being caught in a drug bust at the Josephine.

Then she quickly changed the subject and asked each girl how they came to be at Wyldcliffe Heights, drawing them out with questions until the sad banal stories of truancy, drug use, pregnancies, and suicide attempts became ballads of rebellion and escape.

"You started the fire so your stepfather would stop hitting your mother," she said to LeeAnn after she told her story. "It's not your fault he was too drunk to get himself out."

She told Dorothy that her mother sounded like a controlling bitch and no one should tell her what she should and shouldn't put into her own body.

Donna from Astoria had stopped going to school because the education system didn't work for artists.

Jessica from Rye shouldn't have gotten sent away for sleeping with her high school English teacher; he should have. Together they spun an elaborate revenge plot in which Jayne would lure him to a motel, drug him, and then sacrifice him in the woods like they did in Greek plays.

She coached us, too, on what we should say in our therapy sessions with my father to get the best meds and get out of annoying chores.

"But aren't you afraid you'll let on that you were faking your symptoms when he hypnotizes you?" Dorothy asked.

"Oh, I never go under. I just pretend to." Jayne laughed. "I'd love to watch myself on the tapes he makes."

This was another innovation since we'd come back to Wyldcliffe. My father had bought a fancy camcorder, much like the one Casey had used, to record our sessions.

"But how do you stop from going under?" Dorothy asked. "I always feel sick to my stomach after."

I'd noticed that after her sessions with my father Dorothy would come to dinner as if in a trance and shovel food into her mouth like an automaton. At least she had put on a few pounds and didn't look so skeletal. Truth be told, we were all putting on some weight from the starchy diet and lack of exercise. Even Jayne, who'd always been rail-thin, looked puffy and lumpy under the loose, pajama-like uniform. I wondered if stopping the hypnosis was really a good idea for Dorothy, but Jayne had already moved to sit beside her and taken her hand.

"You're stronger than you think, Dorothy. No one can make you do anything without your consent. When Dr. Sinclair asks if you are ready to be hypnotized say 'yes' out loud but in your head say 'no.' Then when he says, 'Relax your body,' say to yourself, I will not relax my body. My body is mine to control. Repeat that."

"My body is mine to control," Dorothy repeated. So did LeeAnn and Donna and all the other girls. I did, too.

Jayne taught us how to turn around each of the prompts my father used and we all repeated them. At the end Jayne said, "We'll all go out to the woods the next full moon," and we all repeated that, too. Only much later did it occur to me that she was practicing her own form of hypnosis over us.

CHAPTER TWENTY-TWO

D o you think she was?" I blurt out the question not only because I want to know but because I am beginning to feel as if I'm falling under a spell myself. It occurs to me that Veronica herself is practicing a kind of hypnosis on me each day as she spins her tales.

She doesn't answer right away. I can see her jaw clenching and I'm expecting a rebuke for interrupting her and for again conflating fiction with real life. "Have you ever been hypnotized?" she asks instead.

I'm surprised into honesty. "Dr. Husack, the psychiatrist at Woodbridge, tried it once but it didn't work. He said I was too resistant."

"Of course you are," she said. "I imagine you haven't had too many reasons to trust anyone."

I bristle, unsure if that's meant as criticism or praise, but before I can respond she adds, "Sometimes resistance is its own form of trance. That's what Jayne learned . . ." She pauses for a moment, and I realize she's picked up the thread of the story, so I pick up my pen and notebook.

SOME OF THE girls were better at resisting than others. I found it easy. I had grown used to thinking the opposite of each statement

*my father made. I lay on the couch in the tower while he slotted
a cassette in his new fancy camera and then I simply thought the
opposite of each suggestion he made. No, I would not let out the
tension with each exhale; no, my eyes weren't getting heavy; no, I
would not visualize a white light. Instead, I pictured Jayne and me
dancing at the Josephine and recited to myself the lyrics of a song
she liked to sing:*

> *Don't go to sleep, my baby,*
> *Don't rest your head, my darling,*
> *Don't close your eyes, my sweetheart,*
> *Stay awake! Stay awake! Stay mine!*

*As long as I heard Jayne's voice in my head my father's voice had
no power over me. Even when he asked me what happened at the
Josephine the night Anaïs died and I could picture myself lunging at
Anaïs, I was able to tell him I'd slept through it all.*

*LeeAnn said she recited the ABCs to keep his voice out of her
head. She reported that once he thought she was under he kept
taking her further and further back in her childhood, searching for
the moment she first fell in love with fire. "It was always there," she
told him. She loved the smell of matches and the blue flowers that
bloomed on the gas range and the way flames leapt from the burning
leaf piles in fall and the single star of her first birthday cake.*

"And then he asked me if I could remember further back."

*"Further back than your first birthday?" Donna asked. "Like to
when you were in the womb?"*

"I guess—" LeeAnn began, but Jayne cut in.

*"He's talking about past lives," she said. "Haven't any of you no-
ticed the books on his desk?"*

"There's one called Many Lives, Many Masters," I said.

"That's about past-life regression," Jayne said. "He's trying to make you remember something that happened in a past life. Something that explains why you're a firebug."

"That's ridiculous," Donna, who'd been raised by strict Catholics, announced. "There's no such thing as reincarnation."

"No crazier than believing in immaculate conception," Jayne replied. Donna often rubbed her the wrong way, I'd noticed. "Personally, I think I've had many lives. A psychic once told me I was an old soul." She turned toward me. "You are, too, Violet. I knew the first time we met that you and I had known each other in a past life."

"Who did you think you were?" Donna, clearly stung by the immaculate conception remark, asked snarkily. "Antony and Cleopatra? Romeo and Juliet?"

"Romeo and Juliet aren't real," Jayne said, holding my gaze. "That's not who we were." She didn't say then who she thought we'd been but I could tell by the glint in her eye she had an idea. She turned to LeeAnn.

"Tell Dr. Sinclair you were a witch burned at the stake. There's a book about the Scottish witch trials in the library. I'll get you a name and her details that you can use."

"But why would a witch who was burned want to start fires?" Donna asked.

Jayne gave her a withering glare. "If you'd been burnt to death, wouldn't you want to burn down the whole world?"

IN THE NEXT days, Jayne scoured the house for "material," as she put it. We were allowed an hour in the library each day, but we weren't allowed to take the books out. "Besides," Jayne said after she'd found

LeeAnn a witch to claim, "he'll catch on if we use obvious stuff from history. I have a better place to look."

The next time we were outside for our "daily exercise" Jayne waited for the matron to go inside—"She has a stash of liquor," Jayne hypothesized—and took off for the woods. I followed her, half afraid that she meant to run away. I caught up with her at the children's cemetery.

"Who are all these girls?" she asked, walking between the rows of crooked graves.

"These were the Magdalen girls," I told her, "from when the house was a refuge in the 1890s. A lot of them were here because they'd gotten pregnant out of wedlock . . . the little stones are for babies—"

"And they buried them out here in the woods where no one could find them?" Jayne asked, as horrified as if the babies had been left in the woods to die. She stopped in front of a gravestone topped by a statue of an angel, its head broken in half. Jayne cupped her hand around its broken face. "We should use these girls in our sessions with your father, say their names . . . I bet that would freak him out."

The next time we went to the cemetery, Jayne brought a notebook and pencil and wrote down the names of the Magdalen girls and their children. She assigned one for each of us to pretend to be in our sessions with my father. Even after she'd gotten the names, she would still go to the children's cemetery, where, I had begun to suspect, she had a hiding place for her cigarettes and matches. When I asked her where she got them she told me that Gunn came at night and left things for her. "We arranged it beforehand," she told me.

Is that what she had whispered in his ear that last night at the Josephine?

"Isn't he afraid of the dogs?"

Jayne laughed. "He brings a couple of hamburgers for them. He says they're tame as lapdogs after a couple of Whoppers."

One night soon after that I heard Jayne sneaking out of her room, but instead of going outside I heard her creeping past my door. Pressing my eye to the keyhole I saw her stealing through the door to the tower. After a few minutes I jimmied the lock the way Jayne had shown me and followed her. At the foot of the tower I heard voices and froze, but then I realized they were recorded voices. I crept up the tower stairs and found Jayne crouched in front of my father's video recorder. She was watching a tape but her body blocked the screen so I couldn't see it. I took a step closer and my foot hit a creaky floorboard. Jayne spun around. She looked relieved when she saw it was me but she stopped the tape and ejected it before I could see what was on the screen.

"What are you doing?" I asked.

"I wanted to see my sessions," she said. "To review my performance."

"And?" I asked.

She shrugged. "I think I'm getting a bit repetitive. I need some new material. I need—" She focused her laser gaze on me and pointed at my throat. "I need her."

"Josephine Hale?" I asked, touching the locket.

"Her too," she said, grinning. "What would be more natural than for you to be the reincarnation of your grandmother? I bet there are journals of hers somewhere in this heap."

"In the attic," I told her. "Josephine's desk is up there. That's where they would be—"

"And what about Bess?" she asked. "Are her things up there, too?"

When I nodded, she got to her feet. "What are we waiting for? Let's go there."

"Now?"

"Why not?" she said, waving toward the stairs. "Lead on, McDuff."

As I turned to go I saw her slipping the tape she had ejected into her pocket.

I took her to the back stairs that led from the kitchen to the attic. "It's like we're mice scurrying inside the walls," Jayne whispered as we made our way up the narrow twisting stairs, each of us holding a candle that we'd stolen from the pantry to light our way. "Or that children's book about the little people who live under the floorboards."

"The Borrowers," I said. "It was one of my favorite books growing up."

"Of course it was," Jayne said, pausing on the narrow landing and holding her candle up to my face. "You grew up a secret in your own house, Violet. Your father has kept you here like a prisoner."

"It's because my mother went crazy," I said, "or at least my father thought she had and he was afraid I would, too. Now that I've proven him right, he's going to keep me here forever."

"I won't let that happen," Jayne said fiercely, clasping my hand. In the flickering candlelight the shadows under her eyes were so dark against her pale skin that she looked like an apparition—like the ghostly face of Red Bess I'd imagined in the mirror that last night at the Josephine. I knew she meant it, that she always kept her promises, but it made me suddenly frightened of what she might do to keep her word.

The attic had once been where the housemaids slept, and for a while my nursery, but now it held old furniture and boxes of books and papers. Jayne went straight to the old rolltop desk and sat in the spindly chair in front of it. She placed her candle upon it, ran her hands over the accordion-ridged top, and rolled it up. She gasped at all the little drawers and pigeonholes and began exploring them, her long slender fingers darting in and out, pulling out ribbons and seal-ing wax, pen nibs and ink bottles, and, finally, a marbled notebook. She brushed her hand reverently over the cover and then opened it and held it close to the candle. She read aloud the first page.

"'Papa gave me this little book to record my goals for the coming year. So here they are: 1. Make Papa proud—' Ugh." Jayne made a face. "Please tell me your ancestress wasn't a daddy's girl." She flipped through the pages impatiently, riffling them so close to the candle flame that I was afraid she'd set them on fire in her search for something of interest. Then she gasped. "Look," she said, holding the book up for me. "See how the handwriting changes. This isn't written by Josephine."

I looked over her shoulder at the handwriting. Yes, it was dif-ferent from my grandmother Josephine's elegant handwriting. This was rushed and scratchy, almost crude. It felt wrong seeing it in my grandmother's notebook, as if a ventriloquist had taken over her voice. When Jayne read a line out loud, I thought it didn't sound like Jayne, either.

"'My name is Bess Molloy,'" she read, "'whom some have called Red Bess, and this is my confession.'"

"How did she come to write it here?" I wondered out loud.

"What does it matter?" Jayne asked impatiently. "This is it, Vio-let, I can't believe you never knew this was here. This is the true story of Josephine and Bess. We can find out what really happened. This is what's going to get us out of Wyldcliffe Heights."

"How?" I asked, wondering why she thought Bess's story was truer than Josephine's. "I thought you were going to use it in your sessions with my father."

"I am!" she cried, leafing eagerly through the pages. "But we can do more with this. We can write a book about Josephine and Bess *and tell the true story. It will be like* Jane Eyre. *I can already feel it. It will make us rich and famous and then we'll be able to do whatever we want."*

I wanted to be carried away on the tide of Jayne's enthusiasm, but there was something about the hectic flush in her cheeks and the feverish glint in her eyes that made me hold back for once. "What about my father?" I asked.

Jayne smiled and took my hand. "Don't you worry," she said. "I know how to take care of your father."

"Did you know what she meant by that?" I ask.

Veronica shakes her head, no longer pretending that what she's reciting is fiction. "I thought it must have something to do with fooling him into believing that she was the reincarnation of Red Bess. I suppose she meant to reveal at some point that she'd tricked him and use that as leverage to blackmail him. I thought that's why she had stolen her session tape. It wasn't a bad plan. He had ambitions to publish a book on hypnotherapy and past-life regression. Jayne offered him the perfect case. She plunged into reading Red Bess's confession that night, practicing it by reading it aloud to me through the vent between our rooms . . . Are you ready to take it down?"

I startle, unsure for a moment if she's still talking to me or if she's back to reciting the book. "You can't remember the whole thing—"

"I remember every word," she says. "Jayne read it over and over again to memorize it and then passed the journal back to me so I could check that she had it down right. 'It's not like my father has read it,' I told her. 'What does it matter if you know it word for word?' Do you know what she said?"

I shake my head, then, remembering she can't see me, say, "No, what did she say?"

"She said, 'It matters to *her*.' That's when I knew we were in trouble, that Jayne believed that the ghost of Red Bess was real and that she was inside Jayne—are you writing this down, Miss Corey?"

"Are you sure you feel up to going on?" I ask, "It's getting late—" I look out the window but the sky is the same uniform gray it had been when we started. We might be suspended in time, for all I know, stuck in an afternoon in 1993 when one girl read a journal aloud to another, or in 1923 when one wrote her story in another girl's journal.

"I want to tell it now," Veronica replies. "While I still can."

CHAPTER TWENTY-THREE

*M*y name is Bess Molloy, whom some have called Red Bess, and this is my confession. I am writing this in the journal of Miss Josephine Hale because it is the only paper I have at my disposal, but I would like to make clear that she has not coerced or influenced me in what I put down here. I write this of my own free will and take full responsibility for all my actions. May God forgive me.

I was born in Brooklyn, New York, in the neighborhood of Red Hook, of two honest Irish immigrants. My father worked on the docks as a longshoreman and my mother took in sewing. I was the oldest child of six and the only girl. When I reached thirteen, I was needed at home and so, although I loved reading and learning, I no longer went to school. I helped with the young ones and the housework during the day, and at night I helped my mother with the piecework she took in. We made silk flowers—hundreds each night—that were sold in the hat shops and department stores. I made extras to sell on the street. Violets were the most popular. Fresh violets would come down on boats from upstate, where they were grown. I would go early in the morning to the docks and trade silk flowers for real ones and then I would sell them at the restaurants and cafés in Greenwich Village. The men would buy fresh posies for their lady friends, but the women liked the silk ones to trim their hats and keep for later.

One morning the other girls who sold violets were all aflutter at the dock with the news that a violet girl had been found strangled, a violet ribbon tied around her throat, her wares scattered over her body as some kind of perverse tribute. The girls were alarmed, but we all knew we took our chances walking the streets late at night, and the girl who had died, it was whispered, had been selling more than violets.

The next night there was another violet girl killed and then another one the night after that. The newspapers went into a frenzy and called the killer "the Violet Strangler." The preachers said it was God's retribution. The social workers handed out tracts and told us to stay home. Easy for them to say. We had mouths to feed. I took to carrying my sharpest sewing shears with me.

One of the social workers, though, had a practical solution. Her name was Josephine Hale. The first time I saw her speak she was wearing a lilac dress and a corsage of violets. Touching them she said, "They grow them where I live. We have glass houses and the women inmates pick them." This pretty, wide-eyed girl had grown up in a prison. Not as an inmate, of course, but as the daughter of the warden in a place called Wyldcliffe Heights. She said she meant to make things better for us violet girls. She offered us rooms to stay in a settlement house so we wouldn't have to make our way home after selling our wares.

I don't suppose she realized that it would draw the Violet Strangler.

It happened after I'd been at the settlement house for a month. A half dozen of us violet girls had bedded down in the big tower room. I awoke in the middle of the night to see a hooded figure bending over one of the girls. I thought at first that I was dreaming, and then that I was watching the specter of death hovering over the poor girl—and then I saw that he was strangling her. I leapt up and lunged at him, wielding my scissors. He whirled around and raised his hand. The blades went through his hand. I stared at them so stupidly I didn't see his face and I gave him time to strike me with the shears' heavy handle. The blow knocked me to the floor, where I lost consciousness.

When I awoke, I was in a pool of blood—my own, I thought, which would have been better. It was the blood of the violet girls, their throats slit by my own scissors, which lay in my bloody hand. Before I could think to run, a housemaid came in and started screaming. The whole house was roused and came running, including Josephine, whose eyes I could barely stand to meet, so afraid was I that she would look on me as a murderer. Instead, she professed her belief in me.

I was taken to the Women's Detention Center. Josephine got me a lawyer who argued for a plea of mental incompetence and found a doctor, Edgar Bryce, to testify on my behalf. He was a young, good-looking man who spoke compellingly to persuade the jury in my favor. Through his and Josephine's efforts I was remanded to the Wyldcliffe Heights Training School for Women, which she had founded on the grounds of her childhood home.

I was grateful I was spared the hardship of prison, but I would have preferred to be declared innocent. I would forever be "Red Bess," as the newspapers had dubbed me, the slaughterer of innocents. And while Josephine had founded Wyldcliffe Heights to be a place where even a murderer could be treated humanely, I'm afraid she was an innocent in the workings of human nature.

Not long after I arrived, the board of Wyldcliffe Heights demanded that a warden be hired and they appointed Dr. Edgar

Bryce, the doctor who had spoken for me at trial. I think he convinced Josephine that they would be equals in the administration of Wyldcliffe, but it soon became clear that Dr. Bryce planned to make the decisions. Under his direction, we girls were put to work in the greenhouses where the violets grew, which was backbreaking labor. We had to lie on planks laid across the beds to protect the fragile blooms. More care was taken of the flowers than of our bones, which Dr. Bryce insisted were sturdy due to our hearty peasant stock.

He spoke of us as if we were cattle or sheep. Our propensities, he explained in the lectures he delivered at tea gatherings of the board of directors and local women's clubs, were inbred in us from birth. It wasn't our fault. I was present at these gatherings as a prime example of his doctrines. Dressed in the plain muslin uniform of the asylum I would sit on a stool in front for all to see as Dr. Bryce used calipers, his hands always gloved as if he feared contamination from me, to demonstrate the failings of my physiognomy and the consequences of letting the deficient breed.

I learned to pretend that I was not there, to let my soul float up to the ceiling and out the long windows of the library, out across the lawn and into the woods along the meandering paths of the Ramble, as Josephine had taught me to call it. I would pretend that I was there, walking with her, and not in the library being poked at by Dr. Bryce's calipers.

She took me there although the other girls weren't allowed to go on their own. On one of our walks I asked whether she agreed with Dr. Bryce's theory that madness came from poor breeding. She didn't reply right away and I was afraid I'd overstepped. She was nervous, I'd noticed, of having Dr. Bryce's orders questioned. She'd come to rely on him more and more, and he, I had noticed, often used that reliance to make her feel uncertain and small. When she laughed or spoke loudly, he reminded her that excitement was disruptive for the sense of calm "our girls" need. When she took walks with me, he scolded her for singling me out for preference. "The other girls won't like her for it," he told her. Even in her company, I noticed, he habitually wore gloves as if he were afraid that she, too, was contaminated.

When we had reached the stone statue that marked the entrance to the cemetery, she stopped and, laying one hand on one of the horrible hellhound's heads as if he were a beloved pet, said to me, "I don't agree with all of Dr. Bryce's ideas, Bess, but I am hopeful I'll be able to influence his thinking more in the future." And then, with an uncertain smile, she told me that he had proposed they marry. "It makes so much sense, Bess. We'll be able to do more as partners. It will look more proper with the two of us living here together. We must be ever so careful of our reputations, you see, so that we set an example for you girls."

I stared at her. She'd delivered this last bit as a set piece, like the elocution recitations she had us memorize and perform. She didn't sound like herself at all. It was like hearing the puppet master's voice coming out of a marionette's hinged jaw. "Jo," I said softly, laying my hand over hers, "those aren't reasons to marry. You don't love him."

"You don't know that!" she cried, snatching her hand out from under mine. "And you can't be expected to understand—"

"Because I'm mentally deficient?"

"I didn't say that. You're putting words in my mouth. He said you'd be upset—that I've made too much a favorite of you and you've formed an unhealthy attachment to me."

"I'm not the one putting words in your mouth," I cried. "He is! You parrot everything he says. Soon you'll be advocating sterilization for all the girls at Wyldcliffe Heights. Watch out he doesn't recommend the same for you. He treats you as if you're mentally deficient."

She stared at me aghast, her face blushing pink and then turning white. "I think it's time we return you to your quarters, Miss Molloy. You're clearly overwrought."

I bit back the observation that "overwrought" was one of his words. I'd already gone too far. He'd prepared her to expect my objections and I'd put her on the defensive. I turned and started back and she followed three paces behind me, like a guard watching for escape attempts. But there was no escape from the labyrinthine tracks we had laid for ourselves. There was only one path we could take out of here and I knew what it was.

CHAPTER TWENTY-FOUR

After a moment, when it becomes clear she doesn't mean to go on, I say, "Is that it? Is that supposed to be the end of Red Bess's confession? She hasn't confessed to anything!"

"It's all that was in the journal," Veronica says. "The last pages were torn out. We looked for them but we never found them. Jayne said it wasn't necessary. She knew what Bess planned to do."

"So Jayne believed the confession?"

"She swallowed it whole," Veronica says, her voice suddenly hoarse, "as if she had imbibed Bess's story. It was, after all, her story: rich girl saves poor girl then poor girl has to save the rich girl from an evil ogre. Bess had to save Josephine from her overbearing fiancé, Edgar Bryce; Jayne had to save Violet from her father, Dr. Sinclair. At least that's how she saw it. She began the next day slipping into Bess's voice during her sessions. I don't think she had to pretend; I think she thought Bess Molloy was speaking through her."

For a moment I think she means to go on with the story. I hold my pen over the page, ready to take down her words, eager to know what comes next, but then her shoulders slump. "It's tiring to speak in someone else's voice," she says. "I think that will have to be all for today, Agnes."

As I TYPE up the last two chapters—I decide to make Bess's confession its own chapter—that sense of being suspended in time deepens. No wonder Jayne slipped so easily into Bess's voice. As my fingers hit the keys I feel as if *I* might be Jayne or Violet or Bess or Josephine—or any one of the girls imprisoned here.

What if Red Bess's soul is still caught in the Ramble? What if, I wonder, a prison is designed so well—its stone walls and winding staircases, its secret passageways and rambles—it keeps its inmates captive even after they die?

It's such a terrible thought that my fingers freeze on the typewriter keys. In the sudden silence I hear an echo of clatter, like footsteps in the atrium, and I imagine that they are the footsteps of all the girls ever imprisoned here. *Or just Laeticia or Peter,* I tell my own reflection in the darkened window.

I finish typing, gather the pages, shuffle them into order, and then pin them under all the stones on the desk.

Stay there.

When I get up my legs and arms ache. Veronica's right. It's tiring speaking in someone else's voice. I stop in the atrium to pick up my lunch basket and then climb up the curving staircase. In my room I eat half a sandwich and pour a cup of the lukewarm milky coffee from the thermos. Then I open my laptop and retype the last two chapters.

By heart.

I don't need the typescript or my steno pad. My fingers move over the keys as if I'm sitting at a player piano playing a song already punched into its rolls, only pausing to gulp down the sweet coffee to keep myself going. Despite the coffee, by the time I'm done typing I feel as hollow and played out as one of those rolls, my fingers still twitching out their patterns. I lie down on the bed, thinking I'll take a nap, and fall into a deep sleep.

In my dream I'm running in the Ramble. I don't know if I'm chasing someone or being chased, I only know that my life depends on how fast I run. Roots break through the moss to trip me, branches reach out to grab me. Fog hangs heavy as wet sheets on a laundry line between the trees. Figures loom behind them, and I know they're all the girls who were and still are imprisoned at Wyldcliffe Heights. One of those figures lurches out from the trees to block my path, and I see it's Dr. Husack, who's also somehow Dr. Bryce and Dr. Sinclair. A three-headed monster.

"You can't keep running from your problems, Agnes," he says.

I swerve around him and keep running. Ahead of me I glimpse a woman in a long white dress vanishing around the next curve of the path. My mother, I think. She is running toward the cliff. If I don't stop her, she'll run over the edge and die. I run faster but she remains just tantalizingly out of reach, the train of her white gown vanishing around the next bend and the next—

And then, just as I'm closing the distance between us, a snarling beast with yellow eyes leaps out of the fog and tackles me to the ground. My head slams into something hard and my vision blurs, doubles, triples. Three heads snap and slaver over me. I scramble backward in the dirt, and my fingers curl around something hard and rough. I bring it up to bash into the beast's head, but instead of the beast, a robed figure is bending over me, reaching out a hand to help me up. I grasp it, sure the hand is my mother's, but when I look up, I see a woman in a red cloak. She pulls me toward the cliff edge. I try to pull back, but her grip is like a vise. When I look down, I see that the hand gripping mine is a skeleton's hand. I start to scream and she turns on me, revealing the grinning skull inside her hood.

"Better to die than live here as a prisoner," she says. Then we're falling over the edge.

I wake with a start, gripping the bedsheets to keep from falling, morning light streaming in through my bedroom window. It was only late afternoon when I fell asleep, but somehow I slept straight through the night. Every muscle in my body aches, my head is spinning, and the sheets are sticking to my damp limbs. When I push them aside, I see blood. For an excruciating moment I think I've gotten my period and bled all over Laeticia's clean linens. Then I notice the scratches. Thin spidery tracks cover my arms and legs. It looks like an animal has been clawing at me—or that I have been clawing at myself.

Which I haven't done for a long time, not since my first year at Woodbridge. I'd wake up in the middle of the night in the corner of my room scratching at my arms and legs with anything I'd been able to find—a splinter from a floorboard, a nail I'd pried off the windowpane, a shard of glass I'd found in the recreation yard. Dr. Husack asked me what I was dreaming about before I woke up during these episodes. When I told him I didn't remember he said he wanted to try hypnosis. But I'd been too resistant to go under. Eventually, I had stopped "self-harming," and I'd never done it again.

Until now.

Dr. Husack warned me it could happen again in times of stress. I guess living in a haunted nuthouse with a blind writer whose book I'm illicitly sending to her publisher while my crazy mother creeps around the grounds is stressful.

Was it actually my mother I saw from the tower? Had I sleep-

walked into the Ramble and seen her, twisting her into the ghost of
Red Bess in my dreams?

I run a bath, pouring in plenty of the ancient violet bath salts, figuring they'll sterilize my wounds. When I lower myself into the tub, every single scratch flares like a struck match. I'm surprised I don't go up in flames. At least the pain wakes me up and clears my head. I haven't felt this logy since I was on psychopharmaceuticals at Woodbridge. And that dream—it was so vivid—running in the woods, that three-headed beast leaping onto me, the feel of that heavy, rough stone in my hands—

I hold my hand up to the light and see the shadow of a bruise forming in my palm. It looks like I was grasping something tight in my hands. Then I gingerly inspect my scalp. Is that a bump? How did I get that? Was I out wandering the grounds? Did I fall—or did someone hit me? What is happening to me? Am I going crazy? Again?

It's not the first time I've been afraid that I might be going crazy. After all, I saw *crazy* up close with my mother. I might have inherited it from her, even though Dr. Husack assured me that mental illness was not necessarily genetic. *Not necessarily.* He couldn't assure me it wasn't. And although he did assure me that I wasn't crazy when I suffered from delusions, night terrors, and sleepwalking at Woodbridge, that I was just experiencing the impacts of PTSD, he couldn't swear that I wouldn't descend into madness one day.

I slide back in the tub and submerge myself under the water to silence the buzzing voices in my head, but instead I hear the pounding of my own heart, loud as a jackhammer—

Or someone knocking on my door.

I haul myself out of the tub, wrap myself in the terry robe, and answer the door. Laeticia is standing there, her face stern. I expect a lecture on my tardiness but all she says is "You'd better get dressed and come down right away. There's been a break-in."

IT'S EXCRUCIATING TO pull on tights over my scratched legs, but I want to cover every inch of my body and disappear inside my retro-librarian guise. *I am the amanuensis,* I repeat to myself as I descend the curving stairs, clutching my notebook to my chest, my thoughts going round in circles. *Was it my mother who broke in? Will they know it's her? Will they think I brought her here?*

The door to the library is open. As I come in, I look automatically toward the green couch and am reassured to see Veronica there, regal in green velvet. If I just focus on her, if I go straight to her, it will be like all the other mornings. It will be about Jayne and Violet's story, not mine—

Then I look toward the desk. At first, I'm not sure what I'm looking at. The desk is littered with stones—the round gray ones and also smaller, glittering pebbles. It looks like someone has dumped a bagful of loose gravel and stones over the desktop. There are clumps of dirt mixed in—and is that blood?

I approach the mess warily, the scratches on my hands and under my clothes itching. As I get closer I realize what I thought were glittering pebbles are actually shards of glass. Looking up I see that the window over the desk has been broken. *Shattered.*

"It looks like someone threw a stone through the window," I say, remembering my mother's face at the window and her standing below the tower.

"They did more than that."

I turn to find Laeticia right behind me holding a broom and dustpan. Does she expect *me* to sweep up the mess?

"*They*? Do you know who did it?"

"Teenagers from the village, no doubt," Veronica says. "They always get excited about the legend of Red Bess around Halloween."

I notice that there's a larger stone among the debris—a big chunk of marble—that must have been the projectile that broke the window. There are red marks on it—lichen maybe.

"Are the manuscript pages all right?" Veronica asks. "That's the main thing."

"I can't tell," Laeticia says. "I'll have to clean off this mess to see."

"We should leave it," Peter Syms says from library door. When I glance at him I see he's carrying a rifle. "Until the police get here."

"I don't think that's necessary," Veronica repeats, but this time with an edge in her voice. "It's only a prank."

"I found two sets of footsteps outside," Peter says, "and that piece of marble is from the children's cemetery. They climbed up the cliff and came through the woods. We need to tell the police so they're on the lookout tomorrow night at the Halloween parade and the bonfire."

"I don't think that's necessary," Veronica says again. "The police will be busy enough with the parade. You can patrol the grounds as you always do on Halloween and Letty can guard the house."

"Of course," Peter says, "but it wouldn't hurt to let the police know—"

"I SAID NO POLICE!"

The voice sounds too big to have come out of frail Veronica. Peter and Laeticia exchange a look and then Laeticia wordlessly begins sweeping the debris from the desk. I hear Peter mutter "yes, ma'am" as he stomps loudly from the library, his footsteps echoing in the atrium. I hold the dustpan for Laeticia as she sweeps the rocks and glass into it. There are flecks of blood on the glass and clumps of dirt littered among the stones. The hole in the window is bigger than would have been made by the impact of the chunk of marble. Someone punched in the window and cleared the jagged glass away with their bare hands—leaving bloody fingerprints on the top page of the manuscript, visible now that the debris has been removed.

"Are all the pages still there?" Veronica asks, her voice trembling now, not at all the voice of the imperious mistress who'd spoken a moment ago.

Laeticia is staring down at the bloody pages as if afraid to touch them. If Laeticia doesn't want this story told this would be one way of expressing her opinion.

I pick up the pages, turn them over, and leaf through them, checking the page numbers. When I reach the last page, I turn it over to look at the bloody fingerprints again—and notice the writing this time. I have to hold the paper up to the light to make it out.

My silence seems to unnerve Veronica. "What is it?" she demands, her voice querulous and older than her years. An old woman's voice.

I look at Laeticia, sure she'll agree that we should spare Veronica this, but she is already speaking.

"From the numbering it looks like all the pages are here. But one of them has writing on it."

"Well, what does it say?" Veronica asks impatiently.

"Red Bess is coming to take back what's hers."

CHAPTER TWENTY-FIVE

A hoarse rasp comes from the couch, which I'm sure must be Veronica's last gasp and that she's been killed by Red Bess's bloody pronouncement. But when I turn toward her and see her face I realize she's laughing.

"What a sense of humor," she manages, gasping for breath, "the local youth have."

I glance at Laeticia wondering if we should tell Veronica about the bloody fingerprints. This does not look like the work of the local youth. But Laeticia avoids my eye and takes the dustpan from me.

"I'll call the glazier," she says briskly as she leaves the room, "and tell Peter to board up the window in the meantime."

When she's gone I glance back at the desk. The glass and dirt are gone but there's a streak of blood on the wood that turns my stomach. The blood is spotted all over the marble chunk as well, which Peter said came from the cemetery. *How did he know?* I wonder, turning the stone over—

"Are you going to stand there gawking at the wreckage," Veronica asks, "or are we going to get to work?"

I don't answer right away, I'm too busy staring at the face staring back at me. It's the broken angel's head from the cemetery, the one I dreamed about last night. It's covered with bloody fingerprints.

"Miss Corey," Veronica says, her voice softer, "are you all right? Do you need some time to collect yourself?"

"Collect myself?" I parrot dumbly. *It's just a coincidence,* I tell myself, *that the stone is here after I dreamed about it.* I would remember if I broke a window, wouldn't I?

"Do you want to take a break?" she asks me.

"No," I say, shaking myself. *Collecting myself* as if I am in pieces strewn across the desk. I pick up my steno pad and sit down on the chair across from my employer. "I'm ready when you are."

Jayne began "being Bess," as she put it, in the second week of September. We all knew something was different when she didn't come back from her afternoon session with my father. We were in the recreation room, working on one of those interminable puzzles, waiting for our sessions. Matron came and told us that all of the afternoon sessions were canceled.

"Can we go outside, then?" I asked.

I was surprised when she said yes. She must have been distracted by my father's departure from his draconian adherence to schedule. Or perhaps she just wanted us out of her hair. She released us out onto the back lawn and then, instead of keeping an eye on us, went inside.

I walked to the edge of the woods and stood looking up at the tower. I could see my father's silhouette in the window. Usually when he had a patient on his couch he leaned back in his chair and closed his eyes. But now he was leaning forward, poised beside the video camera on its tripod, his eagerness to hear every word evident in the tension of his back muscles.

"He never listens like that in my sessions," LeeAnn said. "What do you think she's telling him?"

I shrugged. "She's probably adding lots of sex," I said, "which is sure to make him uncomfortable."

LeeAnn's eyes widened. "I'd be afraid to do that in case . . . you know . . ." She turned bright red as if there were embers smoldering beneath her skin.

"In case she incites my father's sex drive?" I suggested. "Don't worry. I think my father sees all of us as lab mice in a big maze. He's more excited by the idea of publishing his book than having it off with one of us."

I said it with the casual conviction I'd learned from Jayne, but LeeAnn didn't seem to buy it. "You sound just like her."

"Who?" I asked.

"Jayne," she said with a sly smile. I wasn't sure if she meant it as a compliment or a jab. We all, I think, wanted to sound and look and act like Jayne. All the girls had started tying off their uniform tops at the waist and leaving the top buttons unbuttoned when the matron wasn't looking. Donna filched a pair of blunt scissors from the rec room and gave herself an approximation of Jayne's choppy haircut, which made her look like a Yorkshire terrier, and was given a week of solitary confinement as punishment. LeeAnn had borrowed Jayne's kohl and rimmed her eyes until she looked like a raccoon and the matron called her a slut.

The more we became like Jayne, though, the less she seemed like herself. I expected her to be satisfied by my father's attention and gullibility but she wasn't. "He buys it all," she told me one night through the vents. "He even asked me why I think I came to the Josephine and I told him I thought I was drawn there to find you. And he said"—Jayne's voice grew husky and the next sentence sounded uncannily like my father—"'Is that because my daughter is the reincarnation of her grandmother?'"

"What did you say?" I asked, my cheek cold against the linoleum floor.

"I told him yes, of course," she said, yawning. "So you'll have to do your bit tomorrow. We can practice by writing our book. Did you get a notebook?"

I had snuck into the pantry and taken three composition notebooks, which the housekeeper used for keeping accounts. "I've got it here. Do you want it?"

I started to slide it through the vent but she said, "No, why don't you write. Your handwriting is better and I feel so sleepy. I'll just close my eyes and start us out with our heroine arriving at Wyldcliffe Heights. What shall we call her?"

"Jayne," I said with a sudden inspiration. "The stranger who comes to Wyldcliffe Heights should be Jayne like Jane Eyre, only we'll spell it like you do."

When she didn't answer right away, I thought that I'd said something wrong. Maybe you weren't supposed to use real names in a novel. It had been a silly idea, born of a fear that if the real Jayne was becoming Bess, then at least I could have my Jayne here in this book. "You can probably think of a better idea—" I began.

"No," she said, her voice echoey and remote, as if the walls were talking. "I like that it will be Jayne . . . you know I added the y myself. It's not really how my name is spelled."

"Now it will be," I said. "In our book our stories will be just what we want them to be."

"I like that," she said, her voice husky with sleep. "And we'll call the girl in the tower Violet, for you."

And so we began The Secret of Wyldcliffe Heights that night, Jayne dictating the story as if from memory, as if it had all happened already, and me taking it down. The story she told was like one of those old books Mrs. Weingarten loved—a young woman comes to a mysterious old house and discovers its secrets—but it was also somehow our story. When Jayne would get tired she would say, "It's tiring talking in someone else's voice, you go on now." And I'd pick up the story, reciting it aloud while I wrote as if someone else was telling it to me.

That voice stayed with me when I had my sessions with my father. I let him think he had hypnotized me. He tried to take me back to the night Anaïs died at the Josephine but instead I told him in a deep, sepulchral voice I'd practiced with Jayne: "I am Josephine!" I told him about Red Bess and warned him that she was still angry and seeking vengeance. I could hear him scratching away on his pad beneath the whirring sound of the camera. It felt good to be the one dictating to him. For the first time in my life I was the one in control.

Being Bess, though, did not seem to have the same effect on Jayne. She was alternately tired, falling asleep at the puzzle table during recreation hour, and agitated, pacing up and down the lawn like a caged tiger. Whenever the matron would leave us alone, she would bolt for the woods. I'd follow her to make sure she didn't get lost—or as I feared when I saw the restless look in her eyes, that she didn't run away. I'd find her in the children's cemetery crouched in front of the grave of a baby girl who'd died a hundred years ago. Jayne would leave flowers there and notes that she pinned beneath round stones. One day I found her there crying.

"What is it?" I asked.

"All these children," she said between sobs, "dying with their mothers because no one cared about them! You know what a Magdalen refuge is, don't you? It's where they put girls they think aren't fit to be mothers because they're whores and then they let them and their babies die."

"*That was a long time ago*," I told her gently. "*Josephine Hale reformed the refuge—*"

"*Did she?*" Jayne demanded. "*I was talking to your father and he said that Josephine's idea was to separate girls from their families so they wouldn't be tainted by their bad influences. And then she went and married Edgar Bryce, who was a eugenicist. He wanted to keep women here for the rest of their lives so they wouldn't spread their defective genes. He wanted to sterilize them. That's why Bess killed him—*"

"*You don't know that*," I said. "*It wasn't in the journal—*"

"*I know it* here," she said, thumping her hand against her chest. "*She did it to save all the other girls and she did it to save Josephine because he wanted to put her away, too—*"

"*That's not true*," I said, but in too weak a whisper for her to hear. All my life I'd grown up hearing tales about my grandmother and Red Bess, tales that had an unsavory edge to them as if it was Josephine's fault that Red Bess had killed Edgar Bryce and hung herself in the tower. There must have been something wrong with Josephine to inspire such bad luck. After all, look at how her daughter, my mother, had turned out—unstable, mentally ill, crazy. I'd seen my father looking at me as if examining me for the taint that ran through my blood. That was how Jayne was looking at me. Like I was the crazy one when it was her kneeling before the grave of a child dead a hundred years, her fingers caked with dirt from digging up stones to weigh down her notes to the dead.

"*It was Bess who was mad*," I said, "*not Josephine.*"

Her eyes went so wide I could see the whites of them and her fingers spasmed around a stone—a rough chunk of marble that must have broken off one of the statues—and for a moment I thought she would throw it at me. But instead, she looked down at the stone *in her hands as if she'd forgotten she was holding it and shook her head. I saw a face looking up from the stone and realized it was the head of an angel broken off from a child's grave. Looking at it made my stomach twist but Jayne was smiling.*

"It's not really you saying these things; it's Josephine. She's still under Dr. Bryce's influence even in the afterlife. But don't worry. I know what we have to do. We have to summon Red Bess to break her—and us—free. And to do it, we have to have a bonfire on Halloween night.

As I WAIT for Veronica to go on, I feel like Violet standing over Jayne in the cemetery watching Jayne grasping the marble angel head. *Was it the same one that's on the desk?* I wonder. Is it a coincidence that the same angel head appears in today's installment after being thrown through the library window? Could Veronica herself have thrown it through the window last night? But it's hard to imagine blind Veronica wandering through the ramble at night. She could have had Laeticia or Peter do it for her and now she's included it in the story to . . . what? To taunt me? But why? My head is spinning in ever-tightening circles.

Finally, Veronica says, "I think we should leave the fire until next time. We should clear the room so Peter can board up the window. I'll have him move the typewriter up to your room so you can type up the pages this afternoon. Feel free to take off the rest of the morning."

I wait until she's out the door and then rush to the desk to study the chunk of marble. It looks just like the one Jayne was holding in the story and like the one I dreamed about. I stare at it, afraid to touch it and leave my fingerprints on it—

Unless they're already on it.

My fingers itch with the remembered feel of it in my dream, the smooth bit that fit so neatly in my palm and the rough part I wrapped my fingers around. The smooth part is a face, a mysterious half smile on its curving lips as if it's keeping a secret. It might be a broken angel from the children's cemetery, but that doesn't mean I was in the cemetery last night or that I threw it through the window.

You think it's just a coincidence that you dreamed yourself there last night and then someone threw it through the window?

It wouldn't be the first time I'd done something violent while sleepwalking.

At my last foster home one of the other girls was always *at* me. *Sabrina.* She fancied herself a goth queen, always dressing in skimpy black dresses and torn tights, purple nail polish and lipstick. She had long black hair that she braided with violet ribbons. And she loved *The Secret of Wyldcliffe Heights.* She acted like *she* was the expert on the book and was always telling me what it was really about. I could tell, though, that she was jealous of my hardcover copy with its original dust jacket and sewn-in violet ribbon. One day my copy disappeared. I went to our foster mother and told her I knew Sabrina had taken it. She told me I must never accuse someone without evidence (although she did it to us all the time). She called a house meeting and rambled on about honesty and integrity and trust. Then she told us we were all on lockdown until the missing book had been restored. Me included. It was so unfair! I was supposed to have a visit with my mother but it was canceled. Three days went by with no returned book. I heard Sabrina whispering that I'd made up the whole thing and hidden my precious book myself just to get attention. *She acts like she wrote the book herself.*

That night I had my fog-beast dream again, only in this version when the fog-beast leapt at me, I turned and lunged at it with a pair of scissors I suddenly had in my hand. Just like Red Bess. When I woke, I was standing in the hallway, barefoot in my night-gown. Someone was screaming. I looked down and saw I had two things in my hand: a pair of scissors and a long thick rope of hair braided with violet ribbons. My copy of *The Secret of Wyldcliffe Heights* lay on the floor beside the weeping and shorn Sabrina.

I ran away again the next day, and when I was caught this time I was sent to Woodbridge.

I pick up the marble head. My palm fits around the smooth curve of the angle's cheek, and my fingers slide into the rough grooves where it's broken as if it had been carved to the mold of my hand. I heft it up and down, gauging the weight. It feels famil-iar in my hand. What's more, it feels good.

CHAPTER TWENTY-SIX

It could have been me. I could have sleepwalked to the Ramble, taken the stone, and thrown it through the window. If Veronica changes her mind and sends for the police the fingerprints could match mine. I slip the marble chunk into my backpack along with the bloodied pages and run up the two flights of stairs to my room, the heavy stone banging against my hip. I stuff my clothes in my backpack, add my laptop and my stash of cash—*just in case*. I'm not sure what "case" I'm preparing for, but as I steal down the stairs I feel the familiar fizz in my stomach and itch in my legs that I'd get just before I ran away.

Where will you go? My echoing footsteps ask me.

When has that ever stopped you before? they ask back.

When I reach the atrium, I hear a voice coming from the kitchen.

"I told you it was a mistake letting her come . . ." There's a long pause during which I strain to hear an answer. But there's no answer coming from the kitchen. Laeticia must be speaking on the phone. I'm about to leave when she speaks again, freezing me to the floor.

"She's bringing it all back again and we can't have that . . . she has to go . . ."

Another noise alerts me to someone in the mudroom. From the heavy treads I suspect it's Peter Syms. I don't want to be caught eavesdropping so I sprint out the door, Laeticia's words ringing in my ears. What am I bringing back? Red Bess, as the bloody message suggests? Or is that just a ruse to scare *me* away?

Well, it's worked.

I run down the hill and don't stop until I'm on the other side of the gate. If Laeticia wanted to get rid of me, what better way than make it look like I've taken to committing violent acts in my sleep? But why would she want me gone so badly? Is she afraid that it will come out in this new book that she's LeeAnn? But that seems to be common knowledge—Martha knows—and Laeticia already served time for burning down her family home with her stepfather in it.

But what if that wasn't the last fire she set? Had Laeticia lit the fire that killed Dr. Sinclair and, supposedly, Jane Rosen? I can picture LeeAnn, those embers kindling beneath her skin, growing excited at Jayne's Halloween bonfire and heading for the tower with a blazing torch. The image is so vivid that I can practically smell the smoke—

I *do* smell smoke. I look back up the hill, toward Wyldcliffe Heights, afraid I'll see a blaze above the tree line, but then I hear a crackling sound behind me. I turn and see that it's coming from the orchard behind the farm stand where a woman in a chunky sweater and barn jacket is burning leaves in a tin trash can. She waves cheerily at me when she sees me staring at her.

"Getting ready for the Halloween bonfire!" she shouts. "See you there!"

Is this whole town demented? I wonder as I walk by a poster featuring a witchy-looking woman in a red cape advertising the

Halloween parade and bonfire tomorrow. Sure, a little Halloween celebration is par for the course in most upstate towns. But why has Wyldcliffe deliberately tied their celebration to a madwoman who slaughtered the head doctor of the local asylum and then hung herself a hundred years ago? And if that wasn't bad enough, that same madwoman had inspired a disturbed young woman to set fire to the hospital thirty years ago. And now they celebrated the event with a bonfire!

You'd think they'd rethink their town mascot.

I inhale the aroma of coffee longingly outside Bread for the Masses, but the line is too long so I hurry on to the library, which I find transformed into something that looks like the special effects studio for a B horror movie. Leathery bats swoop through the air, giant papier-mâché witches and jack-o'-lantern heads loom over the stacks. A group of older women sit around a table sewing sequins on red cloth. It could be a homey quilting bee, but as I get closer, I see that the red sequins form a pattern of blood splatter.

"There you are!" a woman in a mask and cat ears exclaims as if I'm late for the coven. When she grabs my arm and sinks her painted fingernails into it, I recognize Martha Conway. "I was hoping you'd be in today. I want to talk to you about something."

She draws me into her cubby-sized office, muttering darkly about sequins in the carpet and papier-mâché fingerprints on the wall. "Every year the costumers and puppeteers promise they'll stay in the community room in the basement and every year they spread upstairs like black mold."

"The parade seems to be a big deal," I say, looking for a place to sit down. Every surface is stacked with books. She clears a chair for me and rolls her eyes.

"It's a total nightmare," she says, sitting behind her desk, stripping her mask off but leaving the cat ears on. I sit down on the chair and hug my backpack in my lap. "It started out as this eccentric little festival, but each year it's grown bigger and bigger. People come in from the city and neighboring towns and mob the sidewalks hours before the parade. Two years ago, the bonfire got out of control and nearly destroyed the marsh. Thank God the fire department took over but still, it's only a matter of time before someone gets killed. It's a kind of mass hysteria . . . speaking of which . . ." She taps on her keyboard and then turns her computer screen around for me to see. "I was wondering if you could explain this?"

I'm afraid she's gotten wind of the break-in at Wyldcliffe, but what's on the screen is worse. It's an image of a woman in a long hooded red cloak and a white skull mask. She's holding up a pair of bloody scissors. The caption below it reads: *Red Bess has returned and is coming for you.*

I try to laugh it off. "It's the same Insta account I showed you a couple of days ago. It's just some rabid fan—"

"Look at the background," Martha says.

I click the enlarge button to make out the dark blurry background. A second Red Bess comes into focus—*she's everywhere!*—but then I realize it's only a reflection. She's standing in the dark outside a lit window. I squint at the blurry shapes and make out a green glob, a hulking black object . . . I scroll to the next photo. The background is clearer because the figure has moved closer to the window. I realize from the camera angle that the figure is taking the picture of herself. The background is clearer here. The green glob resolves into a green-shaded lamp, the hulking black object into a typewriter.

"It's the library of Wyldcliffe Heights," I say. "That's the desk where I've been typing. Someone broke the window last night."

"I know," Martha says. "Scroll to the next picture."

When I do I gasp. The next shot is a reel showing a missile going through a window, glass shattering. The caption reads: *Red Bess takes back her story.*

"Shit," I say. "She filmed her own break-in!"

"Why do you think it's a woman?" Martha asks.

I shake my head. "I don't know . . ." Could it be Laeticia? But somehow I can't picture the housekeeper posting on Instagram. But there's someone else I can picture. "I think it might be someone I work with at Gatehouse Books. Hadley Fisher. I thought she might be behind the Red Bess posts the first time I saw them. She's been working on a true crime book about Red Bess and the girl who OD'd at the Josephine, and I could see her posting as Red Bess as a publicity stunt. I never thought she'd come up here, though."

"You think someone you work with at Gatehouse Books broke into Wyldcliffe Heights?" she asks skeptically.

"I know it sounds crazy . . . would you mind if I wrote a couple of emails from here?" I glance outside her office. A woman is trying on one of the Red Bess robes. It makes my skin crawl.

"Sure. Knock yourself out."

She puts her mask back on and leaves me in her office, which seems awfully trusting of her. I open my email and write first to Atticus, including a link to the latest Instagram post. *What the hell, Atticus? Do you know if Hadley is behind this?*

Then I open an email from Kurtis asking me if I have any more chapters for him. I feel a pang of guilt and regret. He trusted me to come up here and I've made a mess of it. The least I can do is type up today's installment. I glance out the glass door and see Martha engaged with a group of raucous children who are strewing sequins all over the place. She won't be needing her office back any time soon. I type up the last installment quickly and send it to Kurtis. I look up from my laptop at all the Red Besses and recall what Jayne had said: *We have to summon Red Bess to break Josephine— and us—free. And to do it we have to build a bonfire on Halloween night.* What if Jayne succeeded? What if she really did summon the vengeful spirit of Red Bess and she's still here?

I read through the pages again, wondering what was happening to Jayne. Did she really believe she was Red Bess? Is that what started my mother's slide into mental illness? And then something occurs to me—the tapes. Dr. Sinclair taped his sessions. If I could find those tapes . . . But then if they were all in his office they would have been destroyed in the fire.

Except for that one Jayne took. What happened to *that* one?

As I'm pondering this, a notification pings on my phone. "Red Bess" has tagged me on Instagram. It's a selfie of the robed and hooded skull-masked figure holding up a pair of scissors. The caption reads: *See you tomorrow at the parade.*

I feel the same spike of adrenaline as when one of the tough girls at Woodbridge challenged me in the halls. *Fight or flight?* I'd chosen flight if I could, and I can now. I can take out all the money in my account and hop a train to Canada. Start over. It's what I'm good at. It's what my mother taught me.

What was she running from? What had happened to her here?

I'll never know if I run now.

I click on the comment bubble and type out a reply.

I'll be there.

CHAPTER TWENTY-SEVEN

O utside a cold wind has picked up, whisking dry leaves into eddies along the street and catching the purple streamers that have been affixed to every lamppost. There's a hushed expectancy to the town, as if it's waiting for the arrival of an honored guest.

Red Bess.

What happened here one hundred years ago that marked this place so indelibly that it calls the spirit of a murderess back like she's some kind of local hero? What was the pull she had on Jayne that made her want to summon her? And who is pretending to be her now?

As I start up River Road and the fog begins to roll in from the river, the possibilities spin in my head. Could this Red Bess posting on Instagram be my mother? Is this her strange, warped way of reaching out to me?

But my mother loathed and mistrusted the internet. She'd never open an Instagram account.

Could it be Laeticia? She has been hostile to me from the beginning. But would she really expose Wyldcliffe Heights and Veronica by posting on Instagram? Would she even know how?

Hadley, then? She has the social media skills and I can imagine her concocting a publicity scheme for her book in which she turns Red Bess into an internet meme. But would she really have broken into Wyldcliffe last night? And is she really planning to confront me at the parade with a pair of scissors?

Even to my paranoid brain it seems unlikely, but someone broke in—

Unless I did it in my sleep.

I stop on the edge of the road. I'm hugging the stone wall to keep from straying into the center again and reach out for it to steady myself. Beneath a spill of ivy the stones are the same color as the fog, and for a moment I have the horrible notion that my hand will pass straight through, that there's nothing solid in this shifting place, least of all myself. And then my worst nightmare is realized. My hand does go through the wall as if I have no substance. As if *I* am the ghost of Wyldcliffe Heights. Because the scariest thing about my fog-beast nightmare isn't the beast; it's being so lost in the fog I no longer know if anything is real, even myself. Blood roaring in my ears, I pull back my shaking hand and push away the ivy. There's a crack in the wall two feet across.

I peer though it and see that the crack goes straight through. Something is caught in the ivy on the other side. I squeeze my body through, hating the feel of the walls pressing on either side of me, and pluck the bit of cloth from the ivy. It's red and sequined—a scrap of cloth from a Red Bess costume. Just like the one the Instagram poster wore last night.

THERE'S A BASKET in the atrium with a note from Laeticia informing me that Miss St. Clair is retiring early and expects to see me promptly at 8 a.m. tomorrow morning. I'm glad not to have to talk to anyone right now. I climb the curving stairs to my room, my footsteps echoing in the marble atrium as if it's a crypt and all the residents of Wyldcliffe Heights are long dead and I am indeed the ghost in the house.

I lock the door to my room, but there's no lock on the door to the attic so I climb the stairs to make sure no one is lurking in wait up there. I check behind boxes and furniture and then I force myself to open the armoire doors to look inside. The sight of the red cloak startles me even though I know it's there. *Wasn't it hanging further to the right?* Could I have put this on last night and roamed the grounds in it? I run my hands up and down the robe, my skin crawling at the touch of it, searching for a tear that will match the scrap of fabric I found in the wall, but I find none. Besides, this robe is made of fine, soft wool, not the cheap, sequined polyester of the scrap I found. Despite the revulsion I feel touching the robe I'm relieved. This is the only Red Bess robe I have access to. If it's not the one that the intruder who slipped through the wall was wearing then it's probably not the one the Instagram poster was wearing. Which means I'm not the one who broke the window.

I go back down the stairs and shut the door, wedging a chair beneath the knob just in case—

Just in case the cloak comes to life and floats down the stairs to throttle me in my sleep.

Or just in case I wake in the night and sleepwalk upstairs to take on the mantle of Red Bess.

IN MY DREAM I am running through the Ramble pursued by the fog-beast snapping at my heels. I can feel its hot breath on my bare legs and see its exhalations rising from the ground and twining through the trees. I have to reach the cliff before it catches me, but I trip over a branch and land hard on the ground. My hands scrabble in the dirt for purchase and land on a piece of marble that fits in my hand as if molded from it. I turn to face the beast, bringing up the stone to bash its skull—but it's not the fog-beast. A woman leans over me, one side of her face in light, the other in shadow . . . no, I realize as she reaches for me . . . her face is cracked in two. She only has half a face.

I startle awake at the horrible image and realize I'm not in my bed. I'm outside, lying on the cold, hard ground. I look around frantically for the half-faced woman and find instead tilting gravestones, white in the moonlight. I'm in the children's cemetery. How did I get here? I sit up and notice I'm holding the angel head, gripping it so hard my hand spasms when I uncurl my fingers. I must have taken it out of my backpack and sleepwalked to the cemetery. Had I done the same thing last night and broken the library window?

No, no, no. I would remember that.

I get to my feet and look around. There's no one here. I slip the stone into the pocket of my sweatpants—thank God I didn't sleep in a flimsy nightgown—and walk out of the cemetery. I give the Cerberus statue a wide berth, but then I turn back to look at it. Three gaping jaws snarl back at me. Was this the origin of the fog-beast of my nightmares? But how if I'd never been here—

Unless I have been here before.

If my mother *is* Jayne she might have come back here and brought me when I was too young to remember. Much of my early years are a blur of motel rooms and bus stations. I was eight when my mother landed in jail and I ended up a ward of the state in foster care. She could have brought me here and—what? What had she wanted here?

They stole my story.

Had she come back to confront Veronica and demand credit for writing *The Secret of Wyldcliffe Heights*? Had Veronica welcomed her back with open arms? Offered to share the proceeds from the book they wrote together and opened her enormous house to her and her child?

Or did she set the dogs on her and chase her off the property?

I stare at the snarling beast, willing myself to remember running through the woods . . . and I do. I feel my mother's hand in mine, the rough ground beneath my feet, the mist on my face like hot breath. And then I see her, my mother, stopping here, the growling dog leaping up to grab her wrist—

No, she reached into the mouth of the dog, her hand vanishing into its maw.

I take a step forward and reach out my hand, slowly, as if I'm afraid the stone beast will snap it off. I touch its stone snout to reassure myself it's not alive and then, clenching every muscle in my body to keep from bolting, slide my hand down its cold, dark throat. Stone teeth scrape against my wrist and something soft and wet slithers over my hand. My fingertips graze something slick and pulpy that crackles. I grab it and pull, picturing viscera and rotting meat, a bloody stump where my hand used to be, and hold my trophy up in the moonlight.

It's a pack of Marlboro Lights fused into a solid mass.

This is where Jayne hid her cigarettes. I bring it closer and notice there's a slip of paper inside the cellophane wrapping. Water has seeped inside the folded seams of the cellophane, blurring the first and bottom line. But I can read the center part clearly enough.

I just want to come back to explain, it reads in my mother's crooked, childlike script.

CHAPTER TWENTY-EIGHT

I walk into the library the next morning precisely as the clock chimes eight o'clock and sit on the chair opposite Veronica without saying a word. I am burning with so much anger I am surprised the chair doesn't go up in flames. I am sure she will sense my anger without seeing me, that she'll feel the heat rising off me. It's only grown since last night, a fire stoked by each repetition of the thought:

My mother came here to talk and Veronica set the dogs on her.

Veronica stole the book they wrote together and now she's turning Jayne into the villain of the story in its sequel. I flip the cover of my notebook to a fresh page.

"Where were we?" she says without a good morning.

"Jayne was planning a bonfire," I say dryly.

She nods, seemingly unsurprised by my curtness, and begins.

A WEEK BEFORE Halloween I woke to the sound of screams coming from the room next door. It wasn't unusual to hear screams in the night. The girls at Wyldcliffe Heights were prone to nightmares and terrors, and all of Jayne's talk of Red Bess had caused a flurry of sightings: Red Bess's face in mirrors and windows, Red Bess hanging in the closet, Red Bess lying in wait beneath our beds.

But this sounded different. It sounded like an animal in pain. I slid off my bed and crouched at the vent, calling Jayne's name and then Dorothy's, but my voice was drowned out by the screams. Then I heard someone pounding on the door in the next room and calling for help. It sounded like Dorothy, which meant it was Jayne who was screaming. I ran to the door and using a flat laminated card as Jayne had taught me, unlocked it, not caring if the matron or night guard, who would surely be here any second, discovered me. I opened Jayne and Dorothy's door the same way. Dorothy flew out of the room like something was chasing her and I stepped inside.

Jayne lay on the floor, writhing in a patch of moonlight that streamed through the barred windows. She looked as if she were trapped behind the bars in a cage made of moonlight and shadows. My first thought was: Red Bess is inside her, struggling to get out.

And then I smelled the blood.

I knelt beside her and grabbed her flailing hand and called her name. "What is it, Jayne? Where are you hurt?" I ran my hands over her arms and chest and stomach looking for the wound and felt something moving beneath her skin.

It was Red Bess. She'd invited her inside and now she wanted to come out—

"Move away!" someone shouted.

I looked up and saw the matron and the night guard, Syms, in the doorway but I didn't move. What would they do with her when they knew? I grasped Jayne's hand and she squeezed back so hard I could feel my bones grinding together. Suddenly the room was flooded with light. Blinking against the glare, I saw the blood staining Jayne's nightgown and then someone was pulling me away. I heard my father shouting and then the matron said in a disgusted voice, "She's in labor, premature, no doubt, she'll probably lose it."

"No!" Jayne screamed, yanking my hand and pulling my face down to hers. "I can't lose her. Don't let them take her—"

A spasm overtook her but she'd said enough. She knew. She knew she was pregnant all these months, but she hadn't told me. She'd hidden it. And I hadn't seen. I squeezed her hand back. "I won't let them take her," I said.

My father told me to go but I refused. I stayed by her side as the matron declared that the ambulance wouldn't get here in time. She sent Syms and my father out of the room to get towels and hot water and blankets. She spread Jayne's legs and did something that made Jayne swear and spit. The matron leaned forward and slapped her in the face.

"Shut up," she said. "You brought this on yourself and now you have to bring the poor thing into the world dead or alive."

Jayne didn't scream after that. She groaned and labored and grunted for what felt like hours before Matron announced, "It's coming" and then she was bundling something up in towels.

"Is she . . . is she . . ." Jayne spluttered.

I looked at the bundle in Matron's arms. Only a small pinched blue face showed between the folds of the towel.

"It's better this way," Matron said, almost but not quite gently.

I grabbed the bundle away from her, wiped the blood from the baby's face, and chafed its cold limbs. Afterward, Jayne would ask me how I knew what to do, but I couldn't explain. Something outside myself took over. I just knew I couldn't let this tiny spark of life—this part of Jayne—go out to join the babies in the children's cemetery. As I watched, a flood of pink washed over the baby's face and it let out a cry. I stared down at its face and felt something stir in me.

"Give her to me!" Jayne cried.

But now the ambulance had arrived and paramedics filled the room. One took the baby from me and two others swarmed over Jayne. My father grabbed me by the elbow and steered me out of the room.

"Did you know about this?" he demanded.

I shook my head.

"Do you know who the father is?"

I shook my head again even though I was sure it must be Gunn; I'd never seen her with anyone else.

"We'll put 'unknown' on the certificate." Then he looked me over as if he were checking me for signs of pregnancy. But after Jayne had warned me off Casey, I'd never gone with anyone else. My father grimaced at the blood on my pajamas. "Go clean yourself up," he said, leaving me and following the stretcher down the hallway.

I tried to follow as well but Matron ordered me back and told me they wouldn't let me in the ambulance. I went to the hall bathroom and peeled off my bloody pajamas and then stood under the hot shower until the water ran clear and cold and my skin was as blue as the baby's had been. Then I wrapped myself in towels, chafing my skin as I had the baby's as if I were trying to bring myself back to life. When I got back to my room, I found that Dorothy was in my bed.

"She wouldn't go back to her own room," LeeAnn explained. "She said it smells like blood but I think she was just afraid to be alone. You can sleep in my bed if you want."

I shook my head and told her I'd sleep in Jayne's room.

"What do you think will happen?" she asked me as I changed into clean pajamas. "Do you think they'll let her keep it?"

"Her," I said. "It's a girl." I turned at the door. "Do you think Jayne would let them take away anything that belonged to her?"

I SLEPT IN *Jayne's bed each night until she returned three days later from the hospital. And then, instead of coming back to the dorm, she was installed in my old bedroom upstairs. "Until arrangements are made for the infant," my father told me. "You can stay with her if you like, although you won't get much sleep."*

I ran to my old room as fast as I could and found Jayne sitting up in my bed, reading one of my books. "Oh, good," she said when she saw me. "Have you brought the notebooks? We can finish The Secret of Wyldcliffe Heights *while we're here."*

I looked around for the baby, afraid they'd already taken it from her, but it was asleep in a bassinet.

"Careful you don't wake her," Jayne warned. "I just got the little monster down."

The "little monster," swaddled in blankets, looked smaller than she had on her birth day. Was she getting enough to eat? I wondered, longing to pick her up.

"I found notebooks in your desk," Jayne said. "We can start a new one until you can bring up the rest. I'm pregnant with ideas."

I looked at her askance and she burst out laughing, ignoring her own admonition to be quiet. "Your face!" she cried. "Honestly, you'd think you never saw a baby."

"Did you know?" I asked.

She shrugged. "My periods have always been erratic. The doctor at the hospital said I must have been underweight to begin with and she came early. They're waiting for her to be big enough to be adopted."

"You're not going to keep her?"

She shrugged again and I noticed how thin she was beneath the voluminous flannel nightgown—one of mine—she wore. Her bones looked sharp as blades and her eyes had that drugged look again.

"Did they give you anything for the pain?" I asked.

"No such luck," she said. "Not while I'm breastfeeding." She made a face. "Now get out that notebook. Bess wants her story told."

FOR THE NEXT three days I sat with Jayne taking down dictation. She never stopped now to ask my opinion or to give me a chance to write some myself. She poured out the story as if a dam had broken inside her when she gave birth. Maybe, I thought, stealing glances at the unusually quiet baby, she had given birth to Red Bess. When I asked what her name was, she said there was no point naming her since she wasn't hers. When I asked if we should try to tell Gunn she shook her head.

"It's better if he doesn't know. Gunn can get pretty crazy, like he did the night Anaïs died. What kind of person would that be to raise a child with?"

I stared at her. She didn't sound like herself at all. "You mean we're not having the bonfire?" I asked. "We're not leaving?"

"Where would we go? Your father says I'm making progress. In a year I could apply for college—you could, too. In the meantime we can finish our book—"

When she saw me staring at her she snapped at me. "You don't know how lucky you are to have a home like this. I grew up in a crummy house. Why shouldn't I get to live someplace nice for a change?"

The next day the matron told Jayne my father wanted her to come to the tower with the baby. "The nuns from St. Alban's are here," she said.

I looked at Jayne to see if she had any reaction but she only asked me to hand "it" to her. I offered to go with her but Matron told me to join the girls out on the lawn.

It was a cold day—too cold for lingering outdoors—but Matron would want the floor empty so she could stand at the bottom of the stairs to eavesdrop. As soon as I got outside, I headed for the woods, ignoring the looks of the other girls.

I ran through the Ramble until I got to the cemetery. I knew Jayne hid her cigarettes here, but I wasn't sure where. I searched through the rubble around the gravestones, especially around the one where she liked to sit. The head of the angel had broken off so I looked inside, but it was solid marble. I found the broken head—or half of it. Staring into its face I remembered the tint of blue in the baby's face before she took her first breath. How could Jayne let her go? I wondered. It wasn't like her at all. She wasn't like herself at all.

Still holding the marble head, I looked around the cemetery— and noticed the snarling Cerberus, its three mouths gaping wide.

I walked toward the statue, keeping my eyes on the three snarling heads. It had always frightened me. It frightened me then, but I searched each mouth anyhow until I found what I was looking for—a pack of Marlboro Reds with a handwritten note in Gunn's erratic scrawl slipped into the cellophane.

Jay, please tell me what's going on. You haven't replied back to my last message. I told Casey about the tape like you told me and he gave me everything we need. Are we still leaving on Halloween? I'll be here. I've made something for your book that I think you'll like.

What tape? I wondered. The session tape Jayne took from my father's office? What was Jayne planning to do with it, and why had Gunn told Casey about it? And what had Casey given him in return?

I took out a pen from my pocket and scribbled on the reverse side, *I'll be here*, trying to make it look like Jayne's writing. I stuffed it back down the hound's throat and added a handful of stones to weigh it down and make sure it didn't fly away. Our chances felt as fragile as that slip of paper. Even if Gunn came, would I be able to get Jayne to go? And would it be too late to take the baby? At least I could tell him about the baby when he came. Maybe he'd be able to convince Jayne to keep her.

I turned to go back and saw I was still holding the angel's head in my hand. Its smooth cheek fit in the palm of my hand like it was made for it. I slipped it in my pocket and made my way back through the Ramble. When I got back, I noticed the door to the tower was open but Matron wasn't there. I stepped inside, treading softly, and stopped at the foot of the stairs to listen. At first all I heard was a murmur so low it might have been from the pigeons roosting in the battlements of the tower, but then I made out words.

". . . are you sure you want to give up the child for adoption?" I heard my father say.

And then I heard Jayne answer: "I'm sure I want to give up the child."

I grew cold as the stone wall I leaned on. Jayne was going to go along with giving up the baby. I couldn't let that happen. That night I waited until everyone had gone to sleep and then I crept outside, listening for the dogs. When I heard them I tossed a handful of meat scraps I'd taken from the kitchen into which I'd ground the tranquilizers my father had prescribed for me. Then I ran for the woods. Once in the Ramble I knew my way by heart to the cemetery. When I reached Cerberus I stuck my hand in its mouth without hesitation. There was a thick package wrapped in plastic. When I unwrapped it, I saw it was money and an ID card—a Pennsylvania driver's li-

*cense with Jayne's picture on it, one of the photos Casey had taken,
but the name read* Jane Corey.

Meet us in the cemetery midnight on Halloween, *the note read,
this time in Casey's handwriting*. And make sure you bring the
tape.

*I looked through the package twice. But there was no ID card for
me. Jayne had lied to me. She was planning to take the name from
the gravestone and leave without me and the baby—*

"THAT'S NOT TRUE." I'm standing, still clutching my steno pad
even though I stopped writing minutes ago. "Jayne didn't leave
without me."

Veronica tilts her face up to me, a tremor moving beneath the
scar tissues over her eyes as if there were still eyes there trying to
read my face.

Are there? I wonder horribly. *Are her eyes trapped beneath the
scars?*

"The story isn't over, Agnes," she says, not bothering to pretend
she doesn't know exactly who I am. Of course, I realize, she's
known since I wrote that letter and signed it with my name—the
name of a dead baby in the cemetery. That was why she wanted
me to come here. She knew I was Jayne's daughter and she wanted
to tell her own side of the story, but it's all lies.

"It's over for me," I say. "Jayne left with me and she left you
behind. Is that why you're so angry with her? Is that why you're
painting her as heartless—"

"I never said she was heartless," Veronica says. "And I'm not
angry with her—"

"Well, she is with you," I say. "She used to scream that her story
had been stolen from her. You published the book she dictated to

you under your name and when she came back here you set your dogs on her."

"What? I never—" Her face goes ghostly white. "When?"

"I don't know but I remember it. I thought it was a dream—a nightmare—but since I've been here, I remember running through the Ramble, dogs at our heels. And I found her note in the Cerberus head, begging you to see her—"

A strange laugh erupts from her, as jarring as if from a statue. "*See*? I can't *see* anyone, Agnes, because of what she did, but I would still have welcomed her back. That's what I've been trying to tell you."

"You've been trying to turn me against her—my mother, the madwoman—but it won't work. It was all your fault. But she's here now. She's come back, and when I find her, we'll tell the world what really happened."

"She's here?" she says, swiveling her head as if she could sense her presence in the room.

I get to my feet, clutching the steno pad to my chest. "Yes, I've seen her outside the house. She's been afraid to approach me because of how horrible I was to her the last time I saw her but I'm going to find her and when I do, we'll finally know the truth."

Her mouth quivers, trying to form words. I turn and leave her, no longer interested in anything she has to say.

CHAPTER TWENTY-NINE

I go upstairs, holding the steno pad, to get my backpack, still packed with my clothes from yesterday. I add my laptop in case I can't come back. After my outburst it's likely I'm fired. Peter Syms will be instructed to run me off the property. If they still kept dogs, they would set them on me.

That's okay, I tell myself as I go down the winding stairs for what may be the last time. I'm ready to leave. It's not the sequel I came here for, but with what Veronica has told me and my mother's help I can write her side of the story. Kurtis Chadwick will see that and want to publish it. It will be my book that saves Gatehouse Books. Maybe, just maybe, being able to tell her side of the story will save my mother, too.

Laeticia is hovering at the bottom of the stairs, no doubt to inform me that I'm fired. Instead, she asks, "Are you going into town for the parade?"

"Yes," I tell her, remembering Red Bess's challenge. I might as well see who shows up before I leave town. "I hear it's quite the spectacle."

"It's prurient," she says with a sniff, "the way they make a caricature out of the family's tragedy. Peter and I will have our hands full chasing teenagers off the property."

"Maybe you should get a couple of guard dogs, to set on them," I say.

She blanches. "Ms. Corey, we're not trying to hurt anyone; we're just trying to keep them from setting the woods on fire. It's such a cruel reminder to Ms. St. Clair of the fire that took her sight."

"I'm sure there are many things about that night you'd both like to forget." I watch with satisfaction as her cheeks flare red, like embers beneath her skin, and turn to go.

"Just make sure you stay out of the woods tonight," she says to my back. "Peter and I will both be armed and we wouldn't want to accidentally shoot you."

IT's ONLY ELEVEN but already the village is packed for the parade. There are street vendors selling cider and hot chocolate, caramel apples studded with candy corn, and Red Bess Velvet cupcakes. Children—some in store-bought Disney costumes and others in artisanal handsewn fairy and animal outfits—run from store to store collecting candy from harried-looking shopkeepers. There's an edge of sugar-filled energy in the air that makes my teeth ache. Few of the foster homes I stayed in encouraged trick-or-treating. And as for the years I was with my mother—

I stop on the sidewalk so abruptly that a child in a Spider-Man costume runs into me. I remember being on a village street much like this one crying because all the children were in costume except for me. My mother had knelt down to look me in the eye and said, *Be careful of the costumes you put on, Agnes. Some are hard to take off.*

It was a strange thing to say to a child and yet it had worked. I'd stopped crying, terrified by the look in my mother's eyes. I think I'd known then that she was trapped inside a disguise. Now

I realize it's because she'd been forced to flee, abandoned by her own friend.

The parade doesn't start until five so I head to the library to check my email and type up the last installment. The library is packed, too, full of storytelling circles and mask-making workshops. I find a recess in the stacks where I can sit on the floor and look at my phone in private. I see immediately that I have another notification from Red Bess. When my Instagram opens, though, the picture isn't of Red Bess. It's of a blurry figure standing among the gravestones of the children's cemetery. *All the ghosts will rise from the dead on All Hallows' Eve,* the caption reads. The figure is too indistinct to make out. I enlarge the picture to see it better, my hand shaking on the keyboard as the face comes into focus.

It's me.

I'm standing over the grave of Agnes Corey as if newly risen from it, my face blank as a zombie's.

The cold creeps up from my hand until my whole body is numb, and then I'm no longer in my body at all. It's as if I have died and am hovering over my own corpse.

Then I slam back into my flesh. Furious. Someone followed me as I sleepwalked to the cemetery and took my picture. Who would do that? Hadley? But how would she get onto the grounds? Laeticia? For all her no-internet rules, could she be the one posting as Red Bess? It feels like the worst kind of violation, to take my picture when I'm clearly not conscious, but she hasn't just taken my picture, she and Veronica have taken my past. I understand how my mother felt. But I can't let it unravel me the way it unraveled her. I have to expose Veronica and Laeticia and then reclaim our story.

I close Instagram and then open my email. There's one from

Atticus responding to mine from yesterday. *I have no idea who's posting these, Agnes, and neither does Hadley. Frankly, we're both worried about you.*

I close the email without reading to the end then open the last email from Kurtis and reply. *I've got another chapter for you, and I think you'll find it interesting. You'll notice that there's something about a videotape in it. I don't know what was on the tape but I think I'm meeting today with someone who might know more. When I do I think we'll have the missing pieces for a book that will shock everyone.*

I SPEND THE rest of the afternoon hiding in the stacks transcribing the last installment and then rereading what we've got so far. I can see it all so clearly now. Veronica is telling her side of the story and making herself the heroine and Jayne the villain. How it must have galled Veronica that the book that made her name and fortune cast her as the poor madwoman in the attic. *Why,* I wondered, *had she even let it be published?* But then I remember what Peter Syms said about how welcome the money from the book had been. Perhaps Veronica hadn't had any choice but to publish. No wonder she never wrote another book until I came along begging her to write a sequel and she realized who I was. Had it amused her to tell her version in which Jayne was the villain to Jayne's daughter? Or had she had a darker motive? Was there something from the past she didn't want known and she wanted to find out if my mother had told me? I remembered the questions she'd asked me about my mother. Maybe she'd hoped I'd let something slip.

I reread the pages again, looking for I know not what, and then something stops me at the scene the morning Jayne and Violet woke up in the Josephine to find the girl Anaïs dead of an overdose.

What about the thing with the mirror that happened with Violet? They'll see the cuts on her.

And Jayne had said it didn't matter because Anaïs hadn't died from the cuts, she died from the heroin and Casey had brought that—

But they didn't tell the police about Casey. Why not? When Gunn asked why Jayne was protecting him Jayne said, *I'm not protecting him; I'm protecting us.*

Why? Was there something Casey knew that happened after Violet attacked Anaïs? Was she somehow responsible for Anaïs's death? In Veronica's version she didn't know what had happened and she refused to be hypnotized to find out. But what if that was an act and she did know? She had wanted Anaïs dead. She'd lunged for her with a shard of glass. Was that all she did? Or did she wait until Anaïs passed out and . . . what?

I flip back through the pages looking for clues—and then I see it. There was a violet ribbon tied around Anaïs's arm—the same ribbon that Violet had worn earlier that night and that Jayne gave her before they were taken away by the police. Why would Anaïs have Violet's ribbon around her arm—

Unless it was Violet who tied it around her arm and administered the fatal shot of heroin.

Violet—*no, Veronica*—killed Anaïs.

And Jayne knew. And then she ran away. Had Veronica been looking for her all these years, afraid she would one day reveal her secret or blackmail her with it? Is that why my mother always seemed paranoid that someone was searching for her? What might Veronica do now that she knows she's here? I think of Letty and Peter patrolling the grounds with guns. How easy it would be to shoot her as a trespasser.

I send the last installment to Kurtis Chadwick, adding in my message to him, *I think I've also just figured out who really killed Anaïs.* Then I close my laptop and get up. I'm ready to go find my mother.

THE STREET HAS been cleared, but the sidewalks are even more packed than before. Spectators, many with children on their shoulders, line the curb four to five deep, jostling for a good view of the street. The remaining space on the sidewalk is so narrow I can barely walk.

I collide with a tall figure in a black hooded cape and Scream mask and nearly scream myself. It could be anyone, I realize, Laeticia or Peter. Any of the costumed figures wandering the streets of Wyldcliffe-on-Hudson could knife me on the street and no one would even hear me scream over the noise. I don't care about making my date with Instagram Red Bess anymore; I have to get back to Wyldcliffe and find my mother.

The crowd suddenly surges toward the sidewalk and I see that the parade is beginning with a macabre marching band of skeletons dressed in the Día de los Muertos fashion with painted faces and flower wreaths. They're followed by a troupe of dancers in black leotards holding bat puppets on tall poles. The bat puppets swoop and careen wildly, darting at the edges of the crowd, causing children to screech and laugh with the joy of being terrorized while safe in the arms of their parents. The bats are followed by witches carrying cauldrons of candy that they toss to the increasingly hyper children. I feel the hysteria bubbling inside me. The screams of the children, the whoops of the crowd, and the bass beat of the marching band feel primitive, like some ancient rite. An appeasement to the hungry dead who demand each year a sacrifice.

Is that what my mother had been to Veronica and Casey—a disposable girl who entertained them with her antics but in the end wasn't worth keeping? As the red-robed contingent of Red Besses begin their march down Main Street, I wonder if that's what Bess Molloy had been to Josephine and Edgar. A girl from the streets who rich Josephine could pretend to save to make herself feel worthy but who could be abandoned when she no longer fit the role of rescued sinner?

The women marching in their red robes hold batons in their hands like majorettes in a homecoming parade, but at a crash of cymbals the batons burst into flames and the crowd gasps. They spin their flaming batons above their heads, sparks flying, and I feel something ignite in my own blood—a boiling fury that has been simmering my entire life.

If you'd been burnt to death, Jayne had asked Donna, *wouldn't you want to burn down the whole world?*

Yes, I think, feeling the burning weight of the marble head in my backpack. Why should my mother and I run away from Wyld-cliffe? Why should we be forced out when it was my mother who wrote the book that has paid for its upkeep all these years? Why shouldn't I be the one to take my revenge against the woman who cast out my mother and set the dogs on her? Why shouldn't I be the one to set the fire this time?

I turn abruptly to leave—and notice one lone Red Bess stand-ing on the edge of the road. She's not dancing or twirling a baton or wearing a skull mask. This Red Bess is my mother.

CHAPTER THIRTY

"Mom!" I shout, but she's already turning and running from me. I chase after her but I get caught in the last stragglers following the parade. I hear someone shouting my name and look back to see Martha Conway following me, but I keep running. My mother's vanished into the fog of River Road. I hear the plaintive moan of the foghorn and then the flash of the lighthouse beam. It catches my mother on the river side of the road, creeping along the high wall that surrounds Wyldcliffe Heights, as if she's trying to merge into the stone . . . and then she does. She vanishes as if she's melted into the wall.

I rush to keep up with her and see that she's gone through the crack I saw yesterday. I squeeze myself into the gap, the rough stone scraping my arms and face, and pressing so hard against my chest I can't breathe. I push myself forward and suddenly I'm out. It happens so fast, like the wall had spat me out, that I fall on the grass, panting and sobbing. When I look up it's as if I've been born into a transformed world. The smooth-barked trees gleam like bone in the dusk and in between them are sparks, like fireflies, and flitting figures, like ghosts. I can hear voices—shouts and laughter and singing. Then I hear an angry shout and a gunshot.

Shit. Laeticia hadn't been kidding when she said she and Peter were going to patrol the woods. The sparks, I realize, are torches. The flitting figures are costumed locals enacting some weird local rite. Somewhere among them my mother must be disoriented and scared.

Or maybe not so disoriented.

She knew how to get into the estate. She must have a reason for being here.

They stole my story.

Is she here to take revenge? To light her own fire? To find me? Will Peter and Laeticia get to her first?

I start running in what I hope is the direction of the house. The foliage is so thick that I can't see. The hard waxy leaves clatter over my head like the souls of the dead. Then I see a light through the trees—green—like the lamp in the library. I head toward it and come out on the lawn just below the house. I can see straight through the glass doors to the library, where Veronica is sitting on the green couch, beneath the green-shaded lamp, still as a statue, in full view of the woods, visible to all the crazy locals wandering the estate. When I reach the glass door, I see it's wide open, as if Veronica is inviting trespassers in. Her head swivels like an owl in my direction as I step over the threshold.

"Who is it?" she demands hoarsely.

"Just Agnes," I say.

She lets out a breath. "I didn't think you were coming back."

"Neither did I," I say, taking my customary seat. In the circle of green lamplight, I feel like we're actors on a stage. Or targets. "But I followed someone back here."

Her next breath sounds like it has to travel through barbed wire to reach her lungs. "Who?"

"Jayne."

It's what I was about to say, but someone has beat me to it.

Veronica and I both swivel our heads together this time. There in the doorway stands my mother, black hair streaked with gray, her face white as a ghost's, dressed in bloody red. She's even holding the fake scissors that come with the Red Bess costume, only as the lamplight glances off the blades I realize they're not fake.

"Mom," I say, getting to my feet to stop her. I grab her arm and the scissors clatter to the floor. Veronica also rises and reaches out a hand.

"Veronica," she says, "thank God you've finally come back. Please let me explain."

"How you stole my story and then my name and now my daughter? That might be a challenge even for you, Jayne."

I look back and forth between the two women—and settle on the one in green, the spider at the center of the web—and my head spins. The woman in green, the one I have been listening to this last week, isn't Veronica? She's Jayne? Which means that the woman I know as my mother is Veronica?

"Yes, it is," the woman in green—*Jayne?*—says. "And I can't tell it without you, Veronica. Let's tell it to Agnes together. I think we both owe her that."

THEY SIT ON the couch side by side, one in red, one in green. *Like a crazy pair of Elfs on a Shelf,* I think hysterically. I sit on the hard-backed chair opposite them, tempted to take out my steno pad just to have something to hold on to. Jayne—the real Jayne—begins.

"Why did you leave without me, Veronica?" she asks.

"You were planning to leave without *me!*" my mother cries.

"No! I never—"

"Casey only sent one false ID," my mother cuts in. "For Jane Corey."

"I already had yours," Jayne says. "Agnes, will you open the top right drawer of the desk? There's a box of playing cards at the back. Would you bring it to me?"

I do as she says and find the box of playing cards.

"Open it and take out the cards," Jayne says. "There's an ID card in there."

I sift through the dog-eared cards until I find a laminated card. There's a picture of my mother when young above the name Violet Grey. I hand it to my mother wordlessly.

"Do you like the name?" Jayne asks with a small, hopeful smile. "I picked it for you. I thought it suited you."

"I wouldn't have gone with you," my mother says petulantly. "Not without the baby." She turns to me. "*She* was going to abandon you. *I* saved you."

"I wasn't," Jayne says.

"I heard you telling my father—"

"I was just telling him what he wanted to hear until Gunn and Casey could come for us on Halloween . . ." She falters. "Or at least that's what I thought I was doing. I think in pretending to be under hypnosis I finally did fall under your father's spell." She turns to me. "When those nuns came they told me I'd already signed a paper giving you up, Agnes. Which I'd never do. I didn't remember signing it. They would have taken you then but one of the nuns sensed something was off and she insisted I have more time to think."

"I remember that," my mother says grudgingly. "But you told me that you didn't want to leave anymore, and I heard you tell my father that you were ready to give up the baby—"

Jayne shakes her head. "I don't remember. I don't remember anything of that night after I went to my session with your father. You tell me, Veronica." She reaches out and touches my mother's hand. My mother flinches and starts to pull away, but then she looks down at the scarred, crabbed hand and blanches.

"Mom," I say and both heads turn toward me. I look only at the one who raised me. "Mom, you always said that your story was stolen. I want to hear it, whatever it was, whatever you did. I don't care; I still love you."

My mother's eyes fill with tears. Then she looks down and, holding her friend's hand, she begins. "I was listening at the bottom of the tower and I heard you say that you were going to give away the baby. I went up and crouched before you. I showed you the ID that Casey had sent and told you I knew that you were planning to leave. Then I showed you the birth certificate I'd found—the one for the baby who had died whose grave you always went to. I'd found it in the attic. 'Look,' I told you, 'she was born exactly one hundred years before yours. We only have to change the eight to a nine and you can use it for her. I'll help you raise her.' And then I heard my father laughing. 'How charmingly romantic,'" my mother says in a deep voice that sounds wholly unlike her own. I feel a chill as if Dr. Sinclair has entered the room. "'As if you could be trusted with a gerbil, let alone a baby.'" My mother pauses and looks at Jayne. "And then he said, 'Isn't that right, Jayne?' And you said, 'As if you could be trusted—'"

"I didn't!" Jayne cries, shaking her head. "Or if I did it was because he'd hypnotized me to repeat what he said."

"It made me so angry," my mother says. "I wanted to slap you, but instead I reached into my pocket and felt the stone I'd picked up in the cemetery. It was a piece of the angel that stood over

Agnes's grave. As soon as I felt it I knew what I had to do. I hit him. I only thought I'd knock him out so we could escape, but he fell to the floor like a tree felled by an axe and there was so much blood. I knew right away that we had to run, but you wouldn't budge. And I had to go back to get Agnes. I told you to wait and I'd come back for you. I ran up to your room and grabbed Agnes and stuffed my old carpetbag with some things for you and me—I couldn't find my locket but I took the violet ribbon I had given to you—and that you had left behind. But when I got back to the tower it was on fire. I saw Gunn running out of the woods and Casey coming out of the tower and I heard Casey telling him that you were dead . . . and . . . and . . .". My mother shakes her head back and forth, beginning to look agitated. ". . . and I heard Casey tell Gunn that I had killed my father and set the fire! He told him they had to leave before the police got there. I wanted to shout out that yes, I had killed my father, but I hadn't set the fire—but I was afraid that if I stayed the police would arrest me for killing my father and then who would raise Agnes? So I ran. I had to run to save Agnes."

She looks toward me. "To save you."

Jayne nods her head and moves her hand, trying to grip my mother's fingers. "And you didn't start the fire? Accidentally, maybe, by knocking over a lantern when you struck your father?"

My mother whips her head back and forth, her hair flying. "No! I wouldn't have left you in a burning room! Why would you think that?"

"Because that's what Casey told me happened," Jayne says. "When I woke up in the hospital, he said he saw you running out of the tower. He said you left me in there to die and that you didn't—" She gasps and clutches her throat, her shoulders heaving.

I think she's choking but then I realize she's sobbing—a horrible tearless sobbing that sounds like thunder without rain. "He said you didn't have the baby with you. He told me you left us both to die. He said he found the stone you used to kill your father in the cemetery—"

"I did leave it there," my mother admits. "I left in on the grave—it seemed like it belonged there—"

"He told me that you ran away with Gunn."

"No!" my mother cries. "I haven't seen Gunn since that night! I took Agnes, along with the ID and the money Casey had left for you, because I thought you were dead. I thought you were dead until the book—*our book!*—came out under my name. I knew then that you'd tricked me and stolen my story and my name but I didn't care. I had Agnes. I tried my best to raise her—" She turns to me. "But I'm afraid I didn't do a very good job. I've tried to stay away, Agnes, since you asked me to, but I had to know you were safe. Sister Bernadette at Woodbridge told me you were living at the Josephine, so I followed you there and tried to keep an eye on you without letting you know—"

"It was you following me from Gatehouse Books that night," I say. I'm about to ask if she was the one who broke into Roberta Jenkins's office, but I don't want to upset her by accusing her.

"I was alarmed to see you working for the publisher who'd stolen my book. I thought maybe you were trying to get it back for me. But when I saw you come up here—" She turns back to Jayne. "I thought you were trying to steal her back from me the way you took my name and the book for yourself."

Jayne draws in a ragged breath. "When I came to in the hospital everyone was calling me Veronica. I was half out of my mind—blind, in pain. I thought they were talking to someone else. And then Casey came and told me what had happened. He said when he got to the house the tower was on fire and he couldn't get inside. He said he saw you, Veronica, running from the burning house with Gunn. He followed you but at the cemetery you threw a stone at him—the angel's head. He said it was covered with blood and he was afraid you'd used it to kill me and your father. He went back to the house and found out that Laeticia had saved me from the fire and taken me to the hospital. In the confusion everyone thought I was Veronica. He said I might as well *be* Veronica now. I'd have the house—and the book. He'd found the notebooks and read them and he said he'd publish the book—"

"Wait," I say. "What? How could Casey publish your book?" My voice dies in my throat as it all becomes clear. Kurtis Chadwick. K.C. "You meant the initials! I never—"

"Thought to verify the spelling?" an arch voice asks from the door to the foyer. "A rather shoddy mistake for an amanuensis to make, Miss Corey."

I look up to find Kurtis Chadwick standing in the doorway. He's wearing his usual tweedy jacket with its unironic elbow patches accessorized with a Burberry cashmere scarf and a dark gray revolver. I start to rise but he points the gun at me.

"Please stay seated, Miss Corey. Your job isn't quite over yet. You haven't taken down this last chapter, and it's my very favorite so far."

He crosses to the windows and draws the green velvet drapes over the glass, all while keeping the gun trained on us.

"Kurtis," Jayne says. "You've finally decided to join us in person. Does that mean you've been enjoying the book?"

She doesn't know he's holding a gun. But she does know I've been sending the chapters to him. "You knew?" I ask.

"I assumed he'd want to stay informed and that he would have asked you to keep him updated. Kurtis always had a way of playing people against each other."

"And you always had a flare for the dramatic, Jayne. I've been enjoying your version of events from Veronica's point of view. It's an interesting idea for a sequel."

My mother laughs. "What would either of you know about my side of the story?"

"I've spent thirty years trying to understand why you did what you did," Jayne says, "and mostly I've come to the conclusion that I drove you to it."

"She's telling the truth, Mom," I say. "The story she's told doesn't really paint Jayne in the best light. Now that I know you're Veronica I can imagine what it was like growing up here in a mental hospital with the specters of madness and Red Bess hanging over you."

I pause, feeling the weight of it. Of course it was Veronica, the girl who'd grown up victimized by an abusive and manipulative father, who would turn into the unstable, fragile woman I knew as my mother.

"The way your father treated you was criminal," I tell my mother. "Whatever you did to him he deserved. And what he was doing to Jayne—hypnotizing you to give up your baby—to give up *me*—" I say, tears climbing up my throat as it finally comes home to me that the woman in front of me, the one I've sat across from these last days, is actually the woman who gave birth to me. "I wouldn't blame either of you for killing him."

"Oh, but she didn't," Kurtis says. "When I got to the tower Dr. Sinclair was on the floor just regaining consciousness. You'd given him quite a nice tap on the head, Veronica, but he would have survived. He was lively enough to shout at me that he knew I was the one who gave Anaïs the lethal dose of heroin."

"You?" both me and my mother say at the same time. Only Jayne seems unsurprised.

"I thought it was me," my mother says softly. She turns toward Jayne. "You and Gunn said I'd done something, and it was my ribbon tied around Anaïs's arm. I thought I must have waited until she was asleep and given her the lethal dose of heroin because I was so jealous of her."

"You did lunge at her with a shard of glass," Jayne says. "But Gunn stopped you and we took you out of the room to calm down and Casey gave you something to 'settle you.' When we woke up and found Anaïs dead I did wonder if it was you, but then I found Casey's camera. He'd dropped it when you lunged at Anaïs, Veronica, but it was still running. I took the tape because I thought it might incriminate you. I gave it to Gunn because I didn't want the police to find it on me and I asked him to keep it safe until he could bring it to me. I didn't see what was on it until he brought it to me up here and I was able to sneak into your father's office to play it on his machine—"

"That's what you were watching?" my mother asks. "You said it was your session."

"I had to think about what to do with it," Jayne says.

"You mean how to use it against me," Kurtis says.

"What was on it?" I ask.

"Kurtis trying to rape Anaïs," she says, and then turning toward Kurtis she addresses him directly, spitting the words. "She pushed you away and threatened to tell your father what kind of scum you were. You sat there preparing a fix, as if for yourself, but when Anaïs tried to get up you grabbed her and shot it into her arm."

"I was just trying to keep her quiet," Kurtis says.

"I think you knew there was enough there to kill her."

Kurtis shrugs. "Did I? Who's going to believe you, Jayne? A woman who's lied about her identity for thirty years."

"I still have the tape," she says defiantly.

"Do you?" He reaches into his lapel pocket and takes out a cassette tape and rattles it. "That was kind of you to mention the vents between your rooms in your book, Jayne. I've been looking all over for it, but as soon as I read about those grates in your new book I realized where it was."

I stare at the tape in his hand and notice that his hand is bandaged.

"It was you who broke the window, wasn't it?" I say. "You were looking for the tape, but you didn't find it until you read my last email with the newest pages. So you were the one posting as Red Bess. Why did you try to lure me to the parade?"

"I wanted you out of the house while I looked for the tape. Honestly, I hoped you'd stay gone—run away like you always do. But since you came back—" He shrugs again. "You see, Jayne, it's really your fault. If you had just given me the tape years ago none of this would have happened. Or if you had just had the good grace to die in the fire along with Dr. Sinclair—"

"Why did you kill my father?" my mother demands.

"Jayne had told him everything while under hypnosis," he says. "I just finished what you started, Veronica, and burnt all his tapes and notes."

"And me," Jayne says. "You left me there to die."

"I should have waited to make sure," he says. "I won't make the same mistake this time."

"I've kept your secret for thirty years while you kept my daughter and my best friend from me, but now you've returned them," Jayne says. "Shall we call it even, Kurtis?"

Kurtis sighs. I've heard him make the same sound over mediocre manuscripts and weak coffee. "And trust the three of you—a mental patient, an old has-been writer, and a lying, thieving juvenile delinquent—will keep quiet about the events of thirty years ago? I don't think so."

"What are you going to do?" I ask. "Shoot the three of us? How will you explain that?

"I have other plans," he says, smiling. "First, though, I think we need to remove ourselves from the library, where we're so very visible."

"Letty and Peter will be back soon," Jayne says, beginning to look nervous now that she realizes Kurtis has a gun.

"I'm afraid not," Kurtis says. "Peter took a bullet to the arm in the woods—he thinks from a trespasser—and Letty's taken him to the hospital."

The shot I'd heard.

"Now, shall we go?" He waves the gun at my mother. "You help Jayne," he says. "And you—" Before I realize what he plans to do he grabs me by the arm and jams the gun into my side. "Agnes will stay close by me so no one thinks of trying to run. Unless neither of you really care about her."

CHAPTER THIRTY-ONE

He steers us out of the library and up the stairs, Jayne hanging on to my mother's arm, the gun pressed to my ribs. "Where are we going?" I ask.

"The attic," he replies. "Isn't that the favorite motif of you goth girls? The madwoman in the attic? What better place for the three of you—"

"Stop it," I say, "my mother's not mad."

"Which mother do you mean?" he asks, giving me a little prod with the gun.

"She means the woman who raised her," Jayne says, "and no, Veronica's not mad. She survived growing up here and then she saved Agnes when I couldn't and raised her as best she could with limited resources." She turns to my mother. "I just wish you'd come back—"

"I did!" my mother cries. "When Agnes was four, but you set the dogs on us."

"I didn't! It must have been Old Syms. I wouldn't let Peter keep dogs after his father died. I swear, Veronica, I had no idea. I didn't even know Agnes was alive until she wrote to me and then I didn't know if it was really her until she came here."

"Why didn't you tell me you knew who I was?" I ask.

"I didn't know why you were here or how much Kurtis had told you or if he had sent you," she replies.

"Why *did* you let me come here?" I ask Kurtis, coming to a full stop as we reach the second landing. Kurtis is on the side near the railing. If I could edge him closer, I might be able to shove him over before he has a chance to shoot me. I'm still wearing my backpack and I can feel the weight of the marble head in it. I could swing it at him. "You could have thrown out the letter from Ver—I mean Jayne—and just fired me."

"Gloria saw the letter first and showed it to me in front of Diane. How could I explain that I didn't want you to come when it seemed like the perfect answer to our problems? And I wasn't sure how much you knew," he says. "Here you'd infiltrated my publishing house. That seemed like a mighty big coincidence if you didn't know who you were."

"I wanted to work at Gatehouse because I loved *The Secret of Wyldcliffe Heights*!" I exclaim, bringing up my right arm, which nudges Kurtis closer to the banister. "My mother read it to me every night."

"You did?" Jayne murmurs.

Kurtis scoffs. "Really? I've always thought it was trash. When I brought it to my father he said as much, but *I* knew it was trash that would sell. I've always had an eye for that. I knew it would sell to all those goth wannabe groupies and bored Midwest housewives alike. You should have seen my father's face when it made the *New York Times* bestseller list. It was the first time he ever took me seriously."

Kurtis is so enjoying this account of his business acumen that he has relaxed his grip on me and moved a few inches closer to the banister. I use the moment to ease the left strap of my backpack off and grip the other with my right hand. He tilts his head back and crows, "So much for the reading tastes of the American public!"

I swing my backpack at him and feel the satisfying *thunk* of the marble hitting him in the chest and then, for good measure, I put both hands on his stupid tweed jacket and shove. As he stumbles backward his arms come up to regain his balance and he fires the gun, hitting the plaster ceiling. His back hits the banister and I hear a crack, but it doesn't break.

"Run!" I yell to Veronica and Jayne as I lift my leg to kick him. He brings the gun down before I can make contact and shoots. I feel a searing pain in my shoulder that fells me. Before I can move, he grabs the wounded arm, wrenches me to my feet, and hauls me to the banister. The world spins, the spokes of the coiled banisters revolving like a gyre, the weight of the marble head in the backpack pulling me downward. I can see as if from above my body crashing to the marble floor.

"You stupid bitch!" Kurtis spits into my ear. "Did you really think you could beat *me*?" He drags me back to his side, digging his fingers into the place where the bullet went in. The pain is blinding but when my vision clears, I see that we're alone on the landing. I manage a laugh that comes out more like a cough.

"Jayne and Veronica got away."

"They won't get far—a blind woman and a lunatic—and when I kill them, I'll make it extra painful for what you did."

He frog-marches me to my bedroom and kicks open the door. "Are you hiding in here, girls?" he calls.

The room appears empty. He opens the door to the attic and pushes me forward. The stairs are so narrow he has to make me go first, but he keeps the gun jabbed into my back. When I reach the top he pushes me hard and I fall to the floor.

"Here you are," he says as if he's delivered me safely home. "The madwoman returns to her attic at last. I don't think anyone will be too surprised when they read the email you send me tonight confessing your revenge plot against Veronica St. Clair for stealing your mother's book or that you both went up in flames."

"How—?"

"Do you think I'd have given you a laptop and a phone without making sure I had access to your email and social media accounts?" he says smugly. "I've read every email you've written. You've done an excellent job making yourself sound crazy to poor witless Atticus. And those Red Bess posts—I used your email to make that account and downloaded those photos onto your phone. Between your record of petty crime and mental instability, this is clearly the place you were always going to end up."

He heads down the stairs, and I get up to lunge after him, but he's shut the door before I can reach him. I throw myself at the door, knowing there's no lock, but it doesn't budge. I hear a loud scraping noise and realize he's pushing the bed in front to block the door. I shove and hammer my fists and shout, but the door holds and no one comes.

Where are Jayne and my mother?

I go back up the stairs and search behind the boxes and furniture until all that's left is the armoire. I stand in front of it for a second, frozen by my own reflection. My hair is wild and tangled, my face tear and dirt streaked, my clothes torn and bloody. Kurtis was right. I look like the madwoman of my nightmares.

I look like Red Bess.

I wrench open the wardrobe as if daring Red Bess to jump out at me. But there's nothing there but the hooded cloak. I slam the door and sink to the floor in front of the mirror. There's nothing left to do. I'm stuck in this attic while Kurtis Chadwick tracks down and kills my mother and Jayne—

My two mothers.

Everything has happened so fast tonight—including a bullet wound in my shoulder that is making me woozy—that I've had no time to really absorb what I've learned. The woman I thought was my mother is really Veronica St. Clair. The woman who gave birth to me—and who I've been sitting across from for the last week—is Jayne. I try to let it sink in and parse what it means. All my life I've been afraid I would inherit my mother's madness. Does it change anything that we're not connected by blood? I don't feel any less connected to her. If anything, after hearing her story from Jayne, I feel like I finally see her—the woman who's always been in the shadows, standing next to her twin in the light. Together they make a whole. When I look in the mirror I see my own face half in shadow, half in light, both of the women who made me together—

The mirror shudders, blurring my reflection, and then the door swings open. The cloaked figure inside the wardrobe stirs. *Red Bess coming for me at last,* I think. I don't move or scream. I'm ready for her. I close my eyes. She smells like smoke, like the fire she set a hundred years ago. I open my eyes and look up into hers—

And find my mother.

"Are you okay?" she asks. "Can you walk? We have to get out of here."

I blink and look past her. Jayne is crouched in the wardrobe, smoke wisping around her. "How—?" I begin.

"There's a door behind the wardrobe to the back servant stairs," my mother says. "We hid there when Kurtis brought you up here."

"But we waited too long," Jayne says, coughing. "He's lit the house on fire. He must have ignited the gas stove and doused the place with gasoline to get it going so fast. The back stairs have already filled with smoke."

She starts coughing again. I get up and push past her and past the hanging cloak. The back of the wardrobe is open to a stairwell. Smoke is rising up in clouds, like fog coming off the river. "We'll never make it down these," I say, covering my mouth with my hand.

"We have to go up," my mother says, pointing.

I follow her finger and see that the stairs go up another half flight to a glass-covered hatch.

"It opens onto the roof," my mother says. "There's a fire escape down the back of the house. It was put in when my father turned the house into a juvenile facility."

"No one's used it in years," Jayne says between gasps. "It could have rusted away."

"It's our only chance," I say, choking on the smoke. Jayne is coughing so hard her body is shaking. I grab the cloak and wrap it around her, drawing a fold over her mouth. "Help her up the stairs," I tell my mother. "I'll go ahead and open the hatch."

It's only six or seven steps, but it feels like climbing a mountain. When I reach the hatch I push, but it doesn't open. I find a latch, but it's so rusted it breaks in my hand when I turn it. My mother and Jayne are behind me, both of them coughing now. The smoke is snaking around me, gripping my throat. "Cover your heads," I croak.

I reach into my backpack, take out the marble head, and slam it into the hatch. Glass rains down on our heads. I catch a whiff of fresh air but then the smoke, seeing a way out, rushes around me. I strike again, blindly, and again, clearing the glass with my bare hands until there's room to squeeze through. I turn and grab my mom.

"We need to get Jayne out first," she says.

Together we push Jayne through the hatch, trying our best to use the cloak to shield her face from the broken glass. When she gets through, she turns and reaches her hand down and grabs my hand in hers. I try to tell her to let go, to let me get my mother out first but I've got no voice and my mother is pushing me from behind. Jayne pulls, my mother pushes, and I go through the hatch and out into the cold night air that rushes into my lungs. I collapse onto the roof, gasping, face wet with tears and blood while Jayne pulls my mother out and we all huddle for a moment together, our arms wrapped around each other, our bodies shaking with the same sobs.

"You're freezing," Jayne says.

"She's lost too much blood," my mother says.

"Give her the cloak," Jayne says, taking it off. "And let's get to that ladder. I can feel the heat of the fire through the roof."

They wrap the cloak around me and then we both help Jayne cross the rooftop to the far-northwest corner of the house. There's the ancient ivy-covered cast-iron ladder I've noticed clinging to the house. My mother grips the top rung and looks down.

"Does it look like it will hold?" Jayne asks. She's wringing her scarred hands together.

"I don't know," my mother says, giving it a little shake that makes the iron groan. I look over the side of the roof and wish I hadn't. Smoke and flames are pouring out of the lower windows. The ancient stairs look as if the only thing holding them up is the ivy and if the ivy catches fire—

"Right," I say. "Mom, you go first and I'll follow with Jayne."

"Let me stay with Jayne," she says, putting her arm around her.

"Yes," Jayne agrees, "you go first."

I guess that my mother is too scared to go first so I step onto the stairs. Immediately I feel the whole thing tremble. When I grip the rails, rust flakes off in my hand. I can barely use my wounded arm and my hands are cut up from breaking the window. "Just hold on and step . . . lightly," I say, taking a step down. I look up to see that they're following. As each steps onto the ladder I feel the iron shake. "Great!" I say with false cheer. "You're doing great!" I go down the ladder keeping my eye on my mother and Jayne. We make it down the first flight and then, stepping back—

I feel nothing.

I look down and see too late that the landing has rusted through. I swing around so my foot lands on the next rung, the first of the second flight, and feel the metal bolts wrench out of the old stone wall. The cast iron is hot in my hands. I look up and see my mother huddled on the last rung.

"Okay," I say, forcing my voice to sound calm, "you just have to step over that little gap and onto the next flight."

"Veronica," Jayne says, "does it look like it's strong enough for all of us?"

"No," my mother replies, "but it may be strong enough to hold Agnes."

"It'll be fine," I shout, edging back up toward them. "Look! It can hold all of us."

But they aren't looking at me. They've turned their faces to each other, my mother's eyes meeting something in Jayne that can still see. How else do they know to nod at the same time?

"No!" I say, reaching for them.

"It's all right," my mother says. "You go on—"

"And tell our story for us," Jayne finishes.

And then, together, hands clasped, like Jayne and Violet at the end of *The Secret of Wyldcliffe Heights,* they step into the air.

CHAPTER THIRTY-TWO

I'm lost in the fog again. I can hear the baying of the hounds at my heels and when I turn, I see the burning flash of their eyes as I fall at their feet. Then there are hands helping me up and strong arms carrying me out of the fog. I scream and cry to go back. I scream and cry for my mother. I've just found her—I've just found *them*—how can I have two and then none? *It's not fair, it's not fair, it's not fair.* And then I'm falling again, into the fog.

IT TAKES A long time for the fog to clear. "You inhaled a lot of smoke," the nurses tell me, "and lost a lot of blood."

"You hit your head when you fell," the doctor adds.

When I try to talk my voice comes out sounding like a foghorn. I hold up my hands for pen and paper, and I see they're muffled in white like cocoons. *How am I going to be an amanuensis now?* I wonder.

"Thank God!"

I turn my head and find Atticus Zimmerman sitting at my bedside with a notebook and pen. I think he's come to take down the story from me.

"I was afraid you'd never wake up and I'd never get a chance to tell you what an idiot I've been." He launches into a long-winded apology for not believing me, for not taking me more seriously, and for not realizing that Kurtis Chadwick was a murderous maniac. I manage to croak out a question, which he correctly interprets as "Did they catch him?"

"Did they ever!" he crows. "Your friend Martha saw you running from the parade and followed you up to the house. She couldn't get in through the gates but when she smelled smoke she called the police and they caught him fleeing the house reeking of gasoline. He tried to blame you for setting the fire but your mom set him straight—"

I slap my bandaged hands against his chest so hard he yelps. "My mom? Which one? Are they alive?"

"Oh shit," he says, "I guess I should have led with that."

IT TAKES ALMOST an hour to get the full story out of Atticus. When the police reached the estate they apprehended Kurtis Chadwick and called the fire department and ambulances. They arrived just in time to see my mother and Jayne make their leap, which would have killed them but for the giant rhododendrons where they landed. The shrubs broke their fall—and Jayne's right leg and my mother's left arm and three ribs—but they survived. Two firefighters were able to get them out while another rescued me from the fire escape. Jayne and Veronica were rushed by ambulance to Vassar Brothers Medical Center, while I was taken to the closer Northern Dutchess.

"So my mom's alive?" I ask Atticus.

"Both of your moms are alive," he tells me.

ATTICUS VISITS FOR the next few days. "Don't you have to go to work?" I ask.

"What work?" he asks. "Our illustrious boss, Kurtis Chadwick, is in jail facing charges for arson and attempted murder. Veronica and Jayne have made out sworn statements that he tried to kill all three of you and that he started the fire. There's no way he'll get off. So for the time being, Gatehouse Books is closed."

ALTHOUGH I'M GLAD to know that Kurtis Chadwick is not likely to be free anytime soon, I feel a pang recalling that I'd come up to Wyldcliffe to *save* Gatehouse Books, not close it down. "Poor Gloria," I say.

Atticus scoffs. "Gloria's fine. Haven't you heard her brag about buying Microsoft stock in 1986? She and Diane are planning to purchase Gatehouse and restart it under new management. Of course, it will take a while . . . Kayla's jumped ship and taken a job at Amazon. Hadley's using the time to finish her book, which Diane says she wants to publish along with Veronica's—I mean Jayne's. Diane says I've got a job when she reopens the publishing house, and in the meantime I've got some freelance gigs to tide me over. I kind of like it up here . . . which reminds me, your friend Martha told me about an apartment in town. Two bedrooms for half of what I've been paying for a studio in Bushwick. There's another one in the same building if you're interested." He turns bright red as if he'd suggested we share an apartment. Or maybe he's embarrassed by the way he keeps mentioning Martha. Clearly he's taken a fancy to her. I wait for the familiar pang of jealousy but it fails to arrive. Martha saved my life by calling the police. And Atticus has been a good friend sitting by my bedside. If the two of them are together . . . well, it means I'll have two friends here in Wyldcliffe-on-Hudson, which I find myself oddly reluctant to leave.

"I'd take it," I say, "but I don't see how I can afford to since I'm out of a job—"

"You still have a job with Jayne," he says. "In fact, we both do. That's the freelance gig I mentioned. She wants you to finish taking down the sequel to *The Secret of Wyldcliffe Heights*, for Diane to edit, and then for me to copyedit. I'd say we'll both be gainfully employed for the next year."

He grins and I find myself returning his smile. "In that case," I say, "tell Martha I'd like to take that apartment. And tell her thank you."

In the second week of November, Atticus calls a cab to pick us up at the hospital. I'm only half surprised to find the driver is Spike. As he drives us to Wyldcliffe-on-Hudson he fills us in on the town gossip—someone got shot during the annual turkey shoot, the school board voted out the members who'd been trying to ban books from the school library, and the village is planning a Thanksgiving parade to honor the fire department for saving lives at Wyldcliffe Heights.

"What's with this town and parades?" I ask.

Spike chuckles as he parks in front of Bread for the Masses and carries my bag up the stairs to the third floor. When he opens the door I see my mother and Jayne on the couch, both of them in assorted casts.

"Mom!" I say.

"We'd get up—" my mother begins.

"But Letty insists we save our energy for the climb back down," Jayne finishes for her.

Laeticia comes over to fuss—not over them but me. I'm made to sit as if I'm an invalid in a big comfortable easy chair facing the couch. Jayne and my mother share stories about "rehab," as they call it, and all the ways they found to subvert the rules. They sound like teens again, sneaking cigarettes in the Ramble. It's like the last thirty years never happened.

As they talk I notice that Jayne's holding my copy of *The Secret of Wyldcliffe Heights* in her lap, her fingers tracing the embossed design on the cover as if it's braille. Looking from the picture of the girl on the cover to her face I see, once again, the resemblance between them, the thirty years vanishing as she laughs with her old friend.

"Who painted the cover?" I blurt out.

All of those thirty years fall over Jayne like a shroud.

"Gunn," she and my mother say at the same time.

"I realized immediately when I saw it," my mother says. "Gunn was always painting Jayne and he did here, too." My mother guides Jayne's hand to the face of the girl on the cover. "When I saw it I was jealous," my mother admits. "Why should Jayne get to be on the cover?"

For a moment I hear the strident tone that would often herald a manic episode, but then my mother smiles and clasps Jayne's hand. "But then over the years it became the reason I loved the book most because it gave me a picture of my best friend."

"But how did Kurtis get it?" I ask.

"It's what Gunn was bringing to me that night," Jayne says. "Kurtis took it from him and then—" Her voice trembles and I feel something quake inside me.

"What happened?" I demand, all the anger I thought extinguished flaring. "What did he do to—"

Before I can say his name Jayne answers.

"Your father? I never knew. I thought he had abandoned me. I refused to even look. But now, your friend Hadley has been helping me—"

"Hadley found a record of him being arrested for drug use in ninety-three," Atticus says. "He spent three years at the prison in Hudson—"

"So close," Jayne murmurs.

"We'll keep looking for him," Atticus says, then changes the subject, asking what the plans are for Wyldcliffe Heights.

"Jayne and I are going to live in the gatehouse—" my mother begins.

"And we're thinking of renovating the big house and making it a women's shelter," Jayne adds.

"Or a writing retreat," my mother says.

Jayne looks toward her and clasps her hand, hearing, as I had, that my mother's voice is strained. Laeticia suggests that they should be getting back home and Atticus offers to help my mother down the stairs. After the others go Jayne and I sit quietly across from each other for a moment, both of us, I think, imagining all the iterations Wyldcliffe Heights has survived—from Magdalen refuge to progressive training school to a psychiatric treatment center—all with good intentions that somehow went wrong. *Maybe*, I can't help thinking, *some places always revert back to their true natures.*

"You think it will all go bad," Jayne says, as if reading my thoughts.

"From all you've told me," I reply, "yes."

"Everything I told you was how I imagined Veronica saw it," she reminds me. "I wanted you to understand the effect that Wyldcliffe had on her."

"How it drove her mad?" I ask.

She shakes her head. "Your mother's not mad," she says. "I've taken her to see a psychiatrist at Columbia Presbyterian, and she's assured me that all Veronica needs is a loving, supportive environment, a good therapist, and the right medication to treat her bipolar disorder. And I aim to make sure she gets all of that."

"Thank you," I say, meaning it, "but it's not just my mother who's been damaged by Wyldcliffe Heights; it's all of the girls like LeeAnn and Dorothy and Donna—"

"LeeAnn, as you probably guessed, is Letty," Jayne says. "Dorothy is a social worker in Toronto. Donna . . . everyone thought she'd run away, but she's the one who died in the fire. She must have tried to get into the tower to save me after Laeticia had already gotten me out."

"See?" I say, feeling bad for Donna and for making Jayne relive that pain. "Bad things happen in that house. You and my mother could have both died both because I wanted a sequel!" My voice cracks and I begin, surprising us both, to sob.

She puts her arm around me and pulls me closer until I am sobbing on her shoulder. "You were right to want that sequel," she says. "You deserved to know your story, and it's brought Veronica back to me."

"But it almost got you killed! The house is cursed ever since Red Bess—"

"Oh, speaking of Bess," she says, reaching into her pocket, "the ER staff found this in her cloak when they took it off you."

She hands me a packet of paper that's been folded so many times into a tight square it's as if the writer wanted to reduce her missive to its smallest dimensions. It feels weighty as a stone. I'm not sure I'm up for any more revelations from the past.

"Read it later," Jayne says, perhaps sensing my reluctance.

I nod, then put the packet into my pocket. "It's not just Bess either," I say. "It's all the girls, going back to the ones in the cemetery. All the Agnes Coreys—" Again my voice cracks and her hand, shy as a fawn, steals into mine.

"All the Agnes Coreys," she says, "including you, who were brave enough to come here and stand up to the mean old dragon lady and unmask Kurtis Chadwick for what he was—yes, yes, I know, you'll say you weren't brave and it all just happened by chance. You know, I told you Veronica's story because I wanted you to understand that she tried her best—"

"I do," I cut in.

"But I didn't tell you *my* story. It's a bit like yours. A home I couldn't stay in, a series of places I couldn't call home. It makes it hard to trust that anything good will ever happen. It made it easy for Kurtis to fool me all these years by telling me a story that was bad enough—Veronica and Gunn abandoning me, losing you—that I'd believe it. But the worst thing we can imagine isn't always the truth; it's just the easiest thing for people like you and me to believe."

I look away from her as if I'm afraid she'll read the expression on my face. From here I can see that the front windows of this apartment—*my apartment*—face the river. A big ship, majestic as an ocean liner, is moving downriver, carrying with it the gold of the setting sun and filling my new home with light and movement enough for the most restless and least trusting of hearts.

"I'd like to hear it," I say when I can trust my voice. "Your story, I mean."

Her hand flutters in mine, and as she begins, I watch the clouds scudding across the mountains on the other side of the river, like ghost ships sailing through the evening sky.

CHAPTER THIRTY-THREE
The Confession of Josephine Hale

I write this in the same notebook in which my friend Bess Molloy began her own confession. I only read it after her death. She wasn't able to finish it and so I will here, adding my own confession to hers.

Bess was right that I had begun to parrot Edgar's words. Looking back, I see that he had put a spell on me, but that's no excuse. I should have seen.

Bess saw.

Edgar changed after we were married. He no longer asked my opinion in the running of our training school, and when I did venture an opinion, he corrected me and told me I was too soft with the girls. It grew worse when I was with child. He forbade me from conversing with the inmates, as he called them, lest I catch some infectious disease. He was fanatic about hygiene and always wore those soft kid gloves of his, even, horribly, in our bed at night, as if he couldn't bear to touch my flesh with his. He treated me as if I were a leper. Soon I was not allowed to leave my room at all, and when I was finally delivered of a child, she was taken from me because, according to my husband, I had become too excitable.

"I see that you have some of the same inherent weaknesses as the women we shelter," he told me. "Let us pray our daughter will be spared them but to be sure it will be best if she is raised without your influence."

I awoke later that night, hearing the piteous cries of my child. What might Edgar do to her if he thought that she, too, had inherited my weaknesses? I couldn't bear the thought of him harming her. I had to get to her. Although he had locked me in, I knew a way out. I went up to the attic and then down the servants' stairs to the kitchen and from there I followed the sound of my child crying to the tower. I climbed the stairs and came into my husband's office. The child's cries were so loud my husband did not hear me when I reached the threshold. Or perhaps he was too busy. His hands were wrapped around Bess's throat and he was choking the life out of her. I saw her scissors lying on the floor. She must have come to the tower to save my child but he'd been too quick for her. She had tried to free me.

I knelt down and picked up the scissors and stabbed my husband in the back. Only then did he let Bess go and turn to face me. I lunged for his face but he raised his hand and I saw the scar on his ungloved hand, the puncture where Bess had stabbed him once before in the settlement house.

Edgar was the Violet Strangler.

His hands were still shielding his face, so I stabbed him in the heart. Over and over again I plunged Bess's scissors into his cold, cold heart until the cloak I wore was covered with blood and I had wiped that awful smirk off his face and he was lying bleeding his lifeblood out onto Bess.

Poor Bess. Her eyes stared lifeless at the ceiling. She had only wanted to save me—and she still could.

I took off the bloody cloak I wore and switched it with hers. Then I found a rope that Edgar kept in the tower in case of fire and fashioned a noose. Luckily, it was the same knot used to cast on in knitting with some extra loops. I dragged poor Bess up the stairs to the roof and tied one end of the rope around a battlement and slipped the other over Bess's head and pushed her over. Then I went downstairs, picked up my crying baby, and tipped over the lamp to burn away any evidence contrary to the story I would tell. I ran from the tower screaming like the madwoman Edgar had made me out to be and I kept screaming until the housekeeper and night watchman came and then the police. I screamed so long my throat ached as if I were the one who had been hung. Sometimes I think it was me who was hung that night and this has all been a dream. And sometimes when I look in the mirror, I see Bess looking back and I know she's waiting for me on the other side of the glass.

ACKNOWLEDGMENTS

Thank you to my agent, Robin Rue, and her assistant, Beth Miller, of Writers House for their ongoing support and encouragement. Thank you to Liz Stein for shepherding this book through a long and challenging editing process and to Tessa James for seeing it through its final stages. Thanks to Ariana Sinclair, Christopher Connolly, and everyone at William Morrow for all their hard work.

Thank you to my family—Lee Slonimsky, Maggie Vicknair, Nora Slonimsky, and Jeremy Levine—for listening to my stories and making me feel I am not alone in this big world.

Thank you to Ethel Wesdorp for reading an early manuscript and to Andrea Massar who answered questions about social work and read early drafts. Any mistakes are solely of my own making.

I first began thinking of this book when I visited the Dr. Oliver Bronson House in Kingston, on the grounds of the House of Refuge for Women at Hudson, New York, which has been preserved due to the diligence of Historic Hudson. Roberta Andersen, friend and neighbor, shared her memories of a visit to the institution in the 1960s and I learned more about its history in *The Lost Children of Wilder: The Epic Struggle to Change Foster Care* by Nina Bernstein. Some of the names of the girls in the cemetery at Wyldcliffe are the names of the forgotten girls who were at Hudson. This book is dedicated to them.

ABOUT THE AUTHOR

CAROL GOODMAN's rich and prolific career includes such novels as *The Widow's House* and *The Night Visitors*, winners of the 2018 and 2020 Mary Higgins Clark Awards. Her books have been translated into sixteen languages. She lives in the Hudson Valley.

READ MORE BY CAROL GOODMAN
Two-Time Mary Higgins Clark Award Winner

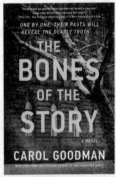

THE BONES OF THE STORY

THE DISINVITED GUEST

THE STRANGER BEHIND YOU

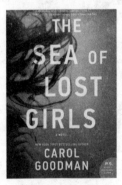

THE SEA OF LOST GIRLS

THE NIGHT VISITORS

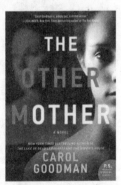

THE OTHER MOTHER